ONE MORE SHOT

Anise Starre is a born and bred Londoner who now travels the world with her husband. She loves writing sweet, fluffy romances featuring Black women being loved on and adored, with a hint of steam and spice to get the heart going. *One Week in Paradise* is her debut novel and the first book in the Flights and Feelings series. The second book is *One Last Job* and *One More Shot* is the third and final novel in the series.

You can follow Anise on Instagram @authoranisestarre and TikTok @anisestarre. Her website is anisestarre.com.

Also by Anise Starre

One Week in Paradise
One Last Job

ONE MORE SHOT

Anise Starre

**SIMON &
SCHUSTER**

London · New York · Amsterdam/Antwerp · Sydney/Melbourne · Toronto · New Delhi

First published in Great Britain by Anise Starre, 2024
This edition published in Great Britain by Simon & Schuster UK Ltd, 2025

Copyright © Anise Starre, 2024

The right of Anise Starre to be identified as author
of this work has been asserted in accordance with the
Copyright, Designs and Patents Act, 1988.

1 3 5 7 9 10 8 6 4 2

Simon & Schuster UK Ltd
1st Floor
222 Gray's Inn Road
London WC1X 8HB

For more than 100 years, Simon & Schuster has championed authors and the stories they create. By respecting the copyright of an author's intellectual property, you enable Simon & Schuster and the author to continue publishing exceptional books for years to come. We thank you for supporting the author's copyright by purchasing an authorised edition of this book.

No amount of this book may be reproduced or stored in any format, nor may it be uploaded to any website, database, language-learning model, or other repository, retrieval, or artificial intelligence system without express permission. All rights reserved. Enquiries may be directed to Simon & Schuster, 222 Gray's Inn Road, London WC1X 8HB or RightsMailbox@simonandschuster.co.uk

Simon & Schuster Australia, Sydney
Simon & Schuster India, New Delhi

www.simonandschuster.co.uk
www.simonandschuster.com.au
www.simonandschuster.co.in

The authorised representative in the EEA is Simon & Schuster Netherlands BV,
Herculesplein 96, 3584 AA Utrecht, Netherlands. info@simonandschuster.nl

Simon & Schuster strongly believes in freedom of expression and stands against censorship in all its forms. For more information, visit BooksBelong.com

A CIP catalogue record for this book
is available from the British Library

Paperback ISBN: 978-1-3985-4416-1
eBook ISBN: 978-1-3985-4417-8

This book is a work of fiction. Names, characters, places and incidents are either a product of the author's imagination or are used fictitiously. Any resemblance to actual people living or dead, events or locales is entirely coincidental.

Typeset in Bembo Std by Palimpsest Book Production Limited, Falkirk, Stirlingshire
Printed and Bound in the UK using 100% Renewable Electricity
at CPI Group (UK) Ltd

For all the eldest daughters out there. Remember to take some time for yourself – you deserve it.

xo

Chapter One

ELIOTT

I have one goal for tonight and one goal only: I, Eliott Rayne, am going to have an orgasm.

Sasha, my flatmate and best friend, cheers loudly. 'That's the spirit, girl!' Some of the Prosecco in her glass spills over onto my sheets as she flops down onto my bed. 'Positive vibes only.'

It feels like I need more than just positive vibes right now, but I appreciate the sentiment all the same. Because, despite having just turned twenty-seven, I've never managed to *get there* with a partner.

Not for lack of trying, mind you.

One-night stands, friends-with-benefits, men, women, both at the same time – I've tried just about every combination possible and not a single one has resulted in the kind of happy little moans I can hear coming from Sasha's bedroom every time her boyfriend, Wes, stays the night.

It's exhausting.

I put the finishing touches on my make-up and step back from the mirror. Sasha has already downed her drink and has swiped mine off the bedside table to sip on. I ignore the blatant theft and turn to face her.

'How do I look?'

She grins. 'Fucking stunning.'

Sasha would stay that if I stumbled out of bed at 5am wearing last night's make-up and a bin bag, but that doesn't mean it's not true right now. Leather pants, corset top, my favourite walkable yet sexy heels – this is a tried and tested outfit. Make no mistake about it – someone is coming home with me tonight.

'So, what's the plan?' Sasha asks, swinging her long legs over to the side so I can drop down onto the bed with her. I snatch my glass away from her and she gives me a pretend pout before reaching for the bottle to refill her own glass.

'No plan,' I say in between sips. 'Unless "*Find someone hot. Bring them back home. Have an orgasm*" counts as a plan?'

Sasha rolls her eyes. 'Yes, that's a given, obviously. But beyond that, what're we looking for? Just because they're hot doesn't mean they know how to fuck, and since we can't just ask them—'

I snort into my drink. 'Oh yeah, that'd go down well. Excuse me, hot person, how would you rate your sexual prowess on a scale of one to ten? One being *couldn't find the clit if I beat you over the head with it* and ten being—'

One More Shot

'*Your sex game is so good; you'll ruin me for everyone else for the rest of my life.*' She sighs happily, and a playful grin tugs at her brown lips. 'I miss Wes.'

'It's been a week,' I tell her dryly. 'And you're seeing him tonight.'

Wes is a DJ and has been on tour with an artist around the country for the last week. As much as I like him, it's been nice not having to hear Sasha's bed-frame rhythmically rocking against our shared wall every other night.

Don't get me wrong. Wes is a great guy and I'm happy that Sasha's found someone who can apparently pinpoint every single one of her many pleasure points in ninety seconds or less, but all it does is remind me that I've never had someone who knows and loves my body like that.

It's not like I've never had an orgasm before. My very well-loved vibrator can always be counted on to get me where I need to go, but it always feels flat. Like I'm on the edge of something amazing but can't quite reach it.

'It's been a long week,' Sasha giggles. 'Shirley has been working overtime.'

Shirley being the vibrator I bought *her* as a joke last year when Wes was overseas for two months.

'But back to you and Mission: Get Eliott Laid.'

'Getting laid isn't the problem,' I say, and God, do I wish it was. If that's all it took, I wouldn't be in this position right now – desperately trying to find someone to, as Sasha so helpfully put it, *ruin me for everyone else*. The trouble isn't finding a willing partner to come back with me.

I'm starting to think that I'm broken, and that's just not the kind of thing *positive vibes* can fix. At this point, I need a divine intervention.

'You're right,' Sasha says, nodding seriously. 'I'm changing the name to Mission: Big O.' She gives me a mock salute and some more of her Prosecco spills onto my sheets. A jolt of irritation pulses through me, but I shove it away. 'I'll be the best wing woman you've ever had.'

Truth be told, Sasha's the *only* wing woman I've ever had. We met at university nearly ten years ago now – two lone black girls in the middle of England desperately trying to find a shop that sold products that worked with our hair types – and we've been pretty much inseparable ever since. When I worked up the courage, about four years into our friendship, to tell her that I'd never had an orgasm with a partner before, Sasha didn't laugh at me or judge me or run and whisper behind my back like I'd feared. She immediately jumped into '*well, let's fix that*' mode and she's been stuck like that ever since.

I think the day I do finally have an orgasm, Sasha might be happier than me.

My phone buzzes, and I glance at it. In the space of about five seconds, my screen lights up with a quick stream of notifications.

LEANNE

ELIOTT!!!!!

PLEASE HELP

EMERGENCY. 999.

ELZZZZZZZZZ

ELIOTT

What? What's happened? Are you okay?
Where are you?

No response.

Oh God.

I feel my Prosecco start to climb back up my throat and my mind starts swimming with worst-case scenarios. My baby sister, injured in a ditch somewhere, alone and afraid.

ELIOTT

Leanne????

Please answer.

LEANNE

soz, jen just sent me a snap and
I had to reply

So not dying in a ditch then. Great.

> **ELIOTT**
> Jesus fucking christ, Leanne. I was worried about you.
>
> You said it was an emergency.
>
> **LEANNE**
> it IS an emergency
>
> can u send me £50 plssssss
>
> promise i'll pay u back
>
> as soon as my student loan drops

A paragraph of about one hundred praying emojis comes through next and I resist the urge to hurl my phone at the wall. Leanne is seventeen and enjoying her last summer before she starts her degree in September. It seems like barely two days can pass without her hitting me up for money, a ride, or some other kind of favour.

> **ELIOTT**
> Ask Mum.
>
> **LEANNE**
> she said to ask u

ELIOTT

Of course she did.

What do you need it for?

LEANNE

travel. i don't have enough in my account to get to work until i get paid next week

can u spare the lecture this once and just let me borrow it???

i PROMISE i'll pay u back

pinky swear

She won't, of course. She never does and I doubt she ever will.

ELIOTT

This is the last time.

And we need to have a serious talk about your money management.

LEANNE

THANK YOU!!!!

lifesaver

> love youuuuuuuuuuuu xoxo

ELIOTT
> Love you too.

I hit send on the bank transfer and then finish the rest of my Prosecco in one gulp, wincing as the alcohol leaves a fiery trail down my throat.

'You good?' Sasha asks, shooting me a sideways look.

'Great.' I try to shake off the sudden wave of irritation I'm feeling, but it lingers. 'You ready to go?'

We're heading to an event hosted by the artist Wes has been DJ-ing for all week. He'll be behind the decks tonight, which means we're guaranteed a good time.

Sasha finishes off her glass and then stands up. Just like me, she's also dressed to impress in a hot pink mini-dress, her long black hair falling in waves to the middle of her back – but Wes is the only man on her mind.

Irritation makes way for a pang of jealously, but I quickly brush it away.

Orgasm first. Then we'll work on the whole loving life partner thing.

Sasha turns to me and grins. 'Mission: Big O has officially started.'

★ ★ ★

As soon as we step through the doors, we're met with chill R&B, the faint smell of smoke mingling in the air, and a crowd that's just the right kind of tipsy.

Sasha immediately spots Wes behind the DJ deck and drags us through the crowd to meet him. I don't mind. It gives me a chance to scope out what I'm working with tonight.

A beautiful girl with braids that fall all the way down to her knees winks at me as we squeeze past her, and my heart does a little flutter. I make a mental note to find her again on the dance floor at some point tonight, along with the tall, broad-shouldered man with the striking green eyes that follow me as we cut across the room.

'He's definitely into you,' Sasha murmurs, her quick gaze darting to Green Eyes for a half a second before it finds me again. 'And did you see the guy giving you the once-over when we walked in?'

I shake my head and resist the urge to glance over my shoulder to see if I can spot anyone else looking at me.

'Well, he was nice. Oh, and there was a guy with locs checking you out. He was hot.'

'You talking about me?'

I can practically see all thoughts of being my wing woman fly out of Sasha's mind as Wes leans over the DJ deck and grins down at her. She doesn't hesitate before diving across the decks and pulling him into a long kiss.

'He was hot, for *Eliott*,' Sasha clarifies as they pull apart. They're both wearing identical goofy grins and Wes doesn't seem to mind at all that Sasha's left a lipstick stain on his cheek.

Wes grins over at me, and I match his smile. Over the last three years we've become friends in our own right, and there's no one I'd trust with my best friend's heart more than him.

'Got your eye on anyone?'

I'm pretty sure Sasha hasn't told him the extent of my bedroom troubles, but Wes has never once judged me for cycling through partners and has even offered to set me up with a friend of his once or twice. I've always declined, too afraid that my inability to orgasm might start to get round our small circle of friends, but I've always appreciated the offer and lack of judgement.

Sasha and I point out the few people we've spotted so far, and Wes wishes me luck and kisses Sasha again before he has to return to the decks.

'All right. Game plan,' Sasha says as we move through the crowd again and head to the bar. 'We'll get some drinks and then start working the room. Give us an hour, and you'll be dragging someone out of those doors and into your bed. How's that sound?'

It *sounds* great, and in theory, it should be.

In practice? Not so much.

Turns out, the girl with the long braids is in a relationship and they're looking for a third. Her partner is as just as attractive as she is, but the one threesome I had a year or two ago didn't do anything for me and it's not an experience I'm particularly eager to revisit anytime soon.

Green Eyes is inexplicably already far too drunk by the time we reach him, despite the event only starting an hour or so ago. The other guy Sasha spotted checking me out seems promising at first, but he keeps calling me *Ellie* – a nickname I've always loathed – even after I ask him to stop, and any thoughts of heading home with him dry up relatively fast.

We can't find the guy with locs she spotted when we first came in, but we do see a few mutual friends about two hours in and agree to momentarily drop the plan for a while to just enjoy the night and dance with them.

It's fun for a while, but then Wes takes the music into an upbeat dancehall segment and the dance floor is suddenly filled with sweaty bodies gyrating against each other. I don't mind dancehall, but I'm more of a reggae girl myself. Sasha, however, *loves* dancehall. She's standing directly in front of the decks, putting on a show for Wes like they're all alone and not in a packed warehouse somewhere in East London.

I consider asking her to come with me, but she looks like she's having a good time (and Wes is definitely enjoying the show), so I leave her to it and step outside to get some air.

The small outdoor space is mostly empty aside from a few smokers in the corner and a tall guy leaning against the nearest wall. He's standing directly below a light, and the warm amber glow illuminates him against the night sky.

And fuck *me*. He's hot.

Warm brown skin, a defined jaw covered in just a little more than stubble, thick brows, full lips, and chin-length locs pulled into a messy bun with a few strands falling in front of his face.

I wonder if he's the guy Sasha caught checking me out earlier. I hope so.

He pays me no attention, his undivided gaze on the phone in his hands, as I inch further into the space. He's wearing a shirt with the first few buttons popped open and I get a glorious glimpse of a well-defined chest.

Sasha's not here, but Mission: Big O is officially back in action.

I casually lean against the wall, leaving enough space between us that it's not awkward, but also not so much that he can't ignore my presence. His thumbs stall against his phone, and I feel a little thrill shoot through me as his gaze slides in my direction.

I pretend to look through my purse, giving him a moment to unabashedly look me up and down. He must like what he sees, because he stuffs his phone into his pocket and clears his throat.

I glance up at him and raise a brow, like I'm not sure why he's bothering me.

He grins and, *wow*. It's a very nice smile. Slightly lopsided, but warm and friendly. The kind of smile that makes you want to smile right back. I don't, though. I keep my expression a careful balance between wary and intrigued, not wanting to play my cards too early.

His grin only widens as he shifts slightly to face me. 'You know . . . I was hoping to bump into you.'

I bite the inside of my cheek to stop a pleased smirk from spreading across my face. He *was* the guy Sasha saw. 'Do we know each other?' I ask, cocking my head to the side.

'Not yet.' He takes a bold step towards me, closing the tactical gap I'd left between us. 'But we can fix that pretty quickly.'

He's hot, and he's smooth. I give him two *ticks* on my mental checklist.

'I'm Dane.' He sticks out a hand.

I pretend to hesitate for a second and then reach out and grab it. 'Eliott.' I linger for a beat too long, letting my fingers trail slowly along his palm as I pull back. 'It's nice to meet you.'

'Likewise.' His grin widens even more, showing off a dimple on his left cheek. 'You're not into dancing?' He nods over his shoulder, back to the still heaving dance floor. Sasha's nowhere in sight and, since she hasn't messaged me, I can only assume that means she's gone behind the DJ deck with Wes.

I shrug. 'Just waiting for the right song.'

He shoots me a curious look. 'And what song would that be?'

'Something a little slower than this. What about you?' I ask. 'How come you're out here all alone?'

'I was actually just about to head out. I only came as a favour to a friend – he's the promoter for tonight – but I'm not a big dancer, so this isn't really my scene.' He looks me up and down again, and then his grin morphs into a small smirk. 'Glad I stayed, though.'

'Oh, really?' I ask, feigning confusion. 'Why's that?'

He chuckles, like he can absolutely see right through me, but is more than happy to play along. Another *tick*. 'Just met a gorgeous girl, and I'd like to see where things go.'

I pretend to giggle and duck my head to disguise my eye-roll.

Dane speaks with the well-practised charm of someone who has said that exact same line about a hundred times before. There's no hesitation in anything he says. No fear of backlash or rejection. It's like he's got it down to a science and he knows exactly what he needs to say and when to have me fawning over him.

He's got *player* written all over him. Not exactly my usual type personality-wise, but his confident gaze sends a shiver down my spine.

The music blaring inside morphs into something slower. I don't recognise the song, but I catch Dane's eye and give him my own well-practised, sultry smile. Dane isn't the only one who knows what he's doing. 'Come on. I love this song.'

He doesn't protest, just threads his fingers through mine and lets me drag him back onto the dance floor. I quite like that. How he's happy to defer to me and let me lead, although it's clear that he's usually the one in charge.

Another tick for Dane.

I pull him to a stop in the middle of the dance floor and press my back up against his chest. He's tall enough that he has to crouch slightly so I can wine my waist against his, but he doesn't complain. Instead, he brings his hands down to my waist and pulls me flush against him.

He wasn't lying when he said he wasn't much of a dancer. His movements are slightly awkward, like he can't quite catch the beat no matter how hard he tries, but he seems content with letting me guide us.

He drops his head onto my shoulder. 'Where'd you learn to move like this?'

I laugh as I roll my hips to the beat. 'It's not hard.'

He hums, his grip on my waist tightening slightly. 'Maybe you'll have to teach me. Do you do private lessons?'

I have to hand it to him; he moves very fast, and I'm not mad at it.

'Is this your game?' I ask, tilting my head slightly so we can make eye contact. 'Pretending that you can't dance and asking for *private lessons* back at some girl's place?'

'I'm not pretending.' He grins, and there's that dimple again. 'But let's just say it is my game. Is it working?'

The song switches and I pull away for a brief moment, only to spin around so I'm facing him. I loop my arms around his neck and he resettles his around my waist.

'Maybe,' I lie. Because it definitely is working. All I need is the Sasha Seal of Approval, and then Dane is coming home with me. 'Tell me more about you.'

'Dane. Twenty-nine. Business owner. Allergic to bananas. Terrible dancer. Great at . . .' He wiggles his brows. '. . . *Other things*.'

I snort and roll my eyes. 'Ugh. And you were doing so well. I've never met a guy who said something like that who could actually live up to the hype.'

He drops his eyes to my lips. 'You've never met me until tonight.'

Fair point.

'Your turn. Tell me more about you, *Eliott*.' He says my name slowly, like it's something to savour.

I pretend to think my answer over as I look around the room, desperate to spot Sasha and get her thoughts on him.

'I'm twenty-seven. I'm a photographer – weddings specifically. No allergies that I know of. But I really hate tomatoes.'

'Tomatoes are like, ninety per cent water,' he scoffs. 'Impossible to hate.'

'They're disgusting. Especially when they're in sandwiches.'

He laughs. 'Noted. Keep tomatoes away from you. Anything else I should know?'

I bite my lip. What about '*I've never had an orgasm and I'm hoping you're going to be the one to change that*'? No. Can't say that. It'll scare him off before we've even really got things started. Instead, I settle for looking up at him through my eyelashes and strategically biting my bottom lip. 'I live about a fifteen-minute Uber ride from here.'

Something flashes in Dane's eyes. 'Good to know.'

We dance like that for a little longer, sharing mundane pieces of information that we'll both most likely have forgotten by tomorrow morning.

I learn that he has his own construction business that he runs with a friend. His favourite colour is blue. He likes to cook and he likes watching quiz shows in his spare time. Doesn't matter the show or the format, he'll get into it somehow. I end up sharing that I'm the eldest of three children, *my* favourite colour is yellow, my favourite food is the soup my grandmother used to make me when I was sick as a child, and I have to wear socks to bed because my feet are always cold.

By the time I eventually spot Sasha sliding out from behind the DJ deck, her gaze inquisitive as she scans the crowd for me, Dane and I have been wrapped in each other's arms for at least an hour.

'I've just seen my friend,' I say, reluctantly unwinding my arms from his neck. 'I'm gonna go and let her know I'm good.'

I move to step away, but he trails his hands up my side, along my arms, and then skims a hand over my jaw.

'Dane—'

Then his lips are over mine and he's swallowing the rest of my question. As first kisses go, it's not half bad. It's great, actually. His lips are soft and surprisingly gentle and I can't help but lean into him as he brings his hand up to cup my jaw, like I'm the most precious thing in the world to him and not some girl he just met in the middle of a sweaty and too crowded dance floor.

He pulls away, hand still on my jaw, and gives me a smile that is somehow a strange mix of both shy and smug. 'Just giving you a reason to come back.'

The probability of me *not* coming back to find him was probably less than five per cent, but that kiss just sealed the deal. 'I'll be five minutes,' I promise before I drift back into the crowd.

When I get to Sasha, she's grinning from ear to ear, clearly having seen the two of us on the dance floor. 'Who's the hottie?'

I give her the rundown on everything that's happened since I first left the dance floor and by the time I'm finished, she's practically vibrating with excitement.

'I *knew* it'd be him,' she says, glancing over my shoulder to get another peek at him. 'When we walked in, I said there was a guy with locs checking you out, didn't I? It was him! You think he's got what it takes?'

'I hope so.'

Dane chooses that moment to look over in our direction. He meets Sasha's gaze and to his credit, doesn't look away. Sasha surveys him for a long moment before giving him a small nod and turning back to me.

'I like him. He's got balls.'

Anticipation shoots through me and I bite down on my lip to try to temper the eager smile I can feel on my face. 'He's got the Sasha Seal of Approval?'

'Hell yeah.' She starts gently shoving me back in Dane's direction. 'Let me know when you get back home and when he leaves.' Her grin widens, and she shoots me an overdramatic wink. '*If* he leaves. And I'm heading back to Wes's after this, so we'll only be ten minutes down the road if you need us.'

Dane quirks a brow as I approach him again. 'I'm guessing your friend gave me the okay?'

Sasha has all the subtlety of a brick to the face and I don't need to turn around to know she's still got eyes on us. 'She did.' It's my turn to raise a brow. 'Is that a problem?' Over the years, I've learned that some guys can get funny about the measures women have to take to stay safe on a night out and if he's one of them – ridiculously handsome or not – then I'm calling it quits right now.

'Nah. You do what you've got to do. And besides—' He reaches for my hand and I let him pull me into his chest. 'I'm assuming her approval can only mean good things for *us*.'

He tilts my chin up and steals another kiss, one I'm more than happy to give. It's been a while since I've been with someone like Dane. Someone who doesn't second-guess themselves and just oozes confidence the way he does. I like it.

'You said your place is only fifteen minutes away,' he murmurs against my lips when he eventually pulls back. 'Is that offer still on the table?'

I nod eagerly, probably too eagerly, but I don't care at this point. I want him. I want him so badly my entire body has begun to tingle with anticipation.

'Good.' His lips are still barely grazing my own and I feel, rather than see, his smile. 'Lead the way.'

Chapter Two

ELIOTT

Dane has my corset top over my head and scattered on the floor within seconds of my bedroom door slamming shut behind us. We stumble in the darkness until the backs of his knees hit the edge of my bed and he drops down onto it, effortlessly pulling me with him as he goes.

His lips find my neck while his hands come up to palm my tits. A shockwave of pleasure shoots through me as his thumb brushes against my nipple, and I arch into his touch.

I'm not under any delusion; there's no romance in any of this. No sweet nothings whispered in my ear, no longing glances or soft touches with hidden meanings. This is just sex.

But *still*.

I can't believe how good this feels already.

Dane works my body like he's touched it a million times before, responding to my every sigh, moan and shudder. I don't think I've ever had a partner pay such close attention to me before, and the realisation snaps me back to reality with annoying clarity.

The orgasm.

Dane is going to give me my first orgasm.

Should I tell him? I nix that idea almost as quickly as it enters my mind. That'd be too much pressure on the both of us. Besides, as long as he keeps doing what he's doing, which is currently sucking on my nipples as another hand fumbles with my pants, there's a chance I might just get there without having to say a word.

'Your ass looks great in these,' he murmurs as he dips his fingers beneath the waistband of my pants. 'But they're a pain to get off.'

I laugh and lift my hips to help him pull them down. 'Good to know they did the job.'

He hums appreciatively as the pants slide down my thighs and wastes no time at all in palming the newly revealed skin there. 'I like what's underneath a little more.'

My heart does a silly little flutter as he sinks his fingers into the soft skin around my hips and pulls me flush against him. Without the extra layer of clothing between us, it's impossible to ignore the unmistakable hardness in his own pants right now. I slide my hands between us and start fumbling with his belt. He's trailing kisses along my collarbone and I feel the way his lips curve upwards into a cocky smirk when I dip below the elastic of his boxer briefs and my breath hitches in my throat.

I curl my fingers around his dick and give him a tentative squeeze.

'*Eliott.*' He groans my name and gives me barely a second to relish in just how low and rough his voice sounds right now, before he leans back onto his haunches. It may be dark, but I can feel his intense gaze burning a pathway down my body as he takes me in.

I resist the urge to place a protective hand over my stomach. I'm not as self-conscious of my body as I used to be, but whispers of my insecurities still linger at times.

'Fuck.'

Fuck? And what exactly am I supposed to take from that? Is it a '*fuck, you're so hot*' or a '*fuck, you're not what I was expecting*'? Or a—

He dives a hand between us and, in one smooth motion, tugs my panties aside.

'How are you already so wet?' he murmurs against my lips.

I blink, jolting back to reality for a second. I hadn't realised he'd got so close again. Before I can respond, he slides a finger inside me, and then another, and then I'm riding his hand while he peppers my neck with kisses.

It feels good.

It feels *so fucking good*. Dane clearly knows what he's doing and I can feel the telltale signs of pleasure building in the very depths of my core.

This is it, I tell myself as Dane circles his thumb over my clit and my back arches off the bed. *This is it.*

My entire body thrums with anticipation.

I'm going to come.

The pleasure builds and builds and builds, like I'm climbing the tallest peak, but instead of reaching the summit, I trip and fall all the way down.

I've lost it.

My back slumps against my sheets as I realise the moment has passed me by.

Again.

Dane is blissfully unaware. His fingers are still pumping in and out of me and although I can recognise a tiny pinprick of pleasure stirring inside me, it's not enough to latch onto.

'—get a condom?'

I belatedly realise that Dane has stopped fucking me with his fingers and is back on his haunches again. He's looking at me curiously, his thick brows knitting together in the middle slightly.

'What was that?'

'I said I'll go grab a condom.' He suddenly looks uncertain, and I realise the look on his face isn't curiosity – it's concern. 'But I don't have to. Not if you're not feeling it.'

I feel myself flush beneath him, and I'm grateful that the

darkness hides how warm my face must be right now. 'I'm fine,' I say as I push up onto my elbows and give him a slow, sweet kiss.

So the foreplay didn't get me there. That's *fine*. The night isn't over yet. We've still got time.

When I pull away, he's got a dopey grin on his face.

I quirk a brow as I lean back down onto my bed. 'Condom?'

He hesitates for half a second, then nods and quickly fumbles for the jeans he discarded earlier. I'm sure he finds the condom and gets it on in record time, and the fact that he's as eager as I am to continue with this sends a burst of confidence shooting through me.

Maybe this time.

He comes to hover over me, his lean and muscular arms bracketing the side of my head as he uses his knee to nudge my legs apart and settle there. 'You sure?'

I feel a spark of pleasure alight in the pit of my stomach as the weight of his dick rests gently against me. 'I'm sure.'

He grins, his dimple making a quick reappearance, before he kisses me again. I get so lost in the kiss – the feel of his tongue against mine, the soft little groans that spill from his lips when I nibble on his bottom lip, how I can feel his heartbeat racing as he presses his chest into mine, like he can't get close enough – that the feel of him slowly sliding into me makes me gasp.

He groans as he sinks into me, and it doesn't take long for us to develop a pace that suits us both. Again, it feels good. But it doesn't go beyond that. It's not great. It's not mind-blowing or life-altering. It's just *good*. And good isn't enough for me, apparently.

I try to focus on the small knot of pleasure I can feel building within me, but it's pointless. I can't hold onto it for long enough for it to build into something worthwhile.

The realisation that I can't get there with someone like Dane – who may just be the most attractive man I've ever brought back home with me – is a depressing one.

It's also a realisation I want to deal with alone.

I need this to be over and I need Dane out of here so I can wallow in my own self-pity until Sasha comes sauntering home tomorrow afternoon and she can commiserate with me.

I squeeze my legs tightly around his waist, close my eyes, and huff out a few loud and well-practised moans. The noises come to me with ease. Too easily.

Sasha thinks that it's terrible that I fake it – '*they should know that they suck*' – but I've come to learn that it's infinitely better than the alternative. For a lot of men, there's nothing more ego-bruising than being unable to make the girl you're sleeping with come. And I've learned first-hand that when a guy's ego gets bruised, they can get mean.

Cruel, even.

I don't need that again. Not tonight.

So I dig my fingers into Dane's skin, arch my back off the bed, and moan like this is the best thing I've ever experienced. Like Dane is shattering my whole world with his well-timed strokes, and I'll never be able to get enough.

Like he's absolutely *ruined* sex for me.

I've done this move plenty of times before and it usually does the job pretty quickly, but when I peek open an eye, Dane has stopped moving and that curious-slash-concerned look is back on his face again.

'What?' I ask, frowning. 'Is everything all right?'

He blinks at me for a few seconds and then slowly – *excruciatingly* slowly – pulls out. 'Are you—' He pushes himself up, leans back and frowns. 'Are you faking it?'

Now it's my turn to blink. I don't think anyone's ever been able to tell that I've faked before. It's a terrible thing to brag about, but I've got my moaning down to an art. 'No,' I lie. 'No, of course not.'

'You were!' His expression flits from offended to amused and back again. 'Was it not good? You weren't enjoying it?'

'You were great!' My voice rises an octave and I'm not entirely sure why I'm suddenly so desperate to spare his ego. '*So* good. I wasn't faking. Come back and finish.'

He shakes his head and, to my relief, his expression seems to settle on amused. 'No, you're not feeling it.'

'I *am*.'

He exhales a deep breath. 'Then let's just say that *I'm* not feeling it anymore.'

I watch, stunned, as he pushes himself off my bed and starts reaching for his clothes.

'Dane—'

A small grin tugs at his lips. 'It's fine, Eliott. You changed your mind, no big deal.' He says it like he really means it, like he's not at all bothered by the strange turn this night has taken. 'I had fun and I hope you did, too. Up until . . .' He trails off and gestures awkwardly in my direction. 'Whatever that was.'

My blood feels like fire under my skin, and I can feel it rushing to my face. 'Yeah. I did.'

He nods, seemingly satisfied with what has to be an incredibly unsatisfying response, and then turns for the door.

'Wait.'

He glances over his shoulder, a brow raised in question. I fidget with the blanket pooled around me. I should tell him that this has nothing to do with him – that this is definitely a *me* thing – but the words won't come. Instead, I give him a sad little smile and he returns it with one of his own.

'Maybe I'll see you around, Eliott.'

'Yeah,' I say as he steps out of my bedroom and lets the door swing shut behind him. 'Maybe.'

Chapter Three

ELIOTT

TWO YEARS LATER

The bride-to-be accosts me as soon as I walk through the door. She's wearing a short, feathery white dress and even the six-inch heels she's wearing can't stop her from launching herself across the space between us and into my arms.

'Eliott!' Bailey cheers my name and wraps her arms around me in a tight hug like we're lifelong friends and she didn't just find me on Instagram a week ago. 'I'm so glad you could make it. You're a lifesaver, you know that?'

'I don't know about lifesaver.' I force a laugh as she unravels herself from me and takes a step back. 'But I'll do what I can.'

Her fiancé – Caspian, if I'm remembering the details of the frantic messages Bailey sent me correctly – comes up behind her and rests a gentle hand on her waist. Her smile softens into something sweeter, something just for him, and she melts into his touch.

I bring my camera up to my face and snap a quick candid shot of the two of them. They don't even notice. That's how lost they are in each other's gaze. It's cute – *nauseatingly* cute – but I'm used to it. Between being a wedding photographer and living with Sasha and Wes, navigating loved-up couples has quickly become my new normal.

I barely even feel the slight pang of longing in my chest as I watch Caspian tilt his head and whisper something in Bailey's ear that makes her giggle.

Barely.

I turn away from them, feeling like I'm intruding on something private, and glance around the room. They've hired out this restaurant to celebrate their recent engagement and the large space is already starting to fill with friends and family.

I always enjoy engagement party jobs. They practically guarantee the couple will book me for their big day, and it's a slightly more relaxed way of getting to know them, understanding how they operate, and seeing how comfortable they are in front of the camera. If any red flags pop up tonight, we've got the chance to iron them out before the big day.

'Thanks so much for fitting us in,' Bailey says, pulling my attention back to the happy couple. 'I know it was late notice, but our first photographer bailed on us.'

'We thought it was a sign that maybe we shouldn't bother with one for tonight,' Caspian says.

'But then we saw your portfolio online and fell in love!' Bailey finishes with a bright grin.

Pride blooms in me, and I bite back a pleased smile. I'd known that Bailey was a fan of my work, given the fact that she liked and reshared almost my entire feed within a span of five minutes one evening, but *still*. I've put a lot of effort into working on my craft over the years, and it always feels good to hear that recognised. 'Have you guys settled on a date for the big day yet?'

They exchange a look and both break out into identical, slightly weary grins. I get the distinct impression that I'm watching a silent conversation play out in front of me. It's the kind of thing Sasha and Wes do all the time. Like one of the side-effects of being so ridiculously in love with someone is developing the power of mind-reading.

Annoying, but also cute. So goddamn cute.

'We're still working on a few things,' Caspian says.

'But don't worry,' Bailey says. 'As soon as we've got it all sorted, we'll be able to confirm a date and get you booked in.'

'Sure,' I say with an easy shrug. I've got no doubt in my mind that I'll take on Bailey and Caspian as a couple. They're friendly, easy-going and open in a way that a lot of couples aren't — and it definitely helps that they're paying double my fee tonight thanks to the late notice. 'I tend to book out pretty quickly, but if you let me know as soon as you have rough dates in mind, I can block out some time in my schedule for you.'

Bailey's smile widens. 'Like I said, Eliott. You're a lifesaver.'

We've gone over the specifics in our messages already, but Bailey and Cash — as I quickly learn he prefers to go by — give me a brief rundown of what they'd like me to do for the night.

'We don't want too many staged photos,' Bailey explains. 'We'll save that for the wedding. Tonight we just want candid photos of the night. Just shots that really capture the atmosphere and the energy.'

'We should probably make sure to get some with Amber and Finn,' Cash cuts in.

'Right. Amber's my best friend and my maid of honour.' A sad look crosses over Bailey's face for a brief second before her smile is back. 'But she's moving abroad soon, so she won't be here in person for most of the wedding planning. It'd be nice if we could get a few photos of us together tonight. For the memories, you know?'

'Should we get Dane in as well?' Cash asks.

The name sparks something in me. A memory I've desperately been shoving to the side for the last two years. I push it right back to the recesses of my mind where it belongs.

Besides, Dane is a perfectly common name.

One More Shot

I think.

'He's my best man,' Cash says, thankfully interpreting the look on my face as one of confusion and not of sudden panic.

'And my brother,' Bailey says cheerfully. 'You're right. Let's make sure to get a couple shots of the five of us together.'

'Just point them out to me and I'll wrangle everyone together at some point to get the shot.' Along with the staged photos, I make a mental note to get as many candid photos of Bailey and Amber as I can throughout the night. If Sasha were moving abroad right before my wedding, I know I'd want as many photos as possible.

'Amber's not here yet,' Bailey says. 'But I'll let you know when they get here. And Dane . . .' She trails off, her brows furrowing slightly as she peers around the room.

'He's definitely here,' Cash says as he surveys the room himself. 'I saw him about ten minutes ago.'

A few more guests spill through the doors of the entrance and immediately make a beeline for Bailey and Cash. Bailey shoots me an apologetic grin, and I wave them both off.

'Don't worry about it. Once you spot him, point him out to me. Amber too.'

Cash's reminder to grab myself a plate to eat later is quickly swallowed up by a squeal of congratulations from their new guests as the happy couple is pulled into a small crowd of cheers and laughter. I get a shot of them, capturing the moment Bailey and Cash are crushed into a five-person hug, and then slink away ready to start doing what I do best.

There's a long table in the middle of the room that's rapidly filling with laughing guests. I take my time circling the room, snapping photos of them all, my SD card rapidly filling with casual candid moments of Bailey and Cash's friends and family celebrating their love.

I lean against a nearby wall and get a photo of Cash and a woman I'm fairly certain has to be his mother on the impromptu dance floor. The look on her face is one of pure adoration as she cups her son's cheeks and says something to him that makes his whole face light up. I watch as his eyes dart over to Bailey across the room before coming back to settle on his mother. He gives her a little nod, and she beams up at him.

This is my favourite part of the job. Getting the candid and unfiltered moments, the quiet moments when people think nobody is watching, and capturing them for a lifetime. They might not remember this conversation ten years down the line, but every time Cash looks at this photo, he'll see the look of love and pride on his mother's face in this moment.

I glance around the rest of the room. Aside from a small cluster of Bailey and a group of friends, most people are settled around the table digging into their plates, and it feels like we've reached a natural lull in the night.

One More Shot

I let my camera swing around my neck and head towards the buffet table, fully intending to take advantage of Cash's reminder to eat before my services are needed again. I'm stopped briefly by a group of screaming children as they sprint across the room, all of them moving in unison like some kind of hyperactive caterpillar.

'Quickly!' the apparent leader of the pack squawks. 'He's gonna get us!'

The other children scream even louder and I bring my camera up just in time to capture the moment a tall man jumps out from behind a corner and scoops the last child up into his arms. The child cackles – somehow both delighted and outraged at having been caught – and my thumb freezes over the shutter button as my heart climbs into my throat.

His hair's a little longer, his beard a little thicker, but he's just as handsome, just as striking, as he was two years ago.

Dane.

'All right, all right,' he drawls as he sets the child back down onto the floor. 'I won.'

'Nuh-*uh*.' The group of kids swarm around him, their faces red, sweaty and grinning. The leader sticks out a hand and points at the recently captured child. 'You only caught one of us.'

Dane heaves an overdramatic sigh. '*Fine*. I'll give you guys a thirty-second head start.'

They all scream again and rush to dart away – even the

one who was just caught, which seems against the rules. But Dane just grins as he watches them sprint off into another dark corner of the restaurant.

'*Dane,*' a reproachful voice calls. An older woman brushes past him and gives him a disapproving look. 'Don't get the little ones so riled up, especially this late at night.'

Dane's grin doesn't waver, like he's completely unbothered by the light scolding he's just received. 'Hey, Aunt Jay.'

His aunt titters but still leans in to give him a kiss on the cheek. He's so tall she just about reaches his shoulders even when he bends over to meet her, and she ends up settling for leaving a red lipstick stain on the collar of his white shirt. 'I mean it, Dane. If Callum's still bouncing off the walls by the time we leave, you're going to have to deal with him.'

He laughs at the threat. I'm starting to realise that he seems to exist in a permanent state of being unaffected by anything. A spark of envy shoots through me, and it's so sharp it's actually startling.

The kids choose that exact moment to run screaming by me again and I watch, in a kind of horrified slow motion, as Dane looks over in my direction.

For a second, I entertain the idea that maybe he won't notice me. That maybe God will do me this one solid and let Dane's gaze slide right over me.

No such luck.

His deep brown eyes settle on me as his brows pinch together in the middle. A hint of recognition flashes across his face, and I know he's combing through his memories, trying to figure out where he remembers me from.

My mind races and only one thought sticks out.

Run.

I turn around quickly and dash for the furthest end of the room, as far away from him as I can manage.

He only got a brief glimpse, I try to reason with myself as I slip into the shadows. *Maybe it won't be enough.*

Maybe he won't remember me at all.

Despite everything, I snort as that thought pops into the forefront of my mind. Given the circumstances, I think I'd be hard to forget.

But that's fine.

There's only an hour or so left to go. I'll just avoid him for the rest of the night and – *Ah.*

He's the best man.

He's the *fucking best man*.

As in, practically impossible to avoid. As in, I've promised to corral them all together at some point to take a photo. As in – *Shit.*

The prospect of being face to face with him again quite literally makes me want to heave. There's only so much embarrassment I can take in one lifetime, and I thought I'd already had my fair share of it two years ago.

My stomach twists and my mind races, playing out for me exactly what's going to happen.

Realisation will dawn on his face as he remembers. His grin will turn sly and mocking as he remembers just who I am. Heat rushes to my face as I realise there's a chance he's already told Cash all about me. He is the best man, after all, so they've got to be close. And Bailey is his *sister*. How close are they? I'd never talk to my brother about my sex life – though I suppose I don't really talk to Josh about anything – but Leanne could probably pry it out of me after a drink or two if she tried.

What if they all already know? What if they've all sat around and laughed about the weird almost one-night stand he had and the girl who couldn't come?

Who *still* can't come.

Bitterness courses through my veins. I may have given up on the whole '*have an orgasm with a partner*' thing – much to Sasha's displeasure – and settled for a life of mediocre, vibrator-induced orgasms, but it doesn't mean I have to be happy about it.

Once I'm sure I'm far enough away, I glance back over at him. My shoulders sag in relief as I realise he's no longer got an eye on me. Instead, he's standing in a small group by the entrance to the restaurant. Bailey's got an arm draped around the shoulders of a woman with warm brown skin and short cropped hair. They've both got megawatt grins stretching across their faces and I know, without a shadow of a doubt, that this must be Amber. There's also a tall blond man standing beside Amber. They're not touching, but his body is angled towards hers in the same kind of way Cash is standing beside Bailey. Like there's a magnetic pull keeping them rooted in place, and there's nowhere else they'd rather be than in Amber and Bailey's orbit.

Bailey flicks Dane's collar, and he responds with something that makes Cash laugh.

I bring my camera up to my face, intent on capturing the moment, but then Dane suddenly looks over in my direction. Through the viewfinder, I watch as his gaze zeroes in on me, and those thick brows furrow again. He steps out of the little circle the five of them have made and I take a reflexive step backwards.

The intent is clear on his face. He's on his way to talk to me.

Panic floods every single one of my senses but I'm saved, momentarily at least, by Cash, who suddenly drapes an arm around Dane's shoulder and drags him towards another group of friends nearby.

I bite my lip, genuinely considering telling Bailey and Cash that an emergency has come up and I need to leave. But then I spot them again, effortlessly finding each other in the crowd of loved ones surrounding them, and my heart softens just a tiny bit. I can't bail on them.

Not now anyway.

Because they're going to be disappointed enough when I tell them I can't photograph their wedding.

I spend the best part of the next hour clinging to the shadows and sticking to the dark corners of the restaurant. It's all very dramatic, but it works. For the most part. I have one near miss when Bailey flags me down to get an impromptu photo of her parents and Cash's mother seated together. As I'm lining up the shot, I can see Dane in my periphery perking up slightly as he glances over at me. I manage to get the photo before he has the chance to cross the room, helped in part by the screeching group of children who try to tackle him to the ground whenever they spy the right opportunity.

I say a silent thank you to the horde of screaming children. They make it very easy to keep an eye on where Dane is at all times, making sure I can avoid him with relative ease. I can't tell if he minds having his own personal alarm system following him around, but it's easy to see that he's clearly the favourite cousin amongst the little ones, and he seems to slip into the role without any complaint.

The end of the night is rapidly approaching and I suppose what happens next is my fault for letting my guard down. I take the opportunity to dip into the bathroom while there's nothing particularly exciting going on and, when I emerge, I'm immediately prevented from darting back into the shadows by a form blocking my path.

One More Shot

It's in that moment that I decide I truly must be the most unlucky woman in the world. Because I'm *so* close to the finish line and this just isn't fair.

My breath catches in my throat. My heartbeat becomes a glacial patter. And Dane – *fucking Dane* – looks down at me and grins.

'I was hoping to bump into you.'

Chapter Four

DANE

For one horrible moment, I wonder if I've made a mistake and just accosted some poor woman as she leaves the bathroom. Because I don't see any kind of recognition towards me flare up in her eyes. Only wariness.

In hindsight, I probably could've handled this in a much less creepy way. One that doesn't scream '*I've been watching you all night*'. But here we are. Can't be undone.

I shoot her what I *hope* is an easy smile and take a step backwards, surveying her properly. It's been about two years, but I'm pretty sure it's her. Her hair is longer, her hips are fuller, her skin is slightly flushed and her plump lips are twisted into a frown. But you don't forget a face like that.

She still looks just as gorgeous as she did that night.

'Eliott, right?' I ask.

Her eyes narrow slightly and I can only describe the

expression that rolls across her face as one of pure irritation. 'Do I know you?'

She practically spits the words out and her voice is sharp and curt, completely void of the warmth and laughter I remember from our almost night together two years ago. Not what I'd been expecting, but fair – maybe she doesn't recognise me yet.

'Dane,' I tell her before waiting a beat to see if I get even a flicker of recognition in her eyes. Nothing. 'We met two years ago at an event. I think your friend was DJ-ing it.'

'Doesn't ring a bell,' she says quickly. Too quickly.

'I'm sure it was you.'

She shrugs. 'I guess I just have one of those faces.'

'It's a gorgeous face.'

Eliott blinks. Her mouth starts to fall open in what I *think* is surprise, before she catches herself and rolls her eyes. 'Smooth.'

I flash her a grin. 'Pretty sure that's what you liked about me last time around.'

She looks me up and down slowly, and when she meets my gaze again, there's a shadow of the girl I met two years ago. Her caramel eyes hold mine and her lips twitch into an almost smile. 'Pretty sure it wasn't just that.'

My grin widens and her face drops as she realises the implication of what she just said. 'So you *do* remember me.'

Regret spasms across her face and she scowls at me. 'Yes.

Fine. You win. I remember you.' She says it through almost gritted teeth, like it pains her to get the words out. 'Honestly? I remember you were a lot better at a taking a hint two years ago.'

I frown, not entirely sure why she sounds so annoyed. But I don't get the chance to find out. Cash and Bailey are cha-cha-sliding their way towards us from the dance floor. She's trying to make it look casual, but I can see the look of warning in my sister's eyes as she spots Eliott standing in front of me.

Again, very much regretting doing this right in front of the toilets.

I catch Cash's eye as they approach, but he just gives me a sympathetic little shrug. I return it with a glare. If I'd have known that setting up my best friend and my sister was going to lead to this kind of betrayal on the regular, I never would've done it.

Probably.

'Oh good, you've met Eliott,' Bailey says dryly. She gives Eliott an apologetic smile before glaring up at me. I grin right back at her, unfazed by the death stare she's currently shooting me. One day she'll realise it doesn't work on me.

'I was just saying hello.'

'*You* don't need to say hello,' Bailey says pointedly, silently reminding me of the conversation we had back at the table earlier. Not that I need reminding.

One More Shot

Eliott is off-limits.

Bailey's made herself very clear. But does off-limits count when you've already trampled right over those boundaries before?

Bailey nudges me aside with her elbow and positions herself between me and Eliott. 'Tonight isn't about you.'

I pretend to clutch at my chest, scandalised. 'I'm the best man *and* the bride's dashingly handsome older brother. If I'm not the star of this wedding, who is?'

'Me, clearly.' Amber swans in, closely followed by her boyfriend, Finn.

Amber and I aren't overly close or anything like that, but you can't help but want the best for someone when you've known them for as long as we've known each other. And Finn is definitely that when it comes to Amber. The best. He looks at her the same way Cash looks at Bailey. Like the world could be burning around them and they wouldn't notice, as long as those two were standing in front of them.

I suddenly find myself feeling very glad that my parents are currently preoccupied with Cash's mum. Ever since Bailey and Cash got together, they've been non-stop with asking when I'm going to find *The One* and settle down too. I've managed to shove most of the comments off with a laugh or a quick redirect, but I'd be lying if I didn't admit that it's getting tiring.

I'm happy for them, but there's an unspoken assumption that everyone wants what Cash and Bailey have. Or even that everyone is capable of finding it in the first place.

But not everyone is.

I know that first-hand, and I'm *fine* with it. I just wish everyone else was too. But dwelling on that during the engagement party for my best friend and sister isn't high on my list of priorities right now. I force a bright smile back onto my face and rejoin the conversation.

'Since we're all here now,' Cash is saying to Eliott, 'why don't we get that photo we were talking about earlier?'

'Sure.' Eliott gives the group a stiff nod. 'If you could all just come over here – better lighting.'

We do as she instructs and form a small cluster with Cash and Bailey in the middle. I slide over to Cash's free side and sling an arm over his shoulder. Amber does the same with Bailey, pulling my sister in so close, their cheeks are touching. Finn hangs back for a second, but Cash quickly calls him over and he joins the cluster behind Amber and deftly wraps an arm around her waist.

Eliott lifts the camera to her face, takes a few shots and then lets it drop again. 'Amber, if you could turn a little this way for me, that way Finn's shadow won't cut across your face. And Cash, can you get a little closer to Bailey and close that gap there?'

'And me?' I ask, as Cash does what she says and happily

slides even closer to his future wife. 'Any notes or am I just nailing this?'

From the way she bites her bottom lip and ducks her head, it's obvious she wants to laugh. I can't decide whether to feel pleased that apparently I can still make her laugh, or annoyed that she's desperately fighting it.

And why *is* she fighting it?

For some reason, she's acting like I'm the last person she'd ever wanted to see again. Admittedly, there are probably a handful of women who'd probably never like to see me again – those unfortunate enough to meet me when I was young and immature. But I don't think the way Eliott and I left things was bad enough to warrant that. Was it? I frown, searching through hazy memories as I try to figure out if I'm forgetting something important about our almost night together.

'You're fine,' Bailey says, saving Eliott from having to answer. 'Just stand there and look cute.'

'Don't I always?'

There's that twitch of her lips again, though this time she brings her camera back up to her face to hide it. She takes a few more shots of us and then gives us a satisfied nod.

'Got it.'

Cash and Bailey are quickly stolen by a group of our cousins coming to say goodbye, and Amber and Finn take the opportunity to glide back to the table for some more food. Finn's hand doesn't leave Amber's side as they walk, and it's impossible to ignore the way she leans into his touch.

I make the grave mistake of catching my mother's eye across the room. She nods her head pointedly in Amber and Finn's direction and then raises an unimpressed brow at me. I glance away, refusing to rise to the bait.

And anyway, Eliott and I are officially alone again. Though she doesn't look pleased about it. I exhale a quiet breath and lean against the nearest wall. She's deliberately not looking at me, instead choosing to fiddle with her camera.

I'm not an idiot and, contrary to what she said earlier, I *can* take a hint. I know when someone isn't into me. Doesn't happen often, but I'm not pig-headed enough to try to force something that isn't there.

Not anymore, anyway.

Maybe there was something between us two years ago, but whatever it was, it's definitely gone now.

'Look.' There's music and laughter all around us, but the sound of my voice makes her snap her head up sharply, like I've just shattered a silence. 'I get it. You're not interested. I can handle that.'

She opens her mouth as if to say something, but then seems to think better of it. Her lips purse slightly and she rocks back onto the balls of her feet, waiting for me to continue.

'But things don't have to be awkward between us. We're both adults. I think we can navigate being around each other without this . . .' I trail off, clicking my tongue as I try to figure out what exactly it is I'm feeling between us. 'Tension, I guess?' I'm still not sure it's the right word, but it's the closest I can get to whatever it is I'm feeling right now.

Eliott arches a brow. 'We don't need to be navigating anything at all. My professional relationship is with Bailey and Cash. There's no need for us to interact directly whatsoever.'

That gets out a low laugh out of me. 'I'm the best man, Eliott. Pretty sure I'll be on "*wrangling all the old aunts and uncles*" duty for photos on the big day.'

Her eyes widen for a second, like she's actually considering the possibility that Bailey and Cash might put me on photo duty. They wouldn't – if anything, that's an Amber job – but Eliott doesn't know that.

Then she shrugs. 'I haven't actually agreed to photograph the wedding. I might not even be available.'

'You'd pass up a job just to avoid me?' It's not funny at all, but I can't help but grin. 'Should I be flattered? I didn't know I made such a big impression on you.'

Her eyes flit downwards for half a second. 'Nothing big about it.'

I laugh, and the sound seems to startle her. 'If I'm remembering correctly, you didn't have any complaints.'

'If you were remembering correctly, you'd recall how I left *unsatisfied* with our last encounter.'

'Through no fault of my own,' I say with a shrug. Call it being cocky or overconfident or whatever, but I know what I bring to the bedroom. The problem definitely wasn't on my end.

'Maybe you're just not as good as you think you are?'

'I've never had any complaints.'

She grits her teeth. 'Consider this your first.'

I laugh again and her eyes narrow, as if the sound annoys her. 'I don't know why you're trying to pretend like we weren't having a good time together before you decided you weren't feeling it anymore—'

Something flashes across her face. For a brief moment, she looks almost pained, like I've said something that cuts to her very core. But before I can comment on it, the look is gone, replaced with one of unbridled irritation.

'Exactly. I wasn't feeling it then and I'm not feeling it now.' She grips her camera a little tighter, the tips of her fingertips going pale as she wraps them around its frame. 'Glad we could both agree on that.'

'Eliott—'

'I'm still on the clock,' she says sharply. The change in topic is so fast, it almost gives me whiplash. 'If you're done bothering me?'

She pushes past me without so much as a second glance and purposefully strides across the room, putting as much space between us as possible.

'Didn't Bailey tell you to leave Eliott alone?'

I scowl as Cash approaches me. He raises a brow as he glances at me, then over to Eliott, still rushing across the room, and then back to me again. 'What'd you do?'

'You know, you're very much Team Bailey these days,' I grumble as Cash leans up against the wall beside me. 'I'm not a fan. Tread carefully, or I might just take back my blessing.'

Cash snorts out a laugh at my pointless threat. 'Definitely too late for that.'

Given the fact that we're currently at their engagement party, I'd say he's got a point there. But still. 'Never too late. Bailey will just have to find someone else to fawn over her every day. Shouldn't be too hard.'

Cash rolls his eyes and bumps me with his elbow. 'Don't change the topic. What's going on with you and Eliott?'

'Nothing.' It comes out with more bite than I'd intended and Cash shoots me a sceptical look. I clear my throat and shrug. 'I mean, I just thought I recognised her from somewhere, but I was wrong. No big deal.'

Cash and I have been business partners for almost a decade now, and best friends for even longer. It's difficult to remember a time when Cash wasn't an integral part of my life, and he's more like a brother to me than anything else at this point. Sometimes I think he knows me better than I know myself. So it's not all that surprising when the look of scepticism on his face doesn't fade. But he doesn't say anything.

Cash is good at that. Letting you come to him in your own time once you've parsed your thoughts and figured out whatever it is you actually want to say.

I think that's probably why he waited so long to tell me he liked Bailey. Really liked her – not the crush he had when we were kids that would send him rushing from the room whenever she walked in. He was sorting through his thoughts, trying to make sure that it was something real before he broached the topic with me.

And so I know he won't force me to tell him what's on my mind right now. He'll wait, trusting that when I'm ready, I will.

I feel a familiar wave of gratitude towards him as I push myself off the wall. 'Let's talk about your stag do.' As segues go, it's not my smoothest, but Cash lets it slide. 'I've got some ideas I need to run by you. Thoughts on a long weekend of debauchery in Amsterdam? No flights,' I add quickly, knowing just how much Cash hates flying. 'We can get the train.'

'Define *debauchery*.'

I grin as we meander back into the crowd. 'That's for me to know and for you to find out. But it *will* include beer, brownies and beautiful women. The latter being for me, of course.'

Cash snorts. 'Right.'

I spot Eliott snapping a photo of Bailey and a group of her friends as we cut through the crowd. From across the room, her eyes catch mine and I offer her a small smile. She stares at me for a few seconds, her face pinching into an expression I can't quite place, before she turns away – smile, unreturned.

Chapter Five

ELIOTT

Sasha doubles over, tears forming in the creases of her eyes as a loud cackle wracks through her. 'You did *what?*'

I groan into the sofa cushion. 'I pretended like I didn't recognise him.'

Even Wes – calm, stoic, typically unflappable Wes – is in hysterics. 'You didn't.'

Another groan. This is truly a new low. 'I did.'

'Why?' Sasha chokes out as she pulls herself back upright onto the sofa. 'What could have possibly possessed you?'

And that's the million pound question, isn't it? What the *hell* possessed me? Because believe it or not, pretending like I didn't recognise Dane wasn't part of the plan. Plan A was to cling to the shadows like some kind of deranged comic book villain and avoid him like the plague and, if that well-thought-out plan didn't work? Plan B was to act like a normal, well-adjusted human being and simply tell him I wasn't interested in talking.

Instead, the second I whirled around to find Dane looming over me, it was like my brain short-circuited. All capability of rational thought vanished as I took in that lopsided smile and did, quite possibly, the dumbest thing I've ever done. I regretted it almost as soon as the words came out of my mouth, and an all-consuming blend of guilt and shame weighed me down the entire drive home from the restaurant. Pretending like I didn't recognise him was one thing, but doubling down and acting like *he* was the problem two years ago?

I groan again into the cushion. 'I don't know.'

Wes gives me a sympathetic pat on the thigh. Sasha dissolves into another fit of cackles. There's a nondescript terrible SyFy movie playing on mute on the TV in front of us, a bowl of popcorn on the coffee table – with copious amounts spilled on the carpet beneath it – alongside an empty, greasy pizza box, and a thick, fluffy blanket awkwardly wrapped around Wes's legs. I've interrupted a movie night, but neither of them seems to mind.

'Well, at least you'll never have to see him again,' Sasha says, once she's finally managed to compose herself. She gives me a sideways look and wiggles her brows. 'Unless—'

'No,' I say sharply. 'I'm not going to accept their wedding request. Absolutely not.'

'But you said they were nice,' Wes says. He's frowning at me and I avoid his judgement by reaching for the popcorn and stuffing a handful into my mouth. 'Kind of shitty to leave them hanging now.'

'I'm not leaving them hanging. I'm sure they'll have plenty of time to find another photographer they like.' Saying it out loud does absolutely nothing to assuage the wave of guilt that hits me. 'They haven't even sent me their date yet. It's not unreasonable that I might already be booked.'

Sasha and Wes exchange a look. It's exactly the kind of look Bailey and Cash gave each other when I asked about the wedding. The kind of look that implies there's some sort of silent conversation going on between the two of them. A silent conversation about *me*.

I should be used to this.

I'm not exactly sure when it happened, but at some point over the last nine months, Wes has gone from simply being my best friend's boyfriend who spends an inordinate amount of time at our house to, essentially, a third housemate. Neither of them have mentioned it officially and sometimes I wonder if they think I haven't noticed how Wes has a shelf in our bathroom cupboard, or that his laundry lines the rack as often as mine, or how – aside from when he has an out-of-town gig – he spends every single night here.

I don't usually mind. I like Wes. I *love* Wes. He's perfect for Sasha – the soothing calm to her endless dramatics – and ends up being a helpful tiebreaker whenever we have a disagreement about what to order for dinner or whose turn it is to take the bins out, even if he does nearly always side with Sasha. Fundamentally, I like having him here. I just would've preferred that they'd asked me about it before just going ahead and moving him in without a word.

But right now, sat squashed between them with the remains of their interrupted movie night spread out in front of us, while they engage in a silent conversation about me, I can't help but feel like a third wheel.

I stand up abruptly, sending another wave of popcorn rolling to the floor. 'I'm not doing the wedding.'

Sasha blinks innocently up at me. 'We didn't say you should.'

'But you should,' Wes adds.

A rare spark of irritation towards the pair of them begins to simmer inside me. 'You wouldn't understand.'

Because how could they? What they have might not have been love at first sight, but it was definitely close. By their second date it was clear that Sasha was head over heels for him, and Wes has done nothing over the last four years to suggest that she was wrong. They just fit together. Like two perfect puzzle pieces who were always meant to find each other.

And me? I'm broken. There's something wrong with me and the last thing I need to do is spend any amount of time with my biggest reminder of that fact.

So, yeah. Maybe it is a shitty thing to do. Maybe I *am*

going to leave Bailey and Cash hanging. But I don't owe them anything. Not really.

Guilt twists my stomach into painful knots.

I can keep telling myself that, but it's clear I don't even believe it myself.

Chapter Six

DANE

'What do you think about orchids?'

'I don't think about orchids.'

From across the counter, Bailey shoots me a withering glare. Her hair is wrapped in a colourful scarf, she's wearing one of Cash's old Great Dane Construction Services T-shirts, and there's a fresh mug of steaming tea by her side. It's still early and, if I had to guess, I'd say she's been up for less than thirty minutes. Which makes the look on her face – a death stare aimed in my direction – definitely something to worry about.

I reach across the counter and ignore her huff of complaint as I tug her laptop towards me. There are about fifty different windows open and they're all wedding-related in some way. Dresses, invitations, decorations, venues, suits, bands and more all fill the screen. The biggest window open is filled with a seemingly endless stream of colourful bouquets, and her orchid question suddenly makes sense.

I raise a brow at my sister. 'Didn't you get engaged all of two minutes ago? Why're you so stressed already?'

'I'm not stressed,' she murmurs. Her phone vibrates by her side and she immediately reaches to snatch it up. She holds her breath as she scans whatever it is that's come up on the screen and, after a few seconds, she deflates slightly. Her shoulders slump and she lets her phone fall back onto the counter with a bang.

'Hey.' Cash is still in the shower – I can hear his slightly muffled voice singing along to what sounds like a medley of 80s hits – which means I can't rely on him to explain whatever it is that's going on with Bailey right now. 'What's happening here?'

Bailey looks at me for several long seconds and then shakes her head and sighs. 'We're not supposed to tell anyone yet. You know, in case it all falls through.'

'I *don't* know, actually.'

Her eyes narrow a fraction. 'After I posted the engagement photos, a really big bridal magazine got in touch. They want to feature and potentially sponsor the wedding.'

'Oh.' I frown. 'That's a good thing, isn't it?'

Bailey's an influencer and even if I still don't understand exactly what it is she does every day, I know she's good at it. Her follower count is close to a mind-boggling million and rising every day and, as far as I can tell, there seems to be a never-ending stream of brands flooding her inbox every day desperate to work with her. Bridal magazines included too now, apparently.

'It's *great*,' she says, her tone a little too forced. 'It's great exposure and it'll introduce me to an entirely new audience. And then there's all the money we'll save. It's just — and I don't want to sound ungrateful or anything — but I just didn't think wedding planning would involve sending a list of potential flowers to a random editor I've never even met so they can approve them.' Her nose wrinkles as she finishes her explanation, and I have to agree.

'Doesn't sound very romantic.'

She huffs out a dry laugh. 'It's not. Can you imagine sending someone a photo of your dream dress and them emailing back with a note that just says, "*I think we can do better*"?'

'I still think you should get the dress.' Cash's voice comes floating from down the hallway and he emerges into the kitchen a few seconds later. He claps my shoulder as he passes me, then walks over to Bailey and gives her a kiss on the cheek.

'You haven't even seen it,' Bailey murmurs, instinctively leaning into his touch. 'What if it's actually hideous, and the editor was right?'

'You chose it and you like it,' Cash says with a shrug. 'You'll look beautiful in whatever you wear, but I'd rather it be something I know you're happy with.' He pulls away from her and makes his way to the kettle. 'Get the dress, love.'

I swear, the smile on Bailey's face right now could light up a small town.

'I don't get it,' I say, interrupting their latest bout of staring lovingly into each other's eyes. 'Why does the editor even need to approve anything? The magazine approached *you*, right?'

Bailey nods. 'They did, but they still need to make sure the wedding fits their brand and is something their audience will connect with. Technically, we do have the final say when it comes to the big decisions, but we risk losing the feature if we do something they really don't like. I even had to send them Eliott's portfolio and all the engagement party photos so they could check they liked her style of photography.'

I tense slightly at the mention of Eliott's name. Out of the corner of my eye, I notice Cash's thoughtful gaze slide over to me for a brief second before he resumes pouring his tea.

'Did she agree to it, then?' I ask casually. 'Photographing the wedding, I mean.'

'Not yet,' Bailey says. 'We're just waiting on the venue to confirm our dates, and then I can book Eliott in.'

'And what if she says no?'

Bailey looks at me like I've just suggested she shave off all her hair. 'Don't even put that out into the universe, Dane.'

I shrug, trying to keep my expression and gestures as light as possible. But it's hard because suddenly Eliott's voice is ringing in my ear.

'I haven't actually agreed to photograph the wedding. I might not even be available.'

I'd laughed it off back at the engagement party, assuming she was just posturing for my benefit. But now I'm not so sure.

'Eliott's actually the only thing we've been able to agree on with the editor,' Bailey continues. 'They love her style just as much as we do. She's the one thing we don't have to worry about right now, and I'd love for it to stay that way.'

Again, Cash glances at me from across the room. He's leaning against the countertop, quietly sipping his tea, watching me curiously.

Contemplatively.

I avoid his pointed stare and clear my throat, eager to shift the conversation towards something a little more light-hearted and far, far away from me potentially ruining my sister's wedding before it's even started. 'Since we're on wedding talk . . . Do I get a plus one?'

'Who do you want to bring?' Bailey asks absentmindedly, most of her concentration already back on her laptop screen. 'Hazel? I liked her.'

I frown. 'Hazel?'

Bailey looks up, one brow arched in disbelief. 'Hazel. Your girlfriend? Or latest one, anyway. We went on that double date with you two to Winter Wonderland just before Christmas.'

Something clicks in my mind. 'Oh.'

'*Oh?*'

I give her a sheepish grin. 'First off, Hazel wasn't my girlfriend—'

'Did she know that?'

'And secondly,' I say, a little louder this time to combat the sarcasm dripping off her every word, 'we're not together anymore. Didn't work out.'

I say that, but it did. It worked exactly like it was supposed to. A few weeks of fun before things fizzled out and we went our separate ways. No hard feelings, no heartbreak. Just two adults who knew exactly what they wanted from each other and didn't ask for anything more. But if you say that to people, they start to look at you strangely. Like everyone's supposed to want what Cash and Bailey have, and like I couldn't possibly be satisfied with anything less.

Bailey's on the verge of saying something similar. She's got this look in her eyes that's halfway between pity and exasperation, and I have no desire to sit here and listen to another well-meaning, but no less annoying, lecture about my love life. I push away from the counter, making a point to cause the stool legs to scrape loudly against the floor. 'We should get going.' I glance over at Cash. 'Don't want to be late.'

We've got a job over on the outskirts of the city and it'll likely take us at least an hour to get there, even without the threat of rush-hour traffic.

Cash nods, seemingly satisfied with my sudden excuse to leave. He doesn't say a word until it's the two of us in the van together. As soon as he slides into the passenger seat, he turns to me and raises an unimpressed brow. 'Eliott's not going to take the job, is she?'

Straight to the point.

Usually that's something I admire about Cash, but right now it's just annoying.

I scowl at my reflection in the rear-view mirror. 'How am I supposed to know?'

'Dane.'

It's a subtle change in a tone, but it's enough. This isn't Cash, my best friend speaking. It's Cash, Bailey's fiancé.

Despite the flicker of annoyance shooting through me, I can't help but feel happy that Bailey has someone like Cash in her corner. Someone who will always fight for her and what she wants.

The thought of being that person for someone is so foreign to me, I can't even begin to comprehend it. I've tried to imagine myself being the kind of person Cash is for Bailey – reliable, constant, all-consuming with his love – but I come up blank every time. Like the idea of *me* and *love* are two parallel concepts my brain just can't get to work together.

I'm glad Cash and Bailey have each other, though. Even if it does result in this. A weird kind of tension between me and Cash that I don't think I've ever felt before.

The van crawls to a stop as we hit a stretch of traffic and I sigh, my fingers tapping restlessly against the wheel. 'I don't know what she's going to do.' Eliott's irritated face swims in my mind and I wince. 'But, yeah. Can't see her agreeing to it.'

Cash groans and he brings a hand up to run through his hair. 'Why? What happened?'

I hesitate. Cash and I don't have secrets. Not when it comes to things like this. I've never had any problem telling him about my dates, and he's always been happy to wingman for me, to give me advice without judging, to let me live my life the way I want to without trying to mould me into being someone else.

'I'm not sure,' I tell him honestly. Because I'm not. I don't know what I'd been expecting from Eliott at the engagement party, but it definitely hadn't been that. 'But we've met before.' I tell him about that night two years ago, about the chemistry Eliott and I had with each other on the dance floor, about how the energy between us felt almost electric as we stumbled back to her home.

Cash exhales a deep breath and shakes his head. 'So, what

happened? You slept together and then didn't call or something? That's why she's pissed?'

'That's the thing. We didn't actually sleep together. Not really.' Cash shoots me a quizzical look and I shrug. 'It was obvious she wasn't feeling it anymore, so I left.'

I think back to that night and try to recall if there was something I said or did that resulted in the abrupt change in her demeanour that night. How she went from being an enthusiastic participant in our evening together to awkwardly trying to end things. At the time, her truly awful fake moaning had been almost funny – keyword *almost* – but now, thinking back on it, I'm pretty sure there was something else in her eyes.

A sadness I hadn't been able to recognise back then.

I suddenly feel guilty for leaving so abruptly. Maybe I should've stayed and talked to her. Found out what was wrong and tried to help her through it. Is that why she's so mad? For some reason, I doubt it. We didn't know each other. Didn't owe her other anything other than an orgasm, and we both ran a zero on that front.

'I don't know what her deal is,' I say, shaking away my memories of that night. 'But I'm definitely not her favourite person.'

'And you think she'll say no to the wedding *just* to avoid you?' Cash is looking at me in disbelief, and I can't say that I blame him.

'I know how it sounds, but this isn't an ego thing or anything like that. I genuinely think she'd rather turn down a job than have to spend another minute in the same room as me.'

And that's a jarring realisation. Especially when I have no idea what I've done to deserve such a visceral response from her.

Cash frowns and the contemplative look is back. I can practically see the cogs turning in his mind. 'You need to fix this.'

'What?'

The traffic ahead of us starts rolling forward, but I don't make any move to follow. A car honks behind us, but I ignore it in favour of staring at Cash incredulously.

'I need to *what*?'

'Fix this,' Cash repeats simply. 'The feature is important. This is Bailey's job.'

Low blow.

I know just as well as he does how important Bailey's work is to her. I know how hard she's worked to build this platform for herself, and just how difficult it's been maintaining it. I wouldn't do anything to jeopardise that. Not after everything she's been through to get to this point.

'And . . .' His voice softens slightly, and he gets that stupid grin on his face that only crops up whenever he's thinking about my sister. 'It's our wedding, and I want it to be everything she's dreamt about. If that means that you have to patch things up with Eliott so Bailey can have her dream photographer, then so be it.'

The car behind us honks again and I hurriedly pull off, racing to catch up with the traffic ahead. 'And how am I supposed to do that?'

Cash grins over at me, and any tension that's been lingering between us dissipates immediately. 'I'm sure you'll figure it out.'

Chapter Seven

ELIOTT

The thing about working freelance is that everyone tells you how good it'll feel to be your own boss and to set your own working hours, but nobody tells you just how little the people in your life will respect those working hours.

Case in point? It's 3pm on a Friday and the plan had been to spend the day at my desk finishing editing the photos from a wedding two weeks prior. And yet, for some reason, I've spent the day playing chauffeur to my grandmother.

I've taken her to the supermarket, the butchers, the dry cleaners, and was even forced into a moderately awkward lunch with a friend of hers from church. A lunch that mostly consisted of the two of them nibbling at their sandwiches and tittering their disapproval about my current state of singlehood.

Even now, I'm currently seated on an uncomfortable plastic chair in the waiting room at the GP's surgery, waiting for my grandmother to finish with her appointment. An appointment that was supposed to only take ten minutes.

I glance at the old clock on the wall opposite and scowl as I realise that I've been here for at least half an hour now and Nan shows no sign of emerging from the room she disappeared into. The elderly gentleman sitting beneath the clock shoots me a look of alarm and I try to school my expression into something a little friendlier in apology. It doesn't seem to land.

To be fair, when Nan called this morning to ask if I could take her to the supermarket because Mum had cancelled on her (again), I hadn't imagined it would devolve into a whole day of errands.

Which – yeah. Admittedly, that's my fault.

Because it *always* ends up like this, and I should definitely know better by now.

Mum promises to help Nan with something.

Mum flakes.

Nan, understandably, turns to her grandchildren for help.

Or to be more accurate, Nan turns to *me*. Because Leanne won't answer the phone unless there's something in it for her, and Josh is about as reliable as Mum is in situations like this.

When I was younger, I used to like the fact that I was the one everyone turned to in a crisis. I liked being reliable. Being constant. Being called the *lifesaver*.

Now? Not so much.

Everyone just expects me to be there, ready to drop everything and help as soon as they so much as glance in my direction. It doesn't matter what I'm doing or what I've got planned.

Everyone's needs trump mine.

The anger that's been slowly brewing inside me while I sit on what has to be the most uncomfortable seat in existence suddenly morphs into guilt as the door finally reopens and Nan comes shuffling out.

It's a strange feeling watching your grandmother age before your very eyes. When you're young, it's not really something you think about and my memories are filled with echoes of my childhood. Nan hoisting me up onto her kitchen counter so I could help her roll dumpling dough into imperfect little balls. Nan shrieking as she chased me and Josh around the garden with a broom because we spilt juice on her nice new white sofa. Nan teaching me how to swim in that tiny patch of sea behind her cottage in Grenada, back when she could still make the flights back home.

It's hard to imagine Nan doing any hoisting or chasing or swimming now. She's small — smaller than she's ever been — with a slight limp thanks to a nasty fall down the stairs a few months ago that's still yet to heal properly. Her hair — thick, black and healthy in my memories — is thin and almost entirely white now, and there's a tiredness in her eyes that seems to come from more than just a bad night's sleep.

Guilt threatens to drown me from the inside and I suddenly hate myself for feeling even the tiniest bit of irritation towards her.

'All right, Gloria,' Nan's doctor says as he helps guide her back towards the waiting room. I immediately hop out of my seat and meet them halfway. 'You make sure you keep off that leg as much as possible. Understood?'

Nan nods over to me. 'That's what my granddaughter's here for.'

I give the doctor a weak smile as Nan swaps over from his arm to mine, wobbling slightly at the brief lack of balance. 'Is it not healing well?'

'It's healing fine,' Nan sighs.

'Not as well as I'd like,' says the doctor at the exact same time. 'If you're still having trouble with it by our next appointment, we may have to look into surgery.'

Nan sighs again, her face twisting into an expression of obvious displeasure. 'I'll be *fine*,' she says, a little firmly this time. 'Thank you, Doctor Patel. I'll see you in six weeks.' She doesn't wait for him to respond before she starts pointedly guiding me towards the exit.

Honestly, she's surprisingly strong when she wants to be.

'That man treats me like a child,' she grumbles as soon as we step through the doors. I brace myself for the regular barrage of complaints that always seem to follow a visit to her doctor. 'You know, he kept trying to pass me a brochure about an assisted living facility. Assisted living!' Nan barks out a humourless laugh as I walk her over to my car and pull the door open for her. 'I said, "*Doctor Patel, I spent thirty years paying off the mortgage on that house and I shall happily die in it if I very well please.*"'

I wince, as I always do when Nan so casually mentions dying. 'Don't stay things like that.'

'It's the truth,' Nan sniffs. 'He didn't listen to me anyhow. Slipped the brochure into my purse when he thought I wasn't looking.' She fumbles around in her comically large bag and pulls out a slim brochure with a cheerful-looking elderly couple on the front cover. Nan glares at it like it's the source of all her problems in the world and then immediately tosses the brochure out the window.

'Nan!'

She blinks over at me, her face a picture of innocence. 'An accident. My finger slipped.'

'You *wound down your window*.'

Nan shrugs. 'I won't need it, anyway. If I ever did need help to that degree – which I won't, thank you very much – then you'd just move back in.'

She says it so simply, so casually, like it's something she's already considered a hundred times before and this is the only logical conclusion she's been able to come to.

'Excuse me?' I ask.

Nan shakes her head at me like I'm being incredibly dim. 'If there ever comes a time where I *do* need some further assistance with my day-to-day life, I wouldn't move into an *assisted living facility*.' She says the last three words like they're poison on her tongue. 'I'd just move you back into the spare room. We'd have to clear it out, of course, but—'

'And when did you decide this?'

Nan waves a nonchalant hand in front of her. 'Your mother and I have already discussed it.'

'*Excuse* me?' I ask again.

'I'm not sure how many times you want me to repeat myself.'

'I *heard* what you said,' I snap and then immediately regret it when Nan narrows her eyes at me. I clear my throat and I try again, my voice a little more measured and composed this time around. 'I just— Don't you think I should've been included in those discussions?'

'Perhaps,' Nan concedes with a somewhat apologetic shrug. I take it. It's the best I'm going to get. 'Well, I've told you now, so no harm, no foul.'

'*Nan*—'

'It's not going to happen anytime soon anyway,' Nan says, cutting across me like she didn't hear the interruption. 'Aside from this damn leg, I'm in tip-top shape. Nothing to worry about. I'm not quite ready to become a burden just yet.'

And there's the guilt again.

'You're not a burden, Nan,' I mumble. Nan might be several inches shorter than me now but, for some reason, I suddenly feel very small. 'You could never be.'

Nan looks at me for a long moment, then, seemingly satisfied, gives me a nod. 'Right. Next on the agenda – I need to go to the bank.'

'You know you can do pretty much everything online these days?'

'I prefer a human touch.'

I glance at the clock on the dashboard in front of us. Nearly four o'clock. Between this and my upcoming evening plans with my sister, my day of catching up with my edits has well and truly been stolen from me. 'Fine,' I say as I start the car up. 'We'll go to the bank, but then I'm taking you home. No other detours.'

Nan purses her lips and looks for a moment like she wants to argue. 'Fine.' There's a beat or two of silence as I start up my car, but then Nan clears her throat and says quietly, 'Thank you, Eliott.'

My lips lift into a reluctant smile. 'You don't have to thank me.'

But I'm glad she does.

★ ★ ★

Leanne's late.

The only confirmation I have that she's actually going to show up and not leave me sitting alone in a bar all evening is the message she sent me thirty minutes ago, promising she was only five minutes away. Though, to be fair, when it comes to Leanne, thirty minutes isn't actually all that bad. She once left me waiting for three hours at the airport because she missed her flight back home and didn't think to message to let me know. I can't take it personally. She's always been like this. So wrapped up in her own little world that sometimes she forgets the rest of us live here too.

My phone buzzes in my purse suddenly and I pull it out, expecting to see another semi-apologetic message from Leanne. Instead, it's an Instagram message request notification sent to my photography account.

Ever since Bailey found me and reshared practically my entire feed to her legion of followers, my Instagram inbox has been swamped with brides eager to book me. I've never had any trouble getting clients – word-of-mouth spreads quickly within the wedding community and I can usually book up months in advance from referrals alone – but this is the first time I've been so in demand from social media. It's new territory for me, but I can't say I mind it. My calendar is filling up almost three years in advance, and I owe that all to Bailey. Which makes the fact I'm going to have to decline her booking even worse.

She sent her request a few days ago, but I still haven't replied. Part of me hopes that if I ignore it for long enough, it'll go away. The smart, rational part of me knows that I have to respond, but I still haven't figured out what I want to say.

'Sorry, I tried to bring your brother home for a night of back-blowing sex, but embarrassed myself so thoroughly that the idea of spending any extended time with him makes me want to hurl.'

Hm. No. For some reason, I don't think that will go down well. But I need to tell her *something*. Ghosting isn't an option, no matter how tempting it might seem. Bailey and Cash have been nothing but kind to me, and I owe them an explanation. Even if it's not exactly the truth.

I pull up the message request, idly wondering if I could pass their booking on to another photographer with a similar style to me, when the username flashing across my screen makes my heart stop for a moment.

@greatdaneconstruction

No.

Surely not.

I tap the profile. It's empty save for one terribly photographed post of a garage extension almost three years ago. The lighting is off and the focus isn't actually on the extension itself, but rather a nearby bush, which makes the whole photo look slightly blurry. But it's not the terrible photography that's got my heart choking in my throat right now.

One More Shot

Great Dane Construction Services.
Dane.

A memory from our almost night together jumps into the forefront of my mind. Us slow wining on the dance floor, sharing random pieces of information about each other. Nothing too deep, but enough to forge some kind of connection between us before we headed back to my place. I remember vaguely Dane telling me that he runs a construction business with a friend.

I swipe back to the message.

> @GREATDANECONSTRUCTION
>
> hey, eliott. it's dane. from the other night.
>
> and also two years ago lol.
>
> hope you don't mind me messaging you out of the blue like this, but i'd really like to talk things over and clear the air if we can. i know bailey's got her heart set on you for the wedding and i don't want to be the reason that doesn't happen.
>
> anyway. let me know.

'Why do you look like you've just found out there's an asteroid heading for Earth?'

I jump as Leanne slides onto the stool next to me, her

brows raised in question. Before she can say anything else, I drop my phone back into my purse and give my sister a once-over. This is supposed to be a casual dinner and drinks, a way for us to catch up in person because we haven't seen each other face to face since her semester started. I take one look at the strappy heels wrapped around her ankles, her short dress, and her full face of stunning make-up and know, without a shadow of a doubt, that I'm only her first stop tonight.

Given how thoroughly my day was monopolised by Nan, I should feel a sense of relief in knowing that Leanne plans to cut our night together short in favour of . . . a boy, I'm assuming? But it irks me anyway. *She's* the one who badgered me endlessly about tonight. The one who spent the better part of a month begging me to find some time in my calendar so we could catch up.

'I miss you, Elz,' she'd pouted on the phone one night. 'Feels like we never get to see each other anymore.'

And so I'd pored through my calendar, looking for a significant chunk of free time where we could do some real sisterly bonding, like we used to before life got so busy and started pulling us in different directions. So yes, it's more than a little annoying that she's already got one foot out the door.

'Earth to Elz.' Leanne prods me sharply in the chest. 'What's got you looking like that?'

'It's nothing,' I say, shaking my head free of any irritation. Just because the night might end sooner than I would've liked, it doesn't mean we can't have a good time now. 'You look nice. What's the occasion?'

She grins and flips her hair over her shoulders. 'Can't a girl dress up to see her big sister?'

I raise a brow in answer and Leanne immediately starts giggling.

'*Fine*. I'm heading to a party after this, but that's not important. We're having *us* time right now. What's new? Tell me everything. Ooh. Do you want to do shots?'

I open my mouth to decline, but Leanne's already waving the bartender down and, before I know it, two small glasses filled with a brown substance and topped with whipped cream are being placed in front of us.

'Two blow jobs,' the bartender says as he pushes them towards us. He gives me a wink and I, for the first time tonight, give him a once-over. Tall, clean-shaven, nice voice. At one point in my life, I probably would've spent the rest of the evening flirting with him, cautiously testing the waters to see if this had any potential. But I'm not in the mood for that right now.

I haven't been in a very long time.

'Ooh, he's into you,' Leanne says, a little too loudly. The bartender glances over his shoulder, grins shyly and then looks away. 'Want me to wingman for you?'

I don't want to go home with anyone tonight, but even if I did, his reaction to Leanne's comment leaves me feeling a little flat. As much as I hate it, I can't help but think about how Dane would've reacted to it. For some reason, I doubt that all I would've got would've been a shy smile before he started pretending to be busy washing glasses. Dane would've been over here immediately, turning that confident grin on me as well-practised lines spilled from his lips.

God.

When did *Dane* become my standard?

I shake my head and tell myself the only reason Dane is in the forefront of my mind is because of his unexpected message and nothing else. 'I'm good.'

Leanne shrugs and lifts her glass, gesturing for me to do the same. 'To sisters!' she cheers.

'To sisters,' I echo before downing the drink in one smooth gulp. It's actually quite nice. The warmth of the liqueur mixes nicely with the coolness of the whipped cream and helps to relax me a little. I can practically feel my lingering irritation rolling off me in waves.

Leanne gulps hers down just as smoothly and uses the back of her hand to wipe away any whipped cream on her face. 'You want another? Ooh, maybe we should do some tequila shots this time?'

'Let's slow it down a bit,' I laugh. 'We'll grab a table, get something to eat, maybe switch to cocktails for a while.'

Leanne suddenly looks uncomfortable. She squirms a little on her stool and her grin quickly turns sheepish. 'Right. Well. The thing is—'

'If you're about to bail on me—'

'I'm *not* bailing!' Leanne squeaks, voice far too defensive for someone who is absolutely about to bail. 'I told you, I've got that party after this, so I thought I could use this as pre-drinks and as a way for us to catch up. Two birds, one stone.'

'We're supposed to be having dinner,' I say, trying my best not to let disapproval lace my every word. I'm always very aware of the ten years between us and just how easy it is for me to fall into that *mother* role. Effortless really. But I hate it and I know she does too. Ninety per cent of our arguments when she was a kid were about how I wasn't her mother and couldn't tell her what to do — usually shrieked at me when she was seconds away from doing something incredibly dangerous, stupid, or an ill-advised combo of the two. I always agreed wholeheartedly, but someone has to do it.

'I know, I know,' Leanne winces. She looks genuinely sorry. 'But I completely forgot about our plans when I RSVP'd to the party, and Jake is going to be there so—'

'Jake? Who's Jake?'

Her eyes light up. 'He's a guy on my course and *oh my God*, have I not told you about Jake? How have I not told you about Jake?'

'That's what tonight was supposed to be,' I remind her. 'Us catching up. Jake probably would've come up at some point.'

'We can still catch up!' Leanne insists. 'We've still got twenty minutes before I have to leave. Thirty-five,' she amends quickly, shuffling a little closer so she can squeeze my hand. 'Don't give me that look, Elz. We can still have a good time. And I promise I'll make it up to you. It's half-term in a couple of weeks. Maybe we can do a girls' night or something?'

I valiantly resist the urge to tell her that tonight was supposed to be our girls' night and instead give her a stiff nod. 'All right. But I want your undivided attention for the next thirty-five minutes.'

Leanne drops her phone into her purse and zips it up with a flourish. 'I'm all yours.'

Two more rounds of shots, one round of cocktails later, and Leanne is in hysterics as I tell her about a nightmare wedding I photographed a month or so ago.

'He did *not* say that in his speech,' Leanne wheezes, tears forming in the corners of her eyes. 'I refuse to believe a grown man could be so obtuse. Absolutely refuse.'

'He did! The poor bride looked like she wanted to melt through the floor. And her father?' I shake my head and click my tongue. 'Let's just say if looks could kill, I'm pretty sure they'd be planning a funeral right now.'

'Unbelievable,' Leanne says, dabbing at her eyes. 'Please tell me you got photos?'

'I stopped taking them about halfway through the speech when I realised there was no redeeming it. But yeah. Managed to capture that initial look of horror from the bride.'

'Poor girl,' Leanne sniffs before her expression turns curious. 'Does seeing that kind of stuff put you off marriage? Or dating in general?'

I huff out a dry laugh. *That's* not what's been putting me off dating recently, but Leanne doesn't need to know that. 'Not really. They're more like cautionary tales, I guess. You get a first-hand idea of what not to look for in a partner. And—' I pause, my thoughts drifting to Bailey and Cash for a surprising second, 'And what to look for. The green flags, you know?'

Leanne nods thoughtfully. 'Speaking of green flags . . .' She trails off and reaches for her purse, pulling her phone out in one smooth movement. Her phone lights up with a flurry of notifications, all from someone saved as 'JAKE <3', and her expression turns sheepish. 'I should really start heading to the party.'

'Go, go,' I say, waving her off.

'Are you sure? I could maybe stay for another . . .' She glances at her phone. 'Ten minutes.'

I nod. As short as tonight was, I had a good time and the last thing I need is for Leanne to start feeling like she *has* to spend time with me. 'Go and have fun.'

She leans in and gives me a brief but tight hug before pulling away to slide off her stool. 'You're the best, Elz. And I *promise* I'll make it up to you.'

'How're you getting there?' I ask, watching as she wobbles slightly on her heels.

'Tube,' she says with a shrug. 'Won't take too long.'

She's definitely not drunk, but I imagine she's got the same pleasant buzz that's currently thrumming through my veins. '*Please* get an Uber.'

She snorts. 'Not in my budget this month.'

'I'll get it.' The idea of her stumbling along underground platforms late at night suddenly fills me with a sense of panic. I reach for my phone and unlock it. Dane's message is still on the screen, but I swipe it away in favour of opening the Uber app.

Leanne doesn't even try to protest.

'Elz, you are a *queen*!' she coos as I hand her the phone so she can plug in the address. 'My queen specifically. A goddess among women.' She hands my phone back to me, then gives me one last hug before she hurries off, noticeably less wobbly now.

It's only as she disappears through the doors that I realise she's also left me with the bill.

It should bother me – this kind of thing usually does – but between the alcohol still working its way through me and the general happiness I'm feeling after our brief but fun evening together, I can't bring myself to care. Just this once, I'll let it slide.

I can't call an Uber for myself until Leanne reaches her party, so I signal the bartender for another drink and scroll through my phone. I'm seconds away from messaging Sasha to see if she wants to come out and meet me, when I remember Dane's message.

I open it up again, preparing to delete it and push him firmly out of my mind for good, but my thumbs stall over the screen.

I don't know whether to blame it on residual guilt from the engagement party or the handful of drinks I've had tonight but, before I can stop myself, I start typing out a reply.

Chapter Eight

ELIOTT

FROM: bailey@thecurlybailey.com
TO: eliott@eraynephotography.com
SUBJECT: Wedding booking request

Hi Eliott! Hope you're well :)

Thank you again for the brilliant work you did with the engagement party photos – I'm truly obsessed. I'm getting in touch again because we've finally got a date for the wedding and, like we discussed, Cash and I would LOVE to book you for it.

It'll be in September in Portofino, Italy! I know, six months' notice isn't great for a destination wedding, but your travel and accommodation will be paid for on top of your standard fee of course. I'm not sure if I've mentioned, but Cash isn't huge on flying so we'll be taking the train –

you're more than welcome to join us but it'll be a long (but beautiful!) journey, so let me know if you'd rather catch a flight. I can share more information later – maybe we can jump on a call?

But let me know your initial thoughts! As I said, we LOVE your work and are so excited about having you photograph our special day.

Speak soon,

Bailey and Cash xo

Chapter Nine

DANE

I'm not actually expecting a response from Eliott. The only reason I bother sending the message is because I know Cash will ask if I've done anything. I fully expect her to ignore me. To delete the message and continue on with her life without any kind of acknowledgment that I've reached out. So when my phone lights up, the last thing I expect to see is:

@ERAYNEWEDDINGS

Hey. I'm gonna be at the Black Cat in Shoreditch for the next 45 mins or so.

If you want to talk, feel free to meet me here.

She also shares her location, sending me a link to a restaurant and bar that's actually not too far from me right now. I tell myself that the deciding factor in all of this is just how close she currently is, and *not* that I'm feeling strangely eager to see and speak to her again.

> @GREATDANECONSTRUCTION
> cool. give me 30 mins

She doesn't respond again and by the time I get to the Black Cat, I'm halfway convinced that she won't be there. That she's either chickened out or this is just some kind of game to her.

But she is there.

I spot her almost immediately, even through the rapidly growing Friday night crowd. She's sat at the bar sipping on a drink, her focus is locked on the phone in her hands. I wonder if she's aware of just how many eyes she has on her currently.

The bartender keeps sneaking glances at her, looking like he's debating asking for her number but can't quite work up the courage to approach her, and both men on either side of her can't seem to tear their gaze away. I don't blame them.

Eliott is gorgeous.

You'd think my reaction to her would have dulled by now, that I'd be immune to the small smile that quirks her lips as she scrolls through her phone, that the sight of her, wearing a strappy vest that shows a delicious amount of skin, wouldn't immediately fill me with the urge to run my hands along her warm skin to find out if it's as soft as I remember.

And yet.

Every time I see Eliott, it's like I'm seeing her for the first time.

I cross the distance between us and slide into the empty space between her and the guy next to her. She jolts slightly as my arm brushes against hers and looks up, meeting my easy smile with a slightly wary one of her own.

Hell, I'll take it.

'Dane,' she says with a nod.

'Glad to see you remember me this time.'

She cringes, her nose scrunching up in a way I can't help but find disarmingly adorable. 'I definitely deserve that.'

I've never been one for holding grudges and it's easy to tell that her even agreeing to meet me tonight hasn't been the easiest of choices for her. 'Consider it forgotten.'

'No, I owe you an apology.' She huffs out a long sigh. 'And an explanation.'

She doesn't owe me anything if we're being honest here, but the guy next to me shifts slightly in his seat and I'm suddenly acutely aware that we've got an audience. 'You want to grab a table and get something to eat?'

She hesitates for a moment and then shrugs. 'Sure.'

One More Shot

It takes us a couple of minutes to flag down a waiter and then we're guided towards a secluded booth towards the back of the restaurant. As soon as the waiter shuffles away, having taken a quick order of some tapas to share between us, Eliott laces her fingers together and clears her throat. 'Thanks for meeting me tonight.'

A bark of laughter bursts out of me before I even register the sound crawling up my throat.

Eliott narrows her eyes, suddenly on the defensive. 'What?'

'You're just – You sound so formal,' I explain, quite enjoying the way she scowls at me. '"*Thanks for meeting me tonight.*" I feel like I'm about to be fired or something.'

'Is that a conversation you're familiar with?'

'Not since I was sixteen,' I say. There's a long pause, and she cocks her head to the side, obviously waiting for me to elaborate. 'I had a summer job posting leaflets through doors for this restaurant and, long story short, I got bored one day and just tossed all the leaflets in a bin, thinking that my boss would never find out.'

Her eyes light up and she immediately looks more like the person I met that night two years ago. 'Is this going where I think it is?'

'If you're thinking that my boss called me in for a meeting the next day, casually unearthed a stack of leaflets and asked me to explain why she found them stuffed in a bin right outside the restaurant, then yes, it's going exactly where you think it is.'

She laughs, and it's the kind of laugh that can get easily stuck on repeat in your mind if you're not careful. Warm and all-consuming, like the sun in sound form. 'Why would you get rid of them *outside* the restaurant?'

'Fuck knows?' I laugh. 'I was sixteen, stupid, and didn't want to spend my summer as an underpaid mail boy. But don't try to change the topic—'

'I wasn't—'

'That's how my boss started the meeting, "*Thanks for meeting me today*," and that didn't end very well for me.'

'You got fired?'

'I got fired *and* she told my parents. Definitely not a fun time to be me.'

She laughs again, a quiet chuckle this time that echoes in my mind for a few seconds after she's finished. 'Well, I'm not about to fire you or snitch to your parents.'

'Good.' I smile at her and I'm relieved when she mirrors it with a small one of her own. 'And, on a scale of one to ten, how well is tonight going to end for me?'

'One being?'

'One being you tell me you're going to decline photographing Cash and Bailey's wedding.'

She winces. 'And ten?'

'You agree to photograph the wedding and—' There's

been a slight shift between us. The air isn't as tinged with awkward tension as before, so I decide to push my luck. 'And we pick up where we left off two years ago.'

Her eyes widen a fraction and I half expect her to look away, but she doesn't. She holds my gaze as her lips curl upwards into the kind of smirk I'd love to kiss off her face. 'We might be able to get to a solid five.'

I lean back into my seat and grin. 'Are you saying that door's closed?'

'I'm saying that I didn't agree to meet you tonight for that.'

'Ah,' I wiggle my brows. '*Tonight*.'

Her lips twitch. 'Can we stay on topic?'

'And the topic is?'

'Right.' She nods and looks, for a second, like she's steeling herself for something. Any hint of a smile has been wiped from her face. 'I wanted to talk – to clear the air. I know I didn't handle things well at the engagement party. It wasn't fair and—' She swallows. 'And I'm sorry about that.'

I blink at her. If I'm being honest, I wasn't expecting an apology tonight.

'I've got some hang-ups,' she says slowly, and I wonder if I'm imagining the way she winces slightly. 'And seeing you there kind of brought them right to the front of my mind again. I guess I just panicked.'

'I won't lie and say it wasn't a little weird.'

'I know, but if it makes you feel any better, it was quite possibly the most mortifying experience of my whole life. I regretted it straight away and I don't think I've ever been so embarrassed. Second only to—' She stops abruptly and laughs dryly. 'Second only to our night together, I guess.'

I raise a brow, not entirely sure if she meant to insult me or not. 'Well, that's a blow to the ego.'

'Not because of you,' she says quickly. 'But because of . . . you know . . . how things ended.'

I frown. 'How things ended?'

'You *know*. How we didn't end up finishing things because—'

Eliott trails off, leaving me to finish the end of her sentence. 'Because you weren't feeling it?' She squirms a little awkwardly in her seat and realisation suddenly dawns on me. 'Because you started faking it and I caught you?' Is that what this has been about the entire time? Why she was so desperate to avoid me at the party? Because she was embarrassed?

It's probably the worst thing to do in a situation like this, but I can't help but laugh.

Eliott's reaction is almost instantaneous. Her eyes narrow, her lips twist into a scowl, and she looks like she's about five seconds away from sliding out of our booth and making a run for it.

'I'm not laughing at you—'

'You sure?' She glares at me from across the table. 'Because it definitely looks that way.'

'I'm not,' I tell her honestly, because I'm genuinely not. 'It's just . . . I don't want to tell you how to react to things, but if I ran away from everyone I've ever had an embarrassing sex experience with, I wouldn't be able to leave my house.'

She rolls her eyes. 'You don't—'

'Once, I ended up slapping myself in the balls – don't ask how, just know it was thanks to a truly Olympic level of acrobatics on my part – and spent the rest of the night curled up in the foetal position holding a pack of frozen peas to my balls. Definitely not an attractive look. I'd say that definitely counts as embarrassing.'

Her brows disappear into the cloud of hair that frames her face.

'Another time, I thought I'd surprise the girl I was seeing and let myself into her place. Long story short, picture me on her bed, in my birthday suit and suddenly she bursts into the room.'

'That doesn't sound embarrassing.'

'Followed by about five of her friends.'

Her lips start to lilt into a smile.

'And then there was the time—'

'I get it,' Eliott interrupts. 'Just get to the point.'

'My point is, "*that time I had to fake an orgasm because the guy I was with was so bad I would've had a better chance at coming watching paint dry and he caught me*" doesn't have to be the humiliating experience you're making it out to be in your mind,' I say with a shrug. 'It can just be a funny story. Life goes on, you know?'

She hums then bites her bottom lip between her teeth and chews thoughtfully for a few seconds. 'You weren't *bad*, you know? In bed, I mean.'

'Your moaning definitely was,' I say with a grin, choosing to ignore the unexpected compliment for now.

She gives me a smile, though it doesn't quite reach her eyes. 'Believe it or not, no one's ever called me out on it before.'

I raise a brow. 'Do you often fake it?'

She's spared from having to answer right away by our waiter returning with our food and drinks. Our conversation lulls into a surprisingly comfortable silence as we pick at the tapas and sip our drinks. I notice how Eliott avoids anything with tomatoes in and I have vague memories of her telling me about her aversion when we first met.

'Always,' she says quietly. It's the first thing she's said in a few minutes and it takes me a second or two to remember what question she's answering.

'Always?'

She nods as she sips her cocktail. For the first time tonight, she's avoiding all eye contact with me. 'I always fake it because—' She takes a huge gulp of her cocktail, almost finishing the drink, and slams the glass back down onto the table. Her next words come out in a flurry, like she's forcing herself to get them out. 'Because I can't come. And sometimes it's easier to just fake it and get it over with.'

'You can't come? Like at all?' It feels weird to be having this conversation in the middle of a restaurant, but we're far enough away from any of the other booths, there's no danger of anyone listening in. I shake my head in disbelief. 'Of course you can.'

She looks up at me and the expression in her eyes is something I've not seen before. A mixture of anger and pain. I don't like it.

'*I* can't,' she says gruffly, leaving no room for argument. 'Not with another person, anyway. I've tried and I've tried, and it just won't happen for me. I thought that maybe, *maybe*, I could get there with you, but even that was a dud. And if I couldn't do it with someone who looks like you—' She waves a hand in my direction, looking halfway between pissed off and turned on. 'Then there's no hope. That's why I faked it, and that's why I was trying to avoid you at the party. You're like a walking, talking reminder of everything that's wrong with me.'

'There's nothing wrong with you, Eliott.' And I mean it too. Where the hell did she get that from? Are these the words she hurls at herself in the mirror late at night, or is she just repeating something she's heard from someone else? I'm not sure why, but I really hope not.

I clear my throat. 'I've heard that a lot of women find it difficult to—'

'Oh God. Stop,' Eliott groans. 'Just stop.' She picks up her glass again and downs the rest of her drink. 'I don't need to hear this from you of all people. Absolutely not. Don't you even dare think about finishing that sentence.'

I mime zipping my lips shut and sit in silence until Eliott gives me a nod of approval.

'Thank you. I'm not here for your sympathy or anything like that. I just wanted to explain.'

We lapse into another silence. Eliott picks at the remaining tapas between us, awkwardly avoiding my gaze, and I try to figure out something to say that won't have her leaping across the table to choke me.

'We could try again.'

She looks up and, for a second, I'm not sure I've made the right choice.

'Excuse me?'

'Let's try again,' I say, trying to sound as casual as possible. 'Me and you.'

I think the noise that comes out of her mouth is supposed to be a laugh, but it doesn't sound right. It sounds strained, like she's forcing it out to try to keep the atmosphere between us light. 'Yes, because that worked out so well last time.'

Fair point, but . . .

'Last time, I didn't know all the facts. We're on an even playing field now.'

Her jaw clenches and I don't miss the way she leans back slightly into her seat, putting some distance between us. 'Can you be serious?'

'I am being serious. What's the harm in trying again?'

She opens her mouth, then closes it abruptly, her brows knitting together in the middle.

'*See*,' I say with a smirk. 'There's no downside here. It'll be a win-win situation for both of us. You have some great sex, come, and learn what gets you going.'

'And you?' she asks. She's leaned forward again, dropping her chin into the palm of her hand as she looks up at me. As much as she's trying to temper it, I can plainly see a flash of curiosity in her eyes. 'What're you getting out of this arrangement?'

I lean in further too and drop my voice to a low murmur. 'I don't know if you've noticed this, but you're gorgeous.'

We're close enough now that I can see the way her pupils widen at the compliment. I'm also pretty sure that if I pressed a hand to her cheek now, I'd feel a warmth crawling up her skin. The desire to do just that hits me with a surprising fierceness and, if this had been any other date, I'd do it without hesitation.

I'd cup her jaw and pull her in for a kiss. The kind of

kiss that would inevitably have us heading back to my place. But this isn't any other date, so I push down the desire and avoid looking at her lips.

Though they are very nice lips.

'Spending time with you isn't exactly going to be a chore, Eliott.'

Her gaze flickers down to *my* lips. It's only for a moment, but she lingers long enough for me to catch the action.

Fuck it.

I bring a hand up and let my thumb trail along her cheekbone. The skin beneath me is warm, just like I'd expected, and still as soft as I remember. 'What do you think, Eliott? You want to try again?'

The restaurant is loud and heaving around us, but every single sound seems to fade away into a distant echo as I wait for her to give me an answer. Her deep brown eyes don't break eye contact with my own as she considers me for several long, silent seconds. Just when I'm starting to think she's not going to answer at all, she leans in even further. There's barely any space between us now.

Her lips part and I bite back a groan.

'One more time?' she whispers, her lips ghosting against my own. Not quite a kiss. More like a brief taste of what's to come.

I nod and I can *feel* the way she grins against me. She hums quietly and then, just as I think she's about to end this unique form of torture and press her lips firmly against mine, she pulls back and laughs.

'No.'

I blink back at her, still dazed. Still feeling the ghost of her lips against mine. 'No?'

Amusement dances in her eyes. 'Hell, *no*.'

Chapter Ten

ELIOTT

I'm not going to pretend like it's not a tempting offer.

Dane is . . . Well, Dane is *Dane*, and there's a reason he caught my eye two years ago. It's the same reason I've even entertained this conversation for as long as I have tonight. I can't decide whether it's his good looks or the effortless charm he oozes, but there's something about him that keeps me rooted in my seat.

We could try again.

We're on an even playing field now.

Those words should have me running for the hills. I've heard them before, and I've been burned by them – drawn into the promise of a second chance, only to find myself right back at square one. I've learned the hard way that the allure of a fresh start doesn't guarantee a better ending. The opposite is more likely.

I haven't left yet, though.

He's still staring at me from across the table, mouth slightly ajar, as if the possibility of me turning him down had never occurred to him.

Idly, I wonder how many women he's used that move on. Admittedly, it was nice – the whole '*eye contact*' and '*caressing my face*' thing – and might've ended up working if he didn't ruin things by opening his mouth.

A waiter accidentally brushes against Dane as they hurry past with a tray, and the movement is enough to jostle him back to reality. He leans back into his seat and the look of surprise on his face slowly melts away, making way for a familiar, confident smirk.

A shame.

If I weren't so incredibly turned off by his comments, I might admit that the brief, uncharacteristically startled look on his face was kind of cute. Very rabbit in the headlights.

'Can I ask why?' Dane says, finally breaking the stilted silence that's blanketed itself over us.

The answer comes to me easily. 'I don't sleep with the same person twice.'

Dane raises an incredulous brow. 'Never?'

'Not anymore,' I clarify. It's easier this way, this boundary I've been forced to set to guard my heart and avoid making the same mistakes time and time again.

Dane nods, his gaze steady on mine. He considers me carefully for a few seconds before he shrugs. 'Fair enough.'

I expect him to push. The last guy I had this conversation with spent the following twenty minutes practically begging me to rethink my decision, convinced that his apparently *magic dick* would be the one to set things right. Unfortunately, that's a conversation I'm very familiar with. I still haven't decided if it's a case of a bruised ego or just a general delusion suffered by an embarrassingly large portion of the male population, but it always reinforces that I've made the right choice.

But Dane doesn't push.

In fact, I'm pretty sure I see a hint of understanding in his eyes. I'm not sure which I'd hate more right now. Dane desperately trying to wear me down, or the sympathetic look in his eyes. I glance away and fumble with my napkin, focusing on tearing it to tiny shreds.

'So, about the wedding?'

The speed at which he's pivoted back to the reason he's even here in the first place is so impressive, it startles a laugh out of me. There's no trace of irritation in his expression – nothing that would suggest he's reeling from having just been rejected.

Sex is off the table and now he's back to business.

I let myself relax a little in my seat. 'Right. Yeah. The wedding.'

Dane swallows and taps a finger against the table in front of him. *He's nervous.* The realisation hits me with a jolt. I hadn't actually considered that someone like Dane, someone who oozes confidence with seemingly little thought, actually had the ability to feel nerves.

But here we are.

'Cash is my best friend,' Dane says after a long moment. 'And Bailey is my little sister.'

'I'm aware,' I say wryly, wondering where this is going.

The corners of his lips lift into the beginnings of a smile I'm increasingly become fond of, but they dip almost immediately downwards back into a contemplative frown. 'I just mean that they're important to me. And if there's anything I can do to make them happy, I'll do it in a heartbeat.'

It's easy to imagine Dane slipping into the protective older brother role for Bailey, and I feel a twinge of unexpected jealousy.

I'm the eldest out of the three of us, but Josh and I are only a year apart and the idea of him doing or saying something like this for me is unfathomable. I don't think we've even said a word to each other in about two months. Though I suppose Mum's birthday *is* coming up, so I'll hear from him soon.

Technically.

What'll actually happen is this: I'll fire up the rarely used siblings' group chat I created five years ago and subtly remind both Leanne and Josh about Mum's upcoming birthday by floating suggestions for a gift. Leanne will enthusiastically participate in the gift selection – but will have no intention of paying – and Josh will leave me on read. If I'm lucky, he'll frantically message me the day before Mum's birthday and ask if I wouldn't mind putting his name on the gift.

And I'll do it.

Just like I do every year.

'That's why I'm here tonight,' Dane continues. 'I wanted to clear the air and make sure that when Bailey officially sends the request for the wedding – and it *is* coming, by the way, if it hasn't already; Bailey's fully aboard the Eliott train – that you don't turn it down just because you can't stand to be in the same room as me.' He clears his throat, and I can't quite place the expression on his face. He looks almost wary, like he's afraid of what I'm going to say. 'Where do we stand right now, Eliott?'

It's a fair question and, if he'd asked it two hours ago, I know exactly what my answer would've been. But now it's two hours later and the embarrassment I've been stoking for the last two years has simmered well below the surface.

I feel an unexpected sense of trust towards Dane, too. His offer to try again notwithstanding, he's been the perfect gentleman about all this. And besides, it'll just be one more time. I'll do the wedding and that'll be it.

No more Dane.

'We're good,' I tell him. 'I swear I'm not going to run away at the sight of you again.'

Dane heaves out a dramatic sigh of relief. 'Good, because I don't think my ego could handle that again.'

He's good at that. Easing the tension with some well-timed humour. I don't even think he realises he's doing it.

'And the wedding?' he asks.

I nod, enjoying the way his entire face lights up. 'I'll do the wedding.'

His smile is infectious, and I find myself matching it almost instantly.

'You're a lifesaver, Eliott.'

Lifesaver.

The word just keeps following me around.

★ ★ ★

FROM: eliott@eraynephotography.com
TO: bailey@thecurlybailey.com
SUBJECT: RE: Wedding booking request

Hi Bailey. It's lovely to hear from you. Glad to hear the engagement photos went down well! September in Italy sounds absolutely beautiful, and I'm sure it'll be a

> wonderful day. I'd be honoured to photograph the wedding.
>
> Let me know your availability for a call to hash out some details.
>
> Best,
>
> Eliott

* * *

Six months.

Six months to push Dane from my mind and make sure I can keep my promise to act like a rational human being at the wedding.

It feels like a simple enough task. Especially given the cordial, almost friendly manner in which we part ways when we leave the restaurant. As soon as I get the notification from Uber that Leanne's arrived at her party safely – accompanied by an eye-watering deduction from my bank account – I leap up from our table and Dane follows me out. He gives me a not entirely awkward half-hug once we exit the restaurant, mutters that he's glad we did this, and then that's it.

The air between us is officially cleared.

By the time we see each other again, six months from now, this entire debacle will be nothing more than a tiny blip in our memories. We might even be able to laugh about it.

There's no reason for Dane's stupidly handsome face to be occupying any kind of space in my head right now.

And yet . . .

'You want to fuck him,' Sasha says, blunt as ever. She's sat on my bedroom floor, several packets of braiding hair sprawled out in front of her. To her credit, she waited ten minutes before barging into my room, bringing her hair supplies with her. 'And I, for one, don't see what the problem is.' She holds up a finger. 'One: he told you he'd be up for it, didn't he?'

'That—'

A second finger. 'Two: he was chill about the whole engagement party thing.'

Very chill.

She grins at my reluctant nod, and then she adds a third finger. 'And finally, once again: *you* want to fuck *him*.'

'It's not that simple.'

'No, I'm pretty sure it is,' Sasha says with a shrug. She resumes braiding her hair, and squints at me in the mirror. 'I mean – and I guess I don't know him – but, after everything you've told me? He's not giving me Connor vibes.'

I wince at the use of the name. 'Yeah, well. Connor didn't give those vibes either, did he?'

Sasha falls silent and, for a moment, I think I've won this little battle between us. But then she rises from the floor and comes over to my desk. She drapes her arms around my shoulders and squeezes gently.

'Connor was a dick,' she says softly.

I snort. 'The worst.'

She hums in agreement. 'But you can't—'

I cut her off, because I know what she's going to say. It's the same thing she's said the hundred other times we've had this exact same conversation. 'I can't write everyone off just because of him?'

'Exactly.'

I sigh and pull away from her touch. 'But it wasn't just him, was it?'

Connor, my last long-term relationship, was just the tip of the iceberg. He might've been the cruellest; the one to spit that I might not be such a *frigid bitch* and actually enjoy sex if I '*just bothered to lose some weight*', but he wasn't unique.

There was Aaron before him, who'd regularly insist that I was withholding orgasms as a way to punish *him* for something and would retaliate by giving me the silent treatment.

And Jamal, who refused to even try to use toys with me because, in some weird and twisted way, he thought it was 'cheating'.

And Jada before him, who was the first — but not the last — to suggest that maybe there is actually something wrong with me because she'd never not made a girl come before.

And too many names before her.

I started enforcing my rule after Connor and, while my

sex life has been thoroughly unsatisfying ever since – not that it was anything to shout about before – the lack of heartbreak or pain has definitely made up for it.

'Dane is off the table,' I say firmly.

But Sasha looks unconvinced, and honestly? I am too.

Chapter Eleven

DANE

Let it never be said that Dane Clarke isn't a good brother and friend.

The *best*, even.

Because I've cancelled a date tonight in favour of sitting at Cash and Bailey's kitchen table, stuffing invitations into envelopes. To be fair to them, I probably would've cancelled the date, anyway. I arranged it more out of habit than anything else — I think it's been literally years since I spent a Friday night alone — but I'm happy to use the wedding invitations as an excuse.

We've been at it for the last two hours, and the pile Bailey unceremoniously dumped in front of me the second I sat down hasn't seemed to decrease in the slightest.

'There's no way you guys know this many people,' I grumble as I seal up an envelope addressed to a *Patrick and Joan Clarke*. 'And who the hell are these two?'

Bailey glances at the invitation. 'I think Patrick is one of Dad's cousins. Maybe a great uncle? I'm not too sure.'

I can confidently say I've never met cousin/maybe-uncle Patrick in my life. And if I haven't, I doubt Bailey has either. 'But you're inviting them to the wedding?'

She shrugs. 'It's more about keeping the peace. We're not expecting everyone to come.'

'Banking on it, actually,' Cash adds with a wry grin.

'They won't,' Bailey says confidently. 'Patrick and Joan aren't going to fly from Canada to Italy for a four-day weekend.' She gestures to my pile. 'Most of those are for family who live abroad. They're just getting invited to keep Mum, Dad and Cash's mum happy. They won't actually come.'

Everything I learn about wedding planning turns me further and further off the idea. That and the fact that the whole '*falling so deeply in love with someone that you actively want to spend the rest of your life with them*' thing is still fundamentally incomprehensible in my mind.

'If I ever get married, don't expect any of this,' I say, reaching for the next invitation and envelope. 'Actually, I might just turn up with a wife one day, and that'll be it. Still send gifts though.'

Bailey snorts. 'If you ever get married, I think Mum'll have a heart attack on the spot.'

'Why?' I ask, pretending to be offended. 'I could get married.'

I don't particularly want to. But I could.

'Getting married means you'll have to stick with someone for more than three weeks,' Bailey says pointedly.

'My record is six weeks, actually.'

I force a smirk as Bailey rolls her eyes. Six weeks isn't strictly true, anyway. I have had two long-term relationships, and neither ended particularly well. But Bailey doesn't know about them. The only person who does is Cash. When they first started dating, I briefly wondered if Cash might suddenly start sharing all my deepest secrets with Bailey but, given her response right now, it's safe to say he hasn't.

I glance over at him and he meets my gaze with an almost imperceptible lift of the brows. It's a silent question.

You good?

I give him a small nod in response. It's been a long time since I let myself wallow in the memories of my failed attempts at love, and I'm not eager to restart now. Some people – the Cash and Baileys of the world – are meant for love. They're meant for weddings and fairy tale happily ever afters.

And then there's the rest of us.

I'm not mad at it. It's just an immutable fact of life.

Love is not for me.

Bailey's phone suddenly lights up and she reaches for it with a grin. 'Nice. Eliott's just sent over her invoice for the deposit payment.'

Eliott.

Love may not be for me, but a little fun? Yeah, that's definitely something I can handle. Especially with someone like Eliott.

It's taken a few years of trial and error, but I've pretty much got it down to a science at this point. A couple of weeks exploring the flame we first lit two years ago before we go our separate ways. No hard feelings. No awkward goodbyes.

Just the way I like it.

Eliott and I could be enjoying each other's company right now, if she hadn't so spectacularly shut me down. There'd been a moment back at the restaurant when I thought she was about to agree. When I was sure our impromptu night together was most definitely going to end in us heading back to my place for round two.

And then she went ahead and did simultaneously the most frustrating *and* sexiest thing I've ever seen in my life.

Or should that be felt?

Because, even a full week later, I can still feel the featherlight pressure of her lips ghosting against mine. Every time I close my eyes I see the little smirk she gave me as she pulled away, and— Fucking hell.

Just the thought of it sends heat rushing straight to my dick.

I don't think I've ever wanted someone as badly as I want Eliott Rayne.

I don't sleep with the same person twice.

A completely irrational twinge of anger hits me. What bastard is responsible for that rule? Because it's obvious that she's been hurt. That someone — someone she probably cared for — has filled her head with the worst kind of bullshit and forced her to put up these boundaries around herself.

A shame. A real shame.

I let myself enjoy the memory of Eliott's half-lidded eyes and that full, sultry smirk one last time before I push it away, banishing it to the recesses of my mind. There's no point in dwelling on what could have been.

Though it definitely would've been fun.

★ ★ ★

The whole '*Forget about Eliott*' thing isn't going as well as I'd like it to.

For one, Bailey can't stop singing her praises. At dinner with our parents on Sunday, Bailey and Mum spend most of it fawning over the engagement party photos. They are, to be fair, pretty amazing. But hearing her name every five seconds doesn't really help with the whole *pushing Eliott from my mind* thing.

And secondly, and I guess this is the most pressing issue right now, she's standing right in front of me.

One More Shot

I've never been one for believing in karma, but I decide that I must have done *something* to rack up some positive points with someone somewhere. Because Eliott has been playing on my mind non-stop since the engagement party and somehow, here she is.

She hasn't noticed me yet, so I get a few seconds of unashamed ogling as she slowly pushes a trolley down the aisle. Her brows are furrowed as she squints at something on her phone. Whatever it is makes her roll her eyes and shake her head before she grabs something off the shelf and tosses it into her trolley.

Even under the almost fluorescent lighting in this supermarket, Eliott makes me stop in my tracks. It's like I've got tunnel vision and she's the light at the end of it all.

Her dark curls are pulled into a bun with a silk scarf loosely wrapped around the front, and the leggings she's wearing are practically a second skin, showing off delicious, soft curves.

Curves I'd very much love to have pressed up against me right now.

She chooses that moment to look up. Her eyes widen as she spots me down the aisle, and her perfect lips drop open in surprise. For a second I think she's about to turn and run, but then she seems to remember the promise she made back at the restaurant and the look of surprise makes way for something else.

It's a weird mix of delight and irritation and I wonder which of the two is going to win.

'Let me guess,' she drawls as she rolls the trolley to a stop beside me. 'You were hoping to bump into me?'

Well.

Yeah, actually. I'd be a terrible liar if I couldn't admit to myself that I've spent the last week trying and failing to come up with an excuse to message her again. If I'd have known all it took was to just rush out to the supermarket for some emergency snacks, I would've done this days ago.

I flash her an easy grin. 'Am I that easy to read?'

Eliott hums and looks me up and down. When she meets my gaze again, she's smiling and I swear my heart forgets how to beat. 'An open book.'

Tension I hadn't realised was thrumming through my body suddenly evaporates.

Delight, it is.

I lean across her trolley and drop my voice just a little. 'So, tell me. What else are you picking up on?'

Eliott's got the kind of face where, every time you look at her – *really* look at her – you notice something new. Like the smattering of dark, tiny moles that crest along her cheekbones. Or the way she bites her bottom lip slightly when she's holding back a laugh.

'What's so funny?' I ask.

'Nothing,' she says, eyes twinkling. 'I just . . . I was just wondering.'

'Wondering what?'

'Do you ever switch it off?'

I blink. 'Huh?'

Eliott leans against the trolley. 'You know . . .' She gestures in the general area surrounding me. 'This whole *shtick*.'

Another blink. Another, 'Huh?'

She looks at me curiously for a few long moments before she shakes her head. 'Nothing. Don't worry about it.' She starts pushing her trolley back in the direction she came from and I follow without hesitation.

'Do you live round here?' I ask, praying I've managed to keep the blatant hopefulness out of my voice.

Judging from the amused look she gives me, I've failed. But she doesn't mention it. Instead, she shakes her head again. 'I don't. I'm closer to where we met that one time . . .' She clears her throat and pointedly looks away. 'The warehouse? Remember?'

That's right. She'd only been a fifteen-minute Uber ride from the party two years ago.

'So, what're you doing here?' I ask. We're a good thirty minutes away from her place, and I'm sure there are closer supermarkets around.

'My grandmother lives down the road from here,' she says, after a brief moment of hesitation. 'I'm heading over to hers now, and she asked if I could grab her a couple of things on my way.'

I glance at the trolley. It's packed to the brim with groceries. Definitely not what I'd call 'a couple of things'.

'What about you?' she asks. 'Do you live close by?'

We've fallen in step with each other as we meander through the aisles. Our arms brush against each other every so often, but neither of us makes any move to put any more space between us.

'Not far from here.' My brain must be running on autopilot, because I don't even have to think about the words that come out of my mouth next. 'Why? You looking for an invitation?'

Because she can have one. An open invite, even. I'd gladly give one to her. All she has to do is ask.

Eliott rolls her eyes. She looks almost disappointed. 'And there it is again.'

'There what is?'

'The *shtick*.'

We've stopped in the cereal aisle, and Eliott whips out her phone again to check her grandmother's list.

'I already told you,' she mutters as she glances up and down the aisle for whatever it is that's on her list. 'I don't go back for seconds. So you can stop whatever this is. You're just wasting your time.'

I frown. There's an edge to her voice that definitely wasn't there before, and I don't like it. 'Whatever what is?'

Eliott sighs like the weight of the world is on her shoulders. 'We're not going to fuck, Dane.'

Later, I'll revisit this moment and wonder why her bluntness is turning me on like this. But right now, all I can do is gape.

'I wasn't—'

She gives me a sardonic grin. 'Open book. Remember?'

Well, *fuck*.

I guess I am easier to reader than I'd like to think. I smile sheepishly, and it seems to melt away some of the sudden ire she's feeling. 'My bad. But we can be friends, right?'

I don't know why I'm clinging onto anything in the first place. Eliott knows, just as well as I do, that my interest in her is purely physical. Without sex on the table, there's no reason for us to have any kind of lingering communication with each other.

Eliott snorts. 'Right. Sure.'

'What's that supposed to mean?'

'You don't seem like the kind of guy who keeps a lot of girlfriends. *Platonic* girlfriends. And I'll be honest with you, Dane,' she shrugs, 'I don't really need you around if all you're going to do is try to get into my pants.'

There it is again. That bluntness that I can't help but find strangely attractive. Thinking back on it, this is what attracted me to Eliott two years ago as well. Aside from the whole *she's gorgeous* thing. It was the confidence she approached me with, and it's back again now.

Although it's definitely not going in my favour this time.

She's giving me an out and every rational part of me knows that I should take it. Just admit that she's right and we can both go our separate ways. At the wedding we'll be like two ships passing in the night. Nothing more. Nothing less.

But I want more.

'I can do friends,' I tell her.

Disbelief is painted over her face, and I can't exactly blame her.

'I'm serious,' I say. I stick out my hand and she eyes it warily. 'Friends. *Just* friends. I can do that.'

She hesitates for a second or two, and then grips my hand and gives it a squeeze. 'Friends.'

I grin as we shake on it, and I try my best not to think about how nicely her hand slots in with mine.

I fail.

Miserably.

Chapter Twelve

ELIOTT

I'm a masochist.

That's the only logical explanation I can come up with as to why I'm leaving the supermarket with Dane's number saved in my phone. Clearly I'm someone who thrives on pain.

Because Dane and I absolutely do not need to be friends. I meant what I said to Sasha.

Dane is off the table.

As much as I can tell he's hoping otherwise, I'm not planning on reneging on my rule. It's in place for a reason. To stop people – people like Dane – from using me like a toy they'll inevitably get bored of once they realise they're not going to get the result they're hoping for.

SASHA
> Lolllllll

> So why'd you give him your number then?

I'm parked outside Nan's house, glaring at my phone. I don't have a rebuttal for Sasha, and I refuse to admit that she has a point.

Why *did* I give him my number?

Ah yes. I'm a masochist.

I shove my phone into my pocket without responding and start hefting Nan's shopping bags out of the car.

Stepping into Nan's house always feels like coming home. Josh and I practically grew up here after our dad dipped out of the picture and Mum realised she needed help raising two young kids.

I never thought twice about it – the extended periods of time Josh and I spent sleeping head to feet in Nan's tiny spare bedroom, blocking out the muffled sounds of Mum, Nan and Grandad arguing about things I was too young to understand.

It was our safe space. Where we'd come when things with Mum's latest boyfriend didn't work out and we had nowhere left to go.

'Just for a few weeks,' Mum would always say when we'd turn up on their doorstep with hurriedly packed bags missing most of our things.

I started making a list after the third time it happened.

Josh's favourite teddy bear.

Mum's EpiPen.

Our passports.

Money.

Anything that could make our lives a hundred times harder if we forgot them inside the home of a man who no longer wanted anything to do with us.

I was seven.

I think two years was the longest time we spent away from Nan and Grandad – when Mum met Leanne's dad and we played happy families for long enough that I thought it might finally be it. Gavin was always nice enough, but *nice* wasn't *enough* for Mum. She got bored.

Restless.

She's a free spirit and can't be tied down for long, and it turned out that two years was her limit, anyway.

Nan and Grandad kept us after that. It was Nan and Mum's biggest argument yet and, at twelve, I was old enough to understand most of it. Mum was free to come and go as she pleased, but there'd be no more new boyfriends for me and Josh.

We both lived here until we went off to university, with Leanne visiting on sporadic weekends, since she lived primarily with her dad. Mum would flit between Nan's house and whatever boyfriend she had at the time.

She's finally got her own place – now that all her kids have grown up and flown the nest – but it's never felt like home to me. I'm always a guest in her house, no matter how many times I've visited.

But Nan's house is different.

You can't take two steps in Nan's house without seeing some memory of my childhood. Her walls are filled with photos of us, documenting every single awkward phase of our lives. There's even one of me and Sasha at our graduation, beaming at the camera as we toss our hats into the air.

It really wouldn't take much for us to clear out the spare room for me if Nan really needed the help.

It would just be like coming home again.

I could do it, and I will if she needs me to. There's no question about it. I just wish she'd asked first.

I wish anyone would ask first.

'Eliott, do you might lending Leanne some money?'

'Is it cool if Wes moves in?'

'How do you feel about helping Nan out a little more?'

Would it really be so hard for them to ask and not just assume that my answer will always be a yes?

A familiar wave of irritation threatens to drown me as I shoulder open Nan's front door.

'Oh hello, love.' Mum pokes her head out of the living room and gives me a wave. 'We were wondering where you'd got to.'

One More Shot

She disappears back inside the living room and I hear the faint sound of laughter and music coming from the TV. I frown as I stomp further into the house, letting the front door slam behind me.

'What're you doing here?' I ask as I unceremoniously drop the shopping bags to the floor.

Mum is sitting on Nan's sofa, a cosy-looking blanket draped over her lower half and a steaming cup of tea on the coffee table in front of her. On the other side of the room, Nan is settled in her favourite armchair and one of her legs is propped up on a footstool. She gives me a smile, but it looks strained. She shifts in her seat and I swear the movement makes her wince slightly.

Panic begins to trickle through me. 'Is everything all right?'

'Everything's fine,' Mum says flippantly. 'Did you get the biscuits I asked for?' She doesn't wait for me to answer. Instead, she leaps up from her seat and starts rifling through the shopping bags. 'Oh, Eliott, you are a *star*.'

'I thought they were for Nan,' I grumble. 'And if you've been here all along, why couldn't *you* do the shopping?'

'You were on the way,' Mum says, with a dismissive wave of the hand.

'I wasn't though,' I mutter, but it falls on deaf ears. Because what does it matter that I was actually working on some edits when Nan messaged to ask if I wouldn't mind picking up a few things for her? At least, I *thought* they'd been for Nan. Mum grabs a few more items from the shopping bags and sets them aside for herself and I realise that I've been played.

But I've got more pressing issues right now. Namely, the fact that the wince on Nan's face has definitely become more pronounced.

'Nan?' I ask. 'What's wrong?'

She sighs and nods to her leg. 'I'm *fine*. I was putting the laundry out and I tripped on the patio. I'm a little bruised, but nothing to worry about.'

A flicker of recognition sparks in me. Nan's patio is nothing short of a death trap. It was Grandad's passion project before he passed. He kept insisting that he'd get round to fixing it up and but he never did.

Five years on and it's never been worse.

Large pieces of the stone tiles are broken or coming loose, making it a game of Russian roulette whenever you step onto one. Even I've twisted my ankle on one of the wobbly tiles more than once. The idea of Nan having to cross it in order to get to her lawn has always made me nervous. Like she's just one ill-placed step away from doing some serious damage.

I glance at her leg. There are no open wounds or any bones jutting out at awkward angles, so I have to trust that she's telling the truth, and it is just a bruise.

'I thought Josh was supposed to get someone in to fix it?' I ask.

Nan rolls her eyes.

'Right,' I say. Stupid question. I don't know why I even left it in Josh's hands to deal with in the first place. Wishful thinking, I guess.

'He's been busy with work,' Mum chimes in defensively. 'I'm sure he'll get round to it once he has the time.'

She's always quick with the excuses when it comes to Josh. There's no point in arguing, because the excuses are endless.

He's busy with work.

His girlfriend's been giving him grief.

You're just better *at dealing with these things anyway, Eliott.*

I've heard them all a million times before and I'm not in the mood to hear them again.

'I'll get someone in,' I tell Nan, already reaching for my phone to do a search for contractors in the area. 'And we should really make a doctor's appointment for you. Just to check that there's no damage.'

'Oh, yes,' Mum says absent-mindedly. 'Good idea, Eliott.'

Nan purses her lips but gives me a reluctant nod.

I'm about two pages deep into a Google search when a notification pings across my screen.

> **DANE**
>
> hey. just checking you got to your grandma's all right?
>
> also. it was nice seeing you. let me know when you're free, we can grab coffee or something

I have to hand it to him, he's persistent. My thumb hovers over the message, ready to swipe it away and ignore. But then I remember Sasha's question. Why did I bother even giving him my number if I wasn't planning on giving this whole *friendship* thing a go?

And besides, it suddenly hits me that Dane could be of particular help right now.

I'm typing out my reply before I have the chance to talk myself out of it.

> **ELIOTT**
>
> Weird one. But do you know anything about patio repair?
>
> **DANE**
>
> pls don't tell me you only agreed to be friends to get construction tips
>
> this can't keep happening to me
>
> **ELIOTT**
>
> It's happened before?

One More Shot

DANE

long story

but yes, i know everything about patio repair

why?

Chapter Thirteen

DANE

For the first time in years, I'm keeping a secret from Cash.

I don't remember the last time I held anything back between us – there's never been any reason to. Cash isn't the type to judge and there's very little that genuinely embarrasses me.

And yet.

'You coming in?' Cash asks, one hand on the door handle. I'm dropping him back home after a long workday and inviting me up for a drink or some dinner – or even just to annoy Bailey for a bit – comes to him as easily as breathing. I take him up on it most times, but not today.

'Can't,' I say, making a conscious effort to keep my voice steady. 'Got plans tonight.'

Cash throws me an intrigued look. 'Are you seeing someone?'

'I have other friends, you know,' I say, pretending to be offended. 'You and Bailey aren't my entire social circle.'

It's not a lie. I do have other friends. But I'm not going to see any of them tonight.

Cash laughs. 'All right, man. Have fun. I'll catch you later.' He hops out of the van and I watch as he disappears into the home he shares with my sister. A little twinge of guilt gnaws at me as I drive away. I haven't lied; just withheld important information. Important information like . . . I'm currently on my way to see Eliott.

The thought brings a smile to my face, even though it absolutely shouldn't. This isn't a date. Eliott's made that very, *very* clear. But I'm excited to see her again, if only to prove that I *can* be just friends.

I don't know who I'm trying to prove it to, though. Her or me?

It doesn't take me long to make the drive over to Eliott's grandmother's house, and it hits me that we've been orbiting each other for probably quite a while. Always just out of reach, without even knowing. I wonder if things would've been different if we'd met in some other kind of way. If our first meeting hadn't been tainted by our awkward bedroom encounter.

Maybe we would've been friends first.

Real friends.

Not whatever we've got going on right now.

An elderly woman opens the door for me. I can see shadows of Eliott in her. They have the same eyes and the way she surveys me, brows furrowed, eyes narrowed in vague suspicion, is so distinctly Eliott-ish, I can't help but smile.

'Name?' the woman asks, her voice sharp and wary.

'Dane,' I tell her. 'Your granddaughter – Eliott? She asked me to come and check out your patio.' I pause and then, for some reason, decide to add, 'We're friends.'

Eliott's grandmother doesn't look any less suspicious, but she does give me a quick nod before she disappears back into the house. I hear the muffled sound of her shouting Eliott's name and then, a few seconds later, Eliott appears.

Her hair is pulled up in a bun away from her face and her arms are wet and covered in rapidly popping soapy suds. 'Sorry,' she pants.

I try very hard not to think about the last time I heard Eliott out of breath. About just how her breathy little pants sounded. About how I'd very much like to hear it again.

'Was doing the dishes and lost track of time.' She wipes her soapy hands on her thighs and gives me a wide grin, like she's genuinely happy to see me. 'Thanks for coming, by the way.'

'Don't mention it,' I say as I step into the house. It's warm and inviting and I immediately get the feeling that this is very much a home.

Rows and rows of family photos line the walls in the hallway. I can't help but stop and stare at the photos as Eliott leads me down the hall. Eliott jumps out in almost all of them. There's a row of school photos, documenting her growth from primary school all the way up to her university graduation.

There's one in particular that catches my eye. She can't be older than twelve in it, and she's chubby-cheeked, wearing braces and awkwardly grimacing at the camera.

Eliott spots me looking at it and rolls her eyes. 'Don't laugh.'

'I wasn't laughing,' I say innocently. Truthfully, too.

She hums, clearly not believing me. 'Just remember, not all of us were born ridiculously good-looking.'

'Straight out of the womb,' I grin. 'That's what they tell me.'

She laughs and I'm once again reminded that her laugh is a sound I never want to forget. 'That explains the ego, I guess.'

Another photo catches my attention. She's a kid in it, with her hair pulled into two thick bunches, and she's sitting on the lap of an older man. They're both beaming widely and Eliott's got a camera in her hands.

'Your first camera?' I ask, nodding at the photo.

Eliott glances at the photo and her expression changes. It's a subtle difference. She's still smiling, but it's tinged with sadness.

'That's Grandad.' She clears her throat. 'He died a few

years back.' She takes a step closer to me, her arm brushing against mine. 'But yeah, that was my first camera. I think I was eight? Maybe nine? He loved taking photos.' She laughs quietly and gestures to the walls surrounding us. 'You can probably tell.'

'Is that how you got started?' I ask. 'Taking photos with him?'

'Mm,' she hums, eyes focused on the photo in front of us. 'He taught me the basics and kind of just let me go from there. We had different styles, but he always liked seeing what caught my eye and how I interpreted it.'

'How'd you land on weddings?'

She shrugs, like she's barely given it any thought. 'I like capturing the quiet moments. There's all the wedding beats you have to hit as a photographer. First look. First dance. The moment they say "*I do*". But I like getting the softer moments too. The little looks and glances. The soft touches. The smiles when they think no one's looking.'

I think back on the photos Eliott sent through from Cash and Bailey's engagement party. Looking back on it, they were filled with quiet moments. I wonder what the quiet moments in Eliott's life look like. And if I'd be able to slot into them.

Eliott clears her throat again. 'Come on. Nan's patience will only last so long.'

I follow her into a bright and hectic kitchen. There are

pots and pans occupying every spare inch of counter space, and a window overlooking the sink shows off a garden that's clearly seen better days.

Eliott's grandmother sits at the small, cluttered kitchen table and narrows her eyes as we walk into the space. 'I was just starting to think you two had got lost.'

Eliott rolls her eyes, clearly used to her grandmother's dramatics, and wrenches open the garden door. The lawn is long and overrun with weeds, there's a slanted tree at the back that looks like it's just one strong gust of wind away from doing some serious damage, and the patio . . .

I let out a low whistle as I follow Eliott out into the garden. Her grandmother stays seated at the table, and I don't blame her. The first tile I step on immediately collapses under my weight and sends me stumbling forwards.

Eliott shoots me an apologetic wince. 'You see the problem? Nan nearly breaks her ankle every time she comes out here.'

'How did it get so bad?' I ask, crouching down to inspect the crumbling tile beneath me.

Eliott sighs and squats down beside me. 'It's a long story.'

I catch her eye. 'I've got time.'

She quirks a brow and, when I don't relent, she sighs again. 'My brother was supposed to sort this out for Nan months ago. But he never got round to it.'

I wait for a beat or two for her to continue. When she

doesn't, I frown. 'If that's what you call a long story, I'm dying to know what you think a short story is.'

She laughs, but it's not the right laugh – the one that makes me smile right back. This one sounds forced. 'Right,' she says simply before pushing herself back up. She gestures to the space around us and cocks her head to the side. 'What do you think? Is it salvageable?'

'I've definitely seen worse,' I tell her. 'Not much worse, but I can work with this.'

Eliott heaves a sigh of relief. 'All right, why don't you let me—'

Her grandmother pokes her out of the garden door and waves a piece of paper in front of her face. 'Eliott, come and help me with this letter from the council. I don't know what they're asking me for.'

'Nan, I'm just—'

Her grandmother disappears back inside the house without so much as a second glance. Eliott scowls at the empty space and then shakes her head, her expression clearing in an instant. 'I'll be right back.'

'It's fine,' I say. 'I can get started out here.'

She nods and then hurries after her grandmother, mumbling something that sounds suspiciously like *'one thing at a time, Goddamn it'*.

There's not much I can actually do tonight, but I make headway by unrolling my tape measure, my fingers moving mechanically as I begin to measure the dimensions of the space. By the time Eliott returns, an apologetic half-smile on her face, I've already figured out how many tiles I'll need to order to replace the broken ones.

'What's the damage, then?' Eliott asks.

I hand her a piece of paper with a quote written on it. She stares at it for a long moment and then shakes her head and tries to shove the quote into my chest.

'Don't be stupid, Dane.'

I bite back a grin. I'd be lying if I didn't admit that I'd expected this kind of reaction from her. 'What? You've never heard of mates' rates?'

'Obviously I have,' Eliott mutters, her brows furrowing as she stares again at the quote I've written. 'I just . . . I don't see how this will be enough to cover even the cost of materials. It's way too low.'

I shrug. 'Like I said, *mates' rates*.'

'But we're not—'

I raise an unimpressed brow. 'Just take the discount, Eliott. It's not a big deal.'

She purses her lips and glares at me, though there's no heat behind it. 'I don't want you to think I'm taking advantage of you. Especially, you know . . . since we've got *history*?'

'Do we?' I ask lightly, feigning ignorance. 'I guess I forgot.'

That gets a laugh out of her. She shifts slightly, pressing

her back against the nearby wall, and looks up at me through hooded eyes. 'Didn't realise I was so forgettable.'

'Ah.' I lean in just a little. I'm still not in her personal space, but it's enough to trigger a shift between us. I can feel it and, from the way her eyes widen slightly, I'm guessing she can feel it too. 'You're the furthest thing from forgettable.'

She swallows. 'Really?'

It would take absolutely nothing for me to lean in and kiss her right now.

Friends.

The word echoes in my mind.

I clench my jaw and take a deliberate step backwards. 'Truthfully?' I ask. Our eyes lock. A small smile tugs at the corner of her lips, and she nods. 'I don't think I could forget you even if I tried.'

She swallows again and this time, her tongue darts out reflexively to run against her lips. 'Likewise.'

The energy between us shifts again.

Before I can act on it though, Eliott clears her throat and deliberately turns away. 'You're sure about this quote?' she says, voice too high, too stilted. 'Because I'm happy to pay your standard fee and—'

'I'm sure.'

I don't think I've ever been more sure about anything.

'Well.' She turns to face me again, but doesn't quite meet my eye. Under the dim light coming from the fluttering garden lamp beside us, it's difficult to make out if her cheeks look more flushed than usual or if I'm imagining it. 'Thank you, Dane. You're a—' She pauses for a second and chuckles, laughing at some unspoken joke that I'm not privy to. 'You're a lifesaver.'

And you know what?

I think I could get used to hearing that.

Chapter Fourteen

ELIOTT

'No Cash?'

It's been a week since our initial consultation and Dane is standing on Nan's porch, a bag of tools slung over his shoulder, his signature lopsided grin etched onto his face.

'Nope. Just me tonight,' he says, grin widening slightly. 'Is that a problem?'

I'm not going to pretend like I know anything about patio repair, but I get the impression that it's definitely the kind of job that would go by much faster with two people on it.

I shrug, matching the nonchalant energy he's bringing. 'Can you handle it by yourself?'

He lifts a brow as he steps past me and into Nan's house, our arms brushing against each other in the narrow space. 'There's not much I can't handle, Eliott.' He says it with a drawl, drawing out each syllable of my name, like he's offering me a challenge.

I don't *think* he's doing it on purpose.

The flirting, I mean.

I'm pretty sure that being an unrepentant flirt is simply a non-negotiable part of his personality. One he doesn't know how to switch off.

And I absolutely shouldn't be falling for it. Especially after I've put up these boundaries between us. But I can't stop my cheeks from warming, the urge to lean right into the moment and throw one of my own carefully crafted lines right back at him is overwhelming.

It would be so easy, too. Natural, even.

Instead, I roll my eyes as he walks past, feigning indifference. 'Well, I guess we're about to find out, aren't we?'

He laughs and shoots me an easy grin. 'I guess we will.'

Everything about Dane is easy and I feel an increasingly familiar twinge of envy towards him. It must be nice to just be able to float through life without having to be in a perpetual state of worry.

Sometimes it feels like I can never just be in the moment, focused on one thing. I'm either worrying about Nan or sorting out something for Leanne, or – and this is the current bane of my life – emailing back and forth with our landlord because Sasha refuses to engage with him and leaves any issues up to me to deal with.

There's always *something*.

Even now, I should be working on edits and most definitely

not following Dane through Nan's house so I can make sure the patio gets sorted and not have to worry about Nan snapping an ankle every time she steps outside.

'Everything all right?'

I blink up at Dane. He's crouched down by the pile of tiles he ordered to the house, watching me curiously.

'Everything's fine,' I sigh.

His brows furrow slightly.

'It's fine,' I say, a little more forcefully this time. 'Just . . . life, you know?'

He opens his mouth immediately, a response already on the tip of his tongue. But then he clamps it shut and gives me an annoyingly sympathetic smile. 'Got it.'

'Pretty sure you don't,' I mutter. It's petty and childish, and Dane doesn't deserve my ire, but the words come out before I can stop myself.

'Try me,' Dane says with another easy shrug. He's started lifting the broken tiles and stacking them in a pile.

I hesitate.

I should really let him get on with it. He knows what to do and definitely doesn't need me lurking around. But there's something in his expression, a kind of earnestness that reminds me of the look he had back at the restaurant. Before I know it, I'm settling down on the garden steps.

'It's a long story,' I say.

His gaze flits over to me for a second, and a teasing grin

tugs at his lips. 'A long story like how the patio was? Or an actual long story?'

I laugh. 'An *actual* long story. The patio's part of it, I guess.'

Dane nods in understanding. 'Cool. So start with that.'

'Do you ever feel like—' I pause. There's a lump forming in my throat. I don't think I've ever voiced this aloud. Not even to Sasha. It's been my own secret burden to bear for as long as I can remember and the fact that I'm telling it to Dane, of all people, is enough to make a nervous laugh bubble out of me.

Maybe it makes sense that it's Dane. Someone I've got no real connection with. Someone who doesn't expect anything from me.

'Do you ever feel like everyone's relying on you?' I ask after a few seconds. 'Like you're the one everyone turns to in a crisis, and you can't let them down?' The words come out and my chest suddenly feels lighter. It's like a weight has been lifted, but I'd become so used to it I hadn't even realised it was there.

Dane frowns. 'Not really.'

The weight settles on my chest again. 'Didn't think so.'

'Why can't you let them down?' Dane asks.

'Because they need me?' My response comes out sounding more like a question than I expect it to.

'Who told you that?' Dane has stopped with the tiles and is staring directly at me, forcing me to hold his gaze.

'Nobody *told* me,' I say. 'It's just – That's just how it is. How it's always been.'

I think I was nine when I finally realised that my relationship with Mum was never going to be the kind of mother–daughter one I watched on television. I was equal parts her therapist and personal assistant before I even hit secondary school. I remember being fifteen when Grandad got officially diagnosed, and knowing that I had to keep the harsh reality – that Grandad was sick, *really* sick – from Leanne. I almost didn't even go to university because Nan and Grandad got really sick at the same time and I didn't know if Mum would be able to handle it by herself.

'That sounds exhausting.' Dane's voice cuts through my memories like a hot knife through butter.

'It is,' I say quietly.

So exhausting.

'So, why do you keep doing it?' There's no judgement in his tone. He sounds genuinely curious. Like he can't possibly fathom why someone would choose to live their life the way I do.

I've told myself this answer so many times, I don't even have to think about it. 'Because I love them. And if I can do something to make life easier for them, then I should do it. Right?'

I expect him to agree. To accept the universally recognised

truth that, when you love someone, you just do things for them if you can.

'Who makes life easier for you?'

'I—' I stare at him. 'What?'

'Who makes life easier for you?' Dane repeats. He's staring me at me so intently, I'm surprised he's not burned a hole through my skin yet. 'You're busy worrying about everyone else, right? Who worries about you?'

The lump in my throat is back and bigger this time. 'I don't need anyone to worry about me,' I manage to choke out.

'That is—' His jaw ticks slightly and he shakes his head, cutting off whatever train of thought he was on.

'No, no.' I stand up and cross the short distance between us. 'Say it. Go on. I'm a big girl. I can handle it.'

The wind whirls around us and sends a few stray curls whipping around my face. I raise a hand to brush one away, but Dane gets there first. His fingers lightly ghost along my cheekbone as he pushes a strand away.

'You shouldn't have to handle it, Eliott,' he says softly, fingers still dancing along my skin. The moment can't last for any longer than a second, but it feels like it stretches out for an eternity. He clears his throat and finally pulls away. 'That's the problem.'

★ ★ ★

Since he refuses to bring Cash, Dane is working on the patio in a kind of piecemeal way. He comes over to Nan's house every Friday evening to work on the patio and I, despite my best intentions, always end up spending the evening sitting on the garden steps watching him work.

Before I know it, we've started to develop a routine of sorts. It's completely unintentional, and I don't even realise we've fallen into it until it's almost over, but I'm not complaining.

Sometimes we sit in silence; me with my tablet working on some edits while Dane methodically tears up broken tiles and replaces them with newer ones.

And sometimes we talk.

The conversation flows like we've been friends for years and . . . It's nice.

It's *easy*.

'I need your opinion on something,' Dane says suddenly. 'As a wedding expert,' he clarifies when I shoot him a wary look.

'I wouldn't say *expert*.'

It's that weird time of the year where it's not quite winter, not quite spring. The sky is a mix of dark blues and purples and the sun is just a tiny orange blip on the skyline. Nan's one pathetically flickering garden lamp is doing very little to illuminate the space between us. This is normally the part in the evening where Dane heads home, mumbling something about it being too dark to work and that he'll be back to finish the job next week.

But not tonight.

I jump slightly as he drops down into the empty spot next to me on the garden steps. Something in the back of my mind vaguely acknowledges that this isn't part of the carefully crafted routine we've put together over the last few weeks.

This is new.

'How many weddings have you been to?' he asks, stretching his legs out in front of us.

'As a guest or . . .'

He shrugs. 'Just in general.'

I lean backwards and my hand brushes against his. It's not quite electricity that shoots through my veins at the contact, it's more like an unexplainable warmth that starts at the tip of my fingers and spreads like wildfire through me.

I snatch my hand back and stare determinedly at the setting sun. 'Probably coming up to about two hundred now,' I murmur. Beside me, I feel Dane shift slightly but I don't look. 'Why?'

He clicks his tongue and even without seeing his face, I can easily picture the teasing grin that's curving his lips right now. 'Let me know what you think about this opener for my best man speech.' He clears his throat dramatically. '*The Oxford Dictionary defines love as—*'

'Absolutely *not*.' A cackle splutters out of me and I finally turn to look at him. I was right. He's grinning down at me. One of his locs has fallen out of the bun he keeps them in and my fingers twitch to reach forward and slide it back into place.

'You don't like it? I thought it was a pretty good opener.'

'If you start your speech with that, I'll drag you out of the wedding myself.'

'That doesn't sound too bad,' Dane laughs, a teasing glint in his eyes. 'Depending on *where* you're dragging me, of course.'

And here we are again. I should start timing how long it takes for Dane to bring a harmless conversation back into flirting territory.

'How about straight into the Ligurian Sea?' I ask, refusing to take the bait.

My reluctance to engage doesn't seem to bother him at all. His grin widens fractionally. 'Will you be joining me?'

'Can't swim,' I throw back.

'That's fine.' Something flashes in his eyes. 'I can hold you.'

That gets a snort out of me. 'Love the enthusiasm, but—'

'But what?' Dane looks me up and down slowly through hooded eyes. At some point during this back and forth, we've shifted slightly and the space between us is minimal. 'If you're about to say that you don't think I can handle holding you up—' He leans in and suddenly there's barely an inch between us. 'I didn't have any problem with it two years ago, and I definitely don't now.'

Memories flash through my mind.

Dane holding me up against the wall, peppering my neck with soft, wet kisses. Me, pushing him onto the bed and climbing on top. The little groan that fell from his lips as he gripped my still hovering thighs and pulled me firmly down onto him with no hesitation. The way his dick, hard and wanting, felt pressed against my thighs.

The grin on his face is irritatingly self-assured as he pulls away and I know, without a shadow of a doubt, that the memories replaying in his mind right now are identical to mine.

'Do you like making this whole *friends* thing difficult?' I ask, because there's no point in pretending like he can't plainly see what's written across my face.

His smile doesn't waver. 'It is fun,' he concedes. 'And I like making you blush.'

'I don't blush.'

'Hm.' He reaches over, closes the gap between us again, and runs a thumb along my cheek.

I've noticed that he likes doing that. Holding my face with a tenderness that always surprises me. I don't think anyone's ever held me like that before.

'Your cheeks are warm,' he murmurs before he pulls away. 'I think that's the very definition of a blush.'

'Maybe it's my turn to make you blush.'

'Shoot.'

There are a lot of things I could say right now. I could follow his lead and lean into the flirtatious rhythm we've struck up tonight. I'm doubtful that it would make him blush, but I'm pretty sure he'd enjoy it.

There's a quip on the tip of my tongue when something else jumps into the forefront of my mind. 'How come you haven't brought Cash here?' I ask, instinctively voicing the question that's been ruminating in my mind for the last month or so.

He goes quiet, the smile wiped off his face, and I can practically see the gears in his brain working overtime as he scrambles for a way to respond.

'Honestly?'

I nod and bump his shoulder with mine. The touch sends that same warmth shooting through me again. 'Honestly.'

Dane shrugs and he's not blushing exactly, but there's something about the expression on his face. Something I can't quite place. 'Maybe I just don't want to share you with anyone else?'

His response is equal parts evasive and flirtatious – very much the Dane I've come to know over the last few weeks. But there's something else to it. A rare air of vulnerability there. Like I've finally caught him with his walls down and he's not quite sure how to proceed, so he's trying to mask it with a joke that's not entirely untrue.

I don't know what to say in response, so I don't say anything. But I do smile.

And then he smiles back and the urge to run and grab my camera and capture this moment – Dane, grinning widely, the setting sun around us making his skin glow even more than usual – is so strong, it startles me.

Chapter Fifteen

ELIOTT

When the final Friday rolls around and Dane puts the finishing touches on Nan's patio, I can't even pretend like I'm happy about it.

I realise, as I watch Nan shuffle around her newly repaired patio inspecting every inch of it with eagle eyes, that I've started to look forward to our Friday evenings together.

They've somehow become the only pocket of time I have where I don't have to worry about anything at all. It's like Dane has neatly slotted himself into this gap in my life I didn't even realise was there. I don't have to think twice when it comes to him. There's nothing niggling at the back of my mind. No work. No family. No crisis that's just waiting on the periphery, ready to break and consume my thoughts.

'A job well done,' Nan says after her third full inspection of the patio. There's a soft smile tugging at her lips, and I know she's more pleased than she wants to let on. I can't imagine how frustrating it's been for her to have her garden inaccessible for so long, and I feel a pulse of guilt for not having sorted it out sooner. 'Thank you, Dane.'

'It's been my pleasure, Gloria.'

I'm not sure when Nan and Dane got on first-name terms, but it's weird. Nan was a teacher back in the day and I've seen her scold adults twice my age for assuming familiarity and using her first name, but she doesn't seem to mind when it comes to Dane.

'Stay for dinner,' Nan orders as she climbs back up the garden steps and into the house.

Dane opens his mouth to, I assume, politely decline, just like he's done every Friday for the last five weeks, but I get there first.

'Yeah.' I lean against the doorframe as casually as I can. 'You should stay. Unless—'

'No "unless",' Nan scoffs. 'He's staying.' She leaves no room for argument and shuffles back inside the kitchen.

As soon as she's out of sight, Dane raises a brow. 'Unless?'

'Unless you've got somewhere else to be?' I say with a shrug. I jog down the steps and come to sit by his side on the patio. 'It's your first free Friday night in over a month. I don't want to assume.'

I'm fishing.

He knows it. I know it. Hell, if Nan was still listening in, she'd know it too.

A laugh rumbles out of him. It's deep, like rolling thunder, and settles in the depths of my chest. '*Somewhere?*'

'Sure,' I laugh with him. 'You've got your Friday nights free again. The legions of women lining up to date you can resume their regularly scheduled programming.'

'A *line?*' he snorts, clearly amused. 'There's no line, Eliott.'

I find that hard to believe. 'Maybe not a physical line, but—'

'There's not a line right now, anyway,' Dane says firmly. He glances at me as he says it and then looks away.

'You're off the market?' I ask. He's not mentioned a girlfriend, but I suppose I haven't asked. Despite the rampant flirting, love and dating have been the only topics we've both seemed to mutually agree to avoid over the last month.

But the month is over now and I can't pretend like I haven't developed a kind of morbid curiosity about Dane's love life. He seems the type to always have a date lined up and, now that I'm done monopolising his Friday, I expect him to get right back into it. Even if the thought of it does irritate me for reasons I'd rather not dwell on right now.

For a moment, the mask slips and the expression on his face is one I'm not used to. He looks almost . . . *hurt*. The moment is fleeting and his trademark grin is back up so fast, I almost wonder if it ever disappeared. 'No. And that's not happening anytime soon.'

'Ah.' Now that's in line with the Dane I've built up in

my head. The one who flits from woman to woman without a second thought.

'Don't say *ah* like that,' Dane mutters, bumping his leg against mine.

'I'm not judging you,' I say quickly. Probably too quickly, because he raises an eyebrow in disbelief. 'I'm *not*. I get it. You like to have fun.'

He appraises me with hooded eyes, and I get the faintest shadow of a smile from him. 'I do.'

'But you don't want anything else?' I push, my curiosity getting the better of me.

A silence settles over us and it feels like, for the first time, I've stepped over an invisible line. I can see the irritation flash across his face at the line of questioning and my apology immediately bubbles up my throat.

'Sorry, you don't—' I offer him a weak grin. 'I was just being nosy.'

Dane leans back onto his arms and looks up at the sky. 'It's not that I don't want anything else.' His voice is muted, like he's thinking out loud rather than purposefully answering my question. 'It's more like I've realised that lifestyle isn't for me.'

'Lifestyle?'

He tilts his head in my direction and gives me a sad smile. 'The Cash and Bailey story. You know? Love? Happily ever after? That kind of shit. It's not for me.'

'You don't think *love* is for you?' I ask, incredulously. 'There's not a cap on who gets to be loved, Dane. It's not a finite resource. You know that, right?'

'In theory.' He breathes out a dry, sardonic laugh. I don't expect him to elaborate. We've strayed way off our usual path and I wouldn't blame him if he wanted to abruptly change the topic. 'I've had two girlfriends,' he says, after an extended beat of silence. 'And I guess you could say neither relationship ended well.'

'What happened?'

'They both cheated,' Dane says with a shrug. I can tell that it's supposed to be light and airy. Like this doesn't bother him anymore. But there's a stiffness to the way he holds himself. The way he clenches his jaw and his gaze won't meet mine.

'I was young for the first one. Only nineteen. And it sucked obviously. Hurt like hell, but I guess I convinced myself that it was an age thing. That maybe I wasn't that great a boyfriend, anyway.'

He shoots me that same sad smile again.

'And then it happened again. I think I was—' He pauses and clucks his tongue, pretending like he's actually having to think about it. 'I was twenty-three. And she blamed me.'

'She blamed *you*?' I feel furious on his behalf, even though this happened close to a decade ago. 'Dane, you know—'

'I know,' he cuts me off with another dry huff. 'It's not

on me. Don't worry. Cash has been through this with me more times than I can count over the years. She cheated because she had her own issues. I get that. But it was what she said. Her reasoning for it. That *I* wasn't enough.' He shrugs again. 'And I tried to be, for her. You know? I did all the things a good boyfriend is supposed to do. I – I *thought* I loved her.'

'And now you're not so sure?'

Another shrug. 'Got nothing to compare it to.'

'So what? You just stopped trying?'

'Pretty much,' he laughs. 'Once sucks. Twice is truly fucking awful. Wouldn't wish it on my worst enemy. And three times?' He gives me a wry grin. 'I'm not enough of a masochist to try.'

'Dane.'

He groans and shakes his head. 'What was it you said back at the restaurant? *I'm not here for your sympathy or anything like that?*'

A memory clicks into place. 'You just wanted to explain?'

He nods. 'You've got your hang-ups, I've got mine.'

He's right. Who am I to offer sympathy or advice when I'm pretty much in the same boat as him? We've both been hurt by people we trusted and we've had to put up walls to protect ourselves. His constant flirting and nonchalant attitude makes a lot more sense to me now.

It's a way for him to take control again. If he's the one

in charge, the one calling the shots and deciding how long something will last or how serious it'll ever be, he can't get hurt again.

I get it.

I truly do understand, but I can't help but feel a wave of sadness towards him. Maybe I'll never have an orgasm, but I haven't abandoned all thoughts of falling in love. Not yet anyway.

But Dane's chosen his path. I can see it in his eyes, the stubborn glint that tells me there's not a thing anyone could say to him to make him change his mind.

I clear my throat. 'When was the last time you had some fun?'

Dane's grin morphs into something a little more natural, more familiar, and he wiggles his brows. 'Are you offering?'

There we go.

'No,' I snort and smack his thigh. There's that warmth again, blooming under my fingertips at the contact. 'But I will be your wingman.'

Dane's brows disappear into his hairline and I don't blame him. The offer comes out of my mouth before my brain really has the chance to register what I'm saying. '*You'll* wingman *me*?'

'I'm great at it.' It's true. The only reason Sasha even gave Wes a second glance was because of me, and look at them now. 'And you deserve some fun.'

He stares at me for a few seconds, chewing the inside of his cheek. 'And what about you? Do you deserve some fun, *Eliott*?'

He's doing it again. Saying my name in that drawn-out kind of way, like he wants to savour it on his tongue.

I force a smile and try not to put too much thought into the disappointment I'm currently feeling.

We're back to our usual status quo.

* * *

Sasha hasn't stopped grinning all night. From the moment Dane turned up at our door, as we piled into our Uber, and even as we stepped through the doors of the venue, Sasha's brown-lined lips have been pulled into a wide smile.

If Dane's noticed anything off about her tonight, he hasn't mentioned it.

'Can you *stop*?' I hiss when the two of us finally get a brief moment alone as Dane and Wes head to the bar to get us some drinks.

'Stop what?' Sasha says, her voice an innocent sing-song.

'You know exactly what you're doing.'

'I'm having a great time with my boyfriend and my best friend and her—' Sasha gives a deliberate and dramatic pause as she pretends to think. 'Hm. How *would* you describe your relationship with Dane?'

'We're *friends*,' I grit out. 'So you can stop all of this now.'

She flutters her eyelashes at me, a picture of innocence. 'Stop what?'

If Sasha wasn't my very best friend in the world, I think I might throttle her. I still might. 'I mean it, Sash. You're making it weird.'

'Sorry,' Sasha says with what looks like genuine remorse. 'It's just. Well. You guys are *cute* together.'

'But we're not together. We're just friends,' I manage to grit out.

Just. Friends.

'Only because you're stubborn as hell,' Sasha mumbles, quiet enough that I can pretend like I didn't hear. She nods at something over my shoulder and gives me an exasperated look. 'Anyone can see that he's all about you.'

I glance behind me just in time to see Dane and Wes pushing through the crowd again, each holding two drinks in their hands. Wes makes an automatic beeline for Sasha, but Dane gets caught up in the crowd.

A tall, pretty girl with long passion twists stops him halfway across the room. I can't hear what she says over the music, but her body language is unmistakable. She leans in, her chest brushing against his, and whispers something into his ear. Dane's face breaks out into a pleased grin, but instead of nodding enthusiastically and quickly disappearing into a dark corner of the club with her like I expect, he just shakes his head.

The girl pouts, says something else that makes him laugh, and then disappears back into the crowd with her friends. As soon as she's gone, Dane looks up and catches my eye.

'That's right,' Sasha murmurs, looking incredibly pleased with herself. 'Like I said, he's all about *you*.'

Wes gives me a look that suggests he's in full agreement with Sasha.

'Traitor,' I mouth in his direction. My phone vibrates in the pocket of my jeans, but I ignore it.

Sasha and Wes quickly dance their way into the crowd, Sasha's hips swaying in time with the uptempo beat blaring from the speakers.

'What was that about?' Dane asks as he appears in front of me again and hands me my drink. 'How come they left you?'

'No idea,' I lie, before taking a sip from my drink. It's a sickeningly sweet cocktail and the bubbly warmth sliding down my throat gives me a little boost. 'And you?' I nod my head in the direction of the girl who had approached him in the crowd. She's trying not to make it obvious, but every so often her gaze scans the room and I know she's on the lookout for Dane. 'What happened there?'

Dane gives me a mischievous grin over the rim of his glass. 'Nothing happened. She just had a question for me.'

The crowd shifts us further into the throng on the dance floor, and we both start moving to the beat. I take another swig of my drink.

'What was the question?'

Dane two steps over to me and slides his free arm around my waist without hesitation. My heart thuds almost painfully against my ribcage as he pulls me flush against him, shifting slightly so my leg can slot gently between his. 'How's my dancing?' he asks, deliberately ignoring my question.

'A lot better,' I admit. Two years ago he struggled to catch the beat, but he's effortlessly keeping up with me now, even taking the lead at some points. 'Someone's been practising.'

He beams down at me. 'For the wedding.'

The song changes to one I'm more familiar with and I join in with the cheer that erupts from the crowd. Out of the corner of my eye I spot Sasha and Wes, so interlinked you can barely tell where one ends and the other begins. Dane pulls me in even closer and, as I instinctively wrap my arms around his neck, I feel a sense of déjà vu. This whole scene is remarkably similar to that night two years ago.

And we both know how that ended.

Another angry vibration from my phone. I move to reach for it, but then Dane discards his drink and both his hands settle on my waist. I try not to think too hard about how nice the touch feels. How right it feels. Like we're just picking up where we left off and there's not two years of lost time between us.

'She wanted to know if I had plans to leave here with

anyone tonight,' Dane says suddenly. His warm brown eyes are fixed on mine, and I can see the beginning flashes of heat sparking in them.

My heart thuds. 'What'd you say?'

'No plans just yet.'

Just yet.

He leans in, his lips brushing against the shell of my ear. 'For the record,' he murmurs, hands still on my waist, gently guiding me to the beat. A shiver wracks through me, but I'm not cold. I don't think I've ever been so hot. 'There's only one person in here I'd be interested in going home with.'

I swallow.

Remember your rule. Remember your rule.

I don't break eye contact. 'Point her out,' I say, my voice no louder than a breathy whisper. It's a miracle he can even hear me over the blaring music.

The song switches again and Dane lets his hands drop. I fight the urge to pick them back up and put them right back on me.

'Unfortunately, she's not down for it.' He pulls away, putting a fair bit of distance between us.

I swallow again. 'How very unfortunate.'

He gives me a half smile. 'Very.'

My phone buzzes furiously one last time and, to give myself an excuse to look away, I pull it out of my pocket.

> MISSED CALLS: Nan (12)

My heart leaps into my throat while my stomach plummets.

'Shit,' I mutter, immediately pushing through the crowd. 'Shit. Shit.'

Nan isn't the kind of person to keep on calling if she doesn't get a response. Something's wrong.

The cool night air slaps me in the face as I break free from the crowd and into the tiny garden people are using as a smoking area. It's noisy out here, but I can at least hear the dial tone as I wait for Nan to pick up.

She doesn't.

I try again.

Nothing.

The world starts to spin. I feel like I'm going to faint or throw up or—

'Eliott.' Dane's voice cuts through the haze I'm rapidly sinking into and, for a second, I can breathe easily. But then the reality of it all sinks in and I'm drowning again.

Nan.

Twelve missed calls.

And now she's not picking up.

Fuck.

My mind swims with worst-case scenarios that I have to furiously shake away before tears start to prick at my eyes.

'I've got to go.' I start pushing my way back through the crowd, but Dane tugs on my arm and holds me in place. 'Dane, let go. I have to—'

He whirls me around and cups my face tenderly in his hands. 'Breathe, baby. Breathe.'

My breath comes out in a dry, choked sob. 'I *can't*, Nan is—'

Nan is what? Crumpled in a heap at the bottom of the stairs? Gasping for breath, unable to crawl out of bed? My mind flickers with images of Nan hurt, injured, and alone in her home.

Breathing gets even harder.

'Have you tried your mum?' His voice is calm and soothing, cutting through the alarm bells that are blaring in my mind. 'Or your sister? Maybe she managed to get ahold of one of them.'

Logic cuts through my panic. He's right. If Nan couldn't reach me, she'd definitely try Mum or Leanne.

Mum doesn't pick up at all, but Leanne answers on the second ring.

'Oh my god, Elz, I was just thinking about you. You know that dress you have, the purple one? Can I—'

'Leanne.' I cut her off abruptly. We don't have time for this. Not tonight. 'Has Nan called you tonight?'

'Nan?' She hums and I can just picture her tapping her chin thoughtfully. 'Oh. Yeah. She called me about twenty minutes ago, but I was in the shower and—'

'Did you call her back?'

'No?' She sounds confused. 'I told you, I was in the shower and I had to do my hair routine and you know how long *that* takes, so—'

I hang up before I say something I know I'll regret.

'What about your brother?' Dane is tapping away on his phone, but he looks up at me when he hears my groan of frustration. 'Try him.'

'Nan wouldn't bother with Josh unless—' I hiccup out a panicked breath. 'Unless it was an emergency.'

I can't decide whether I want Josh to have heard from her or not, as I wait for him to answer the call. That's assuming he even does. Mum still hasn't even texted me to ask why I called.

'Yo.'

Relief floods through me, but it's short-lived. 'Josh, has Nan called you tonight?'

'Yeah.'

I wait a beat until I realise that's as much of a response as I'm going to get without any prompting. 'Did she say what she wanted?'

'Dunno.' In the background, I can hear the sounds of explosions and gunfire. He's playing a video game. I don't know why that pisses me off more than Leanne and her hair routine taking precedence over Nan, but it does.

'You didn't ask?' I grit out. 'You know Nan wouldn't call

you unless it was an emergency and you just – You didn't even think to check in on her?' I see red as anger erupts inside me. 'What the fuck is wrong with you, Josh?'

I hear the sound of wood scraping back and Josh shifting in his seat. 'Listen, yeah—'

I end the call before I have to hear what I assume will be a pathetic attempt at an excuse. 'I need to go.'

Dane nods and immediately starts carving a path through the crowd for me. 'I called an Uber. It's waiting outside.'

Ever since I noticed the missed calls from Nan, I've been drowning in a sea of emotions. Guilt. Worry. Anger. They've been all-consuming and threatening to swallow me whole.

But, as Dane tucks me into his side, leading me out of the heaving club and into the Uber he has waiting, another emotion starts to emerge.

I don't fully realise what it is until the Uber is hurtling down the street and Dane is sitting by my side, giving my thigh gentle and reassuring squeezes every few seconds.

It's gratitude.

Chapter Sixteen

DANE

Eliott hasn't said a word.

Every so often she'll try to call Gloria again, but it keeps going straight to answerphone and I can feel the tension in her building up.

I don't know what to do or say to make this better. All I know is that I desperately want to. The look on her face – the panic, the fear, the anger – I want to wipe it all away and make sure she's never in a situation that makes her feel like this again.

I've never felt like this before. Hopeless. Worried for someone other than myself. At a loss for what to do.

I feel a sudden urge to message Cash. This feels like something in *his* wheelhouse – not mine.

Eliott keeps her gaze fixated on her phone, like she's afraid if she glances away, even for a second, she'll miss something and her world will come shattering down around her.

'We're almost there,' I murmur as our driver takes us down a familiar street. I give her thigh another squeeze and she relaxes, ever so slightly, into my touch.

'What if she's fallen again?' Her voice is something quieter than a whisper. 'What if she's hurt and she's just lying there, waiting for someone?' Her chest heaves and I can tell she's working her way up to tears. 'And we've all just been ignoring her all night.'

'You weren't ignoring her.'

She looks up at me, her expressive, caramel eyes shiny with unshed tears. 'Twelve missed calls, Dane. *Twelve*. She needed me and I was . . . What? What was I doing that was so important?'

'You were living your life,' I say firmly. 'Having a good time. That's not illegal, Eliott. You're allowed to enjoy your life.'

She sniffs and glances away, and I pretend like I don't notice the tear sliding down her cheek. 'Doesn't feel that way sometimes.'

I pull her in close to me and we stay like that; Eliott's head on my shoulder, my hand on her thigh, in a comfortable silence for the rest of the drive.

The second we crawl up beside Gloria's house, Eliott is out of the door and up the pathway before the car even comes to a dead halt. I mutter a thanks to our driver and hurry after her. Her hands shake as she fumbles for her key, but just as she finally gets it in the lock and turns it, the door is flung open.

Gloria blinks up at the both of us, looking thoroughly unimpressed. Her clothes are soaked from the waist down and she has a mop in one hand and a thick roll of paper towels in the other.

'It's about time,' she huffs, and that's the only acknowledgment we get before she turns around and storms back into her home.

Eliott blinks silently at the space where her grandmother was just stood. 'Nan?' She darts into the house after Gloria. I hang back, not entirely sure if this is something I should be here for. 'Are you okay?'

'Do I *look* okay?' comes Gloria's irritated reply from the kitchen.

'Yes!' Eliott sounds borderline hysterical. 'Yes, you do and—' She gasps loudly. 'How on earth—'

I poke my head into the kitchen and the cause for all the panic tonight is suddenly apparent. There's water everywhere and the only thing stopping it from leaking into the hall and the rest of the house is a mountain of paper towels Gloria has propped up by the entrance.

Gloria lifts a brow at me as I step over the towels and wade through the mini lake that's suddenly appeared in her kitchen. 'Any chance you also do some plumbing on the side?'

'Afraid not,' I say with a wince as the water sloshing

around my ankles slips into my shoes. 'But I know a guy. I can give him a call—' I pause and glance over at Eliott, wondering if I'm over-stepping. She's not looking at me, though. Instead, she's crouched down by the sink, pulling anything vaguely bucket-related out from the cupboard beneath it.

Figures.

She's been in here for less than a minute and already she's trying to solve the problem and make things right.

'What happened?' Eliott asks as she begins scooping water from the floor and pouring it out of the open window. I join her, grabbing a bucket from the pile she's made, and she gives me a soft, thankful smile.

It's the kind of smile that makes my heart skip a beat.

'No idea,' Gloria says with a tired shrug. She sinks into a nearby chair and lets the mop in her hands fall to the floor. 'I came in to make a cup of tea before bed and this is what I walked into. I did try to call you.' She says the last part almost accusingly and Eliott stiffens slightly.

'I was out.' She avoids her grandmother's eye. 'And my phone was on silent.'

Gloria makes a grunting sound and I find myself standing a little straighter as her narrowed gaze slides over to me. 'I wasn't expecting to see you again so soon, Dane.'

The statement is innocent enough, but there's something in her tone that's weighed down with implication.

I force an easy grin onto my face. 'Always happy to help.'

I don't know if I'm imagining it, but I'm pretty sure Gloria's lip twitches. 'You're quite the gentleman.'

'Why don't you go and rest, Nan?' Eliott cuts in quickly. 'I'll get the kettle on for you, and we can sort this out.'

She's included me in the rescue effort without even asking, and it doesn't bother me at all. Like it's completely natural for me to be spending a Saturday night with my jeans tucked into my socks, scooping buckets of murky water out of a kitchen window.

Gloria shuffles out of the kitchen and leaves us to it. As she brushes past Eliott, she gives her a quick squeeze on the shoulder. I get the impression that Gloria's not the overly affectionate type, and even Eliott seems to be surprised by the fleeting gesture.

'Thank you for coming,' she says.

Eliott's eyes widen. 'You don't have to thank me, Nan. Of course—'

Gloria waves a dismissive hand in the air and then disappears out into the hall. Once it's just the two of us again, Eliott turns to me and I'm glad to see that she looks a little more like her usual self.

The storm of emotions that had been pasted across her face since we left the club is mostly gone, and she looks much less likely to collapse into tears now.

'You know you don't have to stay?' she says as she resumes

sifting the water from the floor and into the bucket. 'I've got it handled here.'

'I know.'

Her small smile widens slightly when I don't make any move to walk out of the door.

* * *

It takes us a good few hours to get Gloria's kitchen into a vaguely manageable state. We source the leak to her rarely used dishwasher and plug it as best we can, hoping it'll hold until my plumber friend can get round on Monday.

We don't talk much as we work, but it's a comfortable silence. If you'd have told me just three months ago that I'd be spending my Saturday night doing something like this, I'd have laughed in your face.

Typically my weekends are spent with pretty girls doing all kinds of *fun* things in the comfort of my bedroom.

I look up.

Eliott's leaning against the kitchen counter. Not long after we started, she realised that the skin-tight outfit that she'd worn to the club probably wasn't the best for a task like this, and she ran upstairs and changed into some oversized sweats and pulled her thick curls into a bun.

Pretty girl? Check.

Gorgeous girl, if we're being honest.

And maybe we're not in my bedroom and maybe it's not my usual kind of *fun*, but I guess things aren't all that different from my typical weekend plans.

The thought makes me smile. I could get used to spending my weekends with Eliott.

Gloria pops her head back through the kitchen door. Her eyes scan the room and she gives the both of us an appreciative nod. 'I'm going to head up to bed now.'

'Do you need me to walk you up?' Eliott asks, already pushing herself away from the counter.

Gloria hesitates, then gives her granddaughter a reluctant nod. Eliott crosses the room and loops her arm around Gloria's. The action is smooth and well practised, something they've probably done hundreds of times before.

I wonder how often things like this happen. Mini crises that Eliott has to drop everything for because the rest of her family never pick up their phones. It's a lot to put on one person's shoulders, and I can't imagine that being forced to rely on Eliott for everything is pleasant for Gloria either.

'Back in a sec,' Eliott says as she leads Gloria out of the kitchen and up the stairs. Their conversation gets more and more muffled the further away they get from the kitchen, but I manage to catch snippets of it.

'. . . Saturday night?'

'I told you . . .' Eliott sighs loudly. '. . . nothing . . . just friends.'

'You know, your grandfather and I were just . . .'

'Nan! Can you . . .'

Gloria's surprisingly loud cackle drowns out whatever plea Eliott sends her way, and that's all I manage to hear. By the time Eliott makes her way downstairs again, I've already dried myself off as best I can and I'm waiting by the front door for her.

I wonder if I'm imagining the slightly disappointed look on her face when she spots me by the door, but it's gone and replaced with a smile before I can dwell on it for too long.

'You heading out?'

I nod. 'I think that's as good as we're gonna get it. Unless you need me for anything else?'

'No, no.' She jumps off the last two steps and comes to a halt directly in front of me. We're as close as we were back in the club, and my arms itch to wrap themselves around her waist again. 'You should probably—' She clears her throat, shakes her head, and then starts again. 'Sorry I ruined your night.'

'There's nothing *ruined* about tonight, baby,' I scoff. I've never been one for pet names or nicknames – have never been with anyone long enough for it to happen naturally – but with Eliott, the word slips out without me even thinking twice about it.

She quirks a brow, but otherwise doesn't comment on the impromptu name. 'I didn't do a great job at being your wingman.'

'Like I said, there was only one person in that room who

I was interested in going home with.' I inch forward, closing the minuscule gap between us. 'And look where I am now. I'd say that's a pretty good end to the night.'

Her breath hitches, her eyes widen, and her tongue darts out to run over her lips. We stand there in a charged sort of silence for several seconds too long. She's staring at me, head slightly cocked to the side, her brows pinched together in the middle like I'm a particularly difficult puzzle she can't quite figure out.

I lift a brow. 'What?'

She hums contemplatively and then breaks out into a quiet laugh. 'I could ask you the same thing.' She shifts slightly, pressing her chest up against mine as she looks up at me through hooded eyes. 'What's on your mind?'

I let my arms loop around her waist. I don't think I'll ever get bored of this – holding Eliott in my arms. Every time I do it, every time I give in to the urge and pull her into my arms, it's just feels right. Like this is where she's meant to be.

'At this moment?' I ask.

She nods without breaking eye contact.

'I'm trying to figure out how much of a gentleman I want to be right now.'

I *feel* rather than see the blush creep along Eliott's skin. Even under the fabric of her clothes, I can feel the heat spreading through her. You'd never be able to tell by her expression, though.

Her face is a mask of neutrality. *Casual*. Like I'm not really affecting her at all. Except for her eyes. Her eyes are real heavy right now. 'Anything I could help with?'

I can map the path her eyes take from my lips and back up to meet mine again. Heat flashes in them, and I barely have a moment to acknowledge how truly beautiful they are – like little molten orbs of chocolate specked with gold flakes – before I'm leaning in and her lips are finally, *finally*, caressing mine.

Eliott lets out a low moan into my mouth as my hand comes up to fist her hair, my touch equal parts gentle and firm. I'm not sure who takes the first step, but my back suddenly slams against the front door as her hands come up to grip the collar of my shirt.

'*Dane*—' Her voice is halfway between a whimper and a moan as I pull away from her lips and start peppering her neck with soft, hot kisses. '*Dane.*'

'I could get used to hearing that,' I murmur against her neck. She nudges her thigh between my legs and I let my hands drift downwards to palm at her ass. 'Almost forgot how good you felt.'

She laughs as she pulls my face back up to meet her lips again. 'Should I—'

From her room, Gloria coughs suddenly, the sound echoing throughout the house. Eliott stiffens almost immediately and pulls away. My hands fall back to my side, and already I miss the feel of her beneath me.

'Friends,' she murmurs, pulling away. Her hand skims along my arm as she moves, and if I wasn't looking at her, I'd swear she left a trail of fire in her wake. Her chest is still heaving and her eyes are still firmly on my kiss-bruised lips. 'Just friends.'

I don't think I've ever been so hard, but I give her a stiff nod and bite back the groan I can feel building in my throat. 'Just friends.'

Friends.

Really starting to hate that word.

Chapter Seventeen

DANE

DANE
you still good for tonight?

ELIOTT
Seven, right?

DANE
yeah, i'll pick you up

ELIOTT
Cool. See you then.

A shadow looms over my shoulder and I whirl around to find Cash peering at me suspiciously.

'Are you even listening?'

'Of course I am,' I lie.

Cash, understandably, looks unconvinced. 'What did I just ask you?'

I give him a once-over, taking in the too-tight blazer he's currently got one arm stuck in and the frilly white shirt he's half-heartedly tucked into the waistband of his trousers, and make an educated guess. 'You asked . . . What I thought about the shirt, and if you should size up with the blazer.'

Cash's eyes narrow. 'Lucky guess.'

He turns to disappear back behind the curtain and I huff out a quiet sigh of relief. We've been in here for close to two hours now and it's not like I don't *want* to spend time with my best friend and soon-to-be brother-in-law, it's just—

My phone vibrates again.

ELIOTT

Looking forward to it :)

It's just that I've already got plans for tonight, and this wedding tux fitting session with Cash is starting to encroach on my time with Eliott. It's been two months since the flooded kitchen and our kiss, and I can't quite decide if I'm happy or disappointed with the way things have developed between us.

Happy, because Eliott is still very much a part of my life. In the days that followed the kiss, I worried that she'd pull away again and I'd lose an unexpected bright spark in my life almost as soon as I'd got it. But that didn't happen, and as strange as it is to admit it, that's where the disappointment has come in.

Because we are one hundred per cent, resolutely, just *friends*.

There hasn't been another charged moment like that.

No almost kisses.

No lingering glances.

No fleeting touches.

It's like she's placed me firmly in a box labelled 'DO NOT TOUCH' and there's nothing more I want right now than to break free from it.

I want Eliott in a way I've never wanted someone before, and I don't quite understand it.

I know that I'm attracted to her, that I'd love to hear her soft moans and sink myself into the warmth between her thighs again, but it feels like this goes beyond just basic attraction.

There's another layer to it that I haven't quite managed to figure out just yet.

'You got any plans for tonight?' Cash calls from behind the curtain. The too-small blazer comes flying over the railing and narrowly misses slapping me square in the face. 'Bailey's been invited to a restaurant launch. Pretty sure she could get you on the list with us if you want to come?'

Dining out at some of the most ridiculously expensive restaurants and bars in the city for free is one of my favourite perks of Bailey's job and, on any other day, I wouldn't hesitate to say yes. But not tonight.

Tonight, Eliott is coming over. As a *friend*. I have to keep reminding myself that before I do something stupid and ruin everything.

Friends.

Just friends.

As incongruous as it sounds, I can be the type of guy who spends a chill Friday night watching terrible movies on the couch with a friend. Can't I?

'Gonna have to pass on that one,' I say as Cash emerges from behind the curtain in a sleek, black tux that I know Bailey is going to absolutely lose her mind over when she sees him wearing it.

Cash gives me a sideways glance before he turns to face the mirror. 'I feel like you've been really hard to pin down lately.'

That's a fair assessment.

At some point over the last few months, there's been a switch. My free evenings are no longer spent with Cash and Bailey or trawling through various dating apps on my phone. Any nugget of spare time I have has gone straight to Eliott without me even having to think about it.

Sometimes we'll grab dinner, and we'll spend hours

squashed into a booth stealing from each other's plates and talking about anything and everything.

That's how I discover that Eliott's taste in music stems from spending summers in Grenada with her grandparents growing up, and she gets a special light in her eyes when she talks about the island and her memories there.

Or how, when she tries to explain something about photography and all the intricacies that come with it – things like shutter speeds and aperture and something called *chromatic aberration* – she starts to talk really fast and can't stop grinning.

I like that.

Learning which topics will make her whole face light up. I wonder if I'll ever be one of them. If, when she talks about me, her eyes brighten and her mouth splits into the same megawatt grin the way it does when she's talking about her grandmother's cooking or telling me wild stories about her time at university with Sasha.

'Just been busy,' I say with a noncommittal shrug.

Cash glances over his shoulder and I see a flicker of understanding spark behind his eyes. 'You're seeing someone.'

It's not a question.

I force out a laugh. 'Nah. I'm not.'

Cash hums in disbelief and, once again, I can't decide if it's annoying or admirable just how well he knows me. 'Are you going to use your plus one for her?' he asks, completely ignoring my pathetic attempt at denial. 'What's her name? Our deadline for invitation responses is next week, and we need to add her to the name plates for dinner.'

'I'm not seeing anyone.' I pause and then decide to add firmly, 'And I'm not using my plus one.'

Cash's brows shoot upwards. 'At all?'

I shrug again. 'Probably not.'

Truth be told, I didn't even need a plus one in the first place. The wedding is for my sister and my best friend, so I can't imagine there'll be many people on the guest list I don't already know in some capacity. But I'd asked for one anyway as a way to curb the sympathetic stares from my mother and various aunts, or to stop people from trying to set me up with their daughter once they realise I'm currently unaccounted for. The plus one had been a tactical request more than anything else, but I don't even want it anymore.

It doesn't feel right.

And besides, I'm pretty sure I can handle the endless stream of '*Dane, when are you going to settle down?*' from relatives I haven't seen in years for one evening.

'The dating scene hasn't really been all that appealing lately,' I explain, answering Cash's silent stare of disbelief. 'I'm taking a break.'

Cash's expression morphs from suspicion into something that's a little too close to pity for my liking. 'Is everything all right?'

'Everything is *fine*,' I say with a roll of the eyes. What does it say about me that the fact that I'm not actively dating right now can make my best friend worry about me?

There's something on the tip of Cash's tongue, but he swallows it down and shakes his head. 'So, what are you doing tonight?'

'Nothing.' And it's the truth too. When we last saw each other, I offhandedly mentioned needing to get my locs retwisted soon, and Eliott offered to give it a go. So that's the plan for tonight. And maybe it's not technically *nothing*, but I know it's not what Cash is expecting to hear. 'But I do need to head out soon.'

I'm sure Cash is going to continue to press me on it. There's a stubborn look in his eyes that tells me he doesn't believe me in the slightest. That he knows there's more going on than I'm currently willing to admit. If the roles were reversed, I know I'd push it.

Hell, I *did*.

When I first cottoned onto the fact that his feelings for Bailey were genuine and that there could actually be something there between them, I didn't let it go. I was the one who orchestrated the whole '*spend a week together in Jamaica*' thing in the first place.

So I can't exactly begrudge him for refusing to drop it now. Call it karma, I guess.

But Cash doesn't push. He just shrugs and then sticks out

his arms and spins around on the spot. 'What about this one? Think the fit is fine?'

The change in topic throws me for a half second, but I manage to kick myself back into gear quick enough to respond. 'It looks great. Bailey's gonna love it.'

'Thanks, man.' Cash grins that goofy grin at the mention of my sister's name.

I wonder if that will ever stop, or if in twenty years he'll still be smiling and looking at Bailey as if she hung the moon and the stars. I feel a flicker of envy and wonder, for a brief weak moment, if I'll ever feel like that towards someone.

Doubtful.

'How's planning for my stag do going?' Cash asks suddenly, a wary look on his face.

I grin right back at him. 'That's for me to know and for you to find out.'

'It's nothing too wild, right?'

'It's a perfectly acceptable level of wild,' I laugh. 'Don't worry. It'll be Bailey-approved. And Eliott's been throwing some ideas my way, since she's around that kind of stuff all the time.'

I don't catch the slip of the tongue until it's too late.

Cash's mouth splits open into a wide, knowing grin. 'Eliott? As in, my wedding photographer? *That* Eliott?'

I could lie. Pretend that there's another Eliott who has just happened to wander into my life during the last few months.

But there's no point.

'Yeah,' I grit out.

'Is that who you're seeing tonight?' Cash looks ridiculously pleased for some reason. 'And who you've been hanging out with recently?'

'It's not like that,' I say quickly, knowing what he's alluding to. 'We're just friends.'

Cash rolls his eyes as he starts untying the bow tie around his neck. 'Sure.'

'We are,' I insist, much as I hate to admit it. My mind jumps back to that evening. To our kiss. To the way Eliott felt in my arms. To how my heart sank to the pit of my chest when she pulled away. I shake my head. 'Trust me. There's nothing going on there. And don't worry, I'm not jeopardising your wedding or anything.'

Cash laughs at that, but it's not his normal laugh. It's kind of like the laugh you do when someone tells you something ridiculous, but they haven't realised it themselves just yet. 'I'm not worried about the wedding.'

'You're not?'

'Nope.' Cash's grin widens. I don't think I've seen him look this happy since the day Bailey accepted his proposal.

And then he gives me a look. It's the kind of look you give someone when you know something that they don't.

'What?' I ask.

'Nothing,' Cash says, still grinning like a madman. 'Nothing at all.'

Chapter Eighteen

ELIOTT

I know something is up from the way Sasha slides into my bedroom. She's either here to ask for a favour or she's fishing for something.

'You look cute,' she says, a deceptively innocent smile on her face as she plops down onto the bed. 'What's the occasion? Ah!' She pretends to tap her head like she's just remembered something incredibly important. 'That's right. You're hanging out with Dane tonight, aren't you? I'm starting to wonder if I should feel jealous.'

'Jealous?' I snort and drop down onto the bed next to her. 'Why?'

Sasha gives me a look that's somewhere between amusement and exasperation. 'Eliott, babe. Come on.'

'What?' I ask, genuinely confused.

The expression on her face switches to something else.

She looks almost hurt. 'Since when did we start keeping things from each other?'

'You popped a pimple on my ass last night,' I remind her with a raised brow. 'There's literally *nothing* you don't know about me. Our relationship is actually probably a bit unhealthy.'

'Fair,' Sasha concedes, before waving an accusatory finger in my face. 'But that's what I'm talking about. You'll let me pop your ass pimples, but you won't tell me that you and Dane are fucking?'

I freeze and stare at my best friend incredulously. 'Excuse me?'

'I know we had that talk and you were like, "*no, no, Dane is off-limits*". But you don't have to be embarrassed if you changed your mind. I'm not gonna judge you.' She looks genuinely upset. 'I was the one who said you should give him another chance in the first place, so I don't understand—'

'Sash—'

'And you're not even doing a good job at hiding it,' Sasha continues, completely oblivious to my attempt at an interruption. 'You guys are always messaging, and you're always rushing off to meet him randomly. And I don't think *we've* hung out together on a Friday night in weeks.'

I frown. That can't be true.

I comb through my memories of the last few weeks. It hits me with a jolt when I realise that she's right. Ever since that night with Nan's kitchen, I'm pretty sure Dane and I have done something together every week.

I haven't thought twice about it.

Spending this time with Dane has become natural. Second nature. When an artist I've loved for years announces a one-off gig, Dane is the first person I ask to see if he wants to come with me. His response is an immediate *'of course, babe'* and I don't even have the chance to load up Ticketmaster before he's sending me a screenshot of the tickets *he* just bought for us.

When I get a new camera – a beautiful vintage Olympus model that reminds me of the camera Grandad used to use when I was younger – I don't hesitate to ask if Dane wants to wander around the city and be my model for a few test shots. He agrees without hesitation and takes his role as my model seriously, right up until we get to my last two shots of film. That's when he insists that I jump into the shot with him and we spend ten minutes awkwardly trying to prop the camera up on a wall so we can get a shot of Dane resting his chin on my head, his arms wrapped loosely around my waist.

When I'm heading back from a late night wedding down dark and unfamiliar country roads, I don't think twice about calling Dane to keep me company on the long ride home. He stays on the call for three hours straight, and doesn't hang up until I close my bedroom door behind me and he knows I'm home safely.

When did Dane become that person for me?

It was always Sasha who came with me to gigs when I didn't have anyone else to go with; Sasha who acted as my model whenever I ordered some new film or wanted to try a new technique; Sasha who always dutifully stayed up and kept me company on the phone when I drove home late at night.

When did that change?

And how did I not notice?

'I'm just saying,' Sasha continues with a shrug. 'You don't have to keep hiding it from me.'

'We're not,' I say quickly. 'We're not fucking or anything like that.'

Sasha quirks a brow in obvious disbelief.

'We're *not*,' I repeat firmly. 'We're just friends.'

She stares at me for a few long seconds and then bursts into laughter. 'No, you're not.'

'We *are*.'

'No, I get that you *think* you are,' Sasha says in between giggles. She's laughing like this is the funniest thing she's ever heard. 'But you're not. You're absolutely not.' She leans back against my pillows and grins. 'You guys are definitely going to fuck.' Sasha, completely undeterred by my silence, happily continues on. 'One hundred per cent you two are going to fuck. I bet my entire Fenty collection on it.'

That gets a snort out of me. 'We're not going to sleep together. Like I said, we're just friends.'

Friends who sometimes share passionate kisses. The kind

of kiss that lingers in your mind and provides several nights' worth of *fun* material to think back on.

We've not kissed since. Haven't even spoken about it. But I'd be lying if I didn't admit that I wouldn't be mad if it happened again.

But it *can't* happen again, because we're friends.

Just friends.

Sasha just hums as she jumps off my bed and flounces towards the door. 'Can't tell if you're just being stubborn or if you're genuinely an idiot.'

'Can't it be both?' I ask with a weak laugh.

Sasha shakes her head once last time before she disappears out the door. 'Pretty sure it is.'

★ ★ ★

I can't get Sasha's words out of my head. Every time I close my eyes, I see her smug face grinning at me as she mouths the words *I told you so*. She hasn't been proved right, not yet anyway, but I'm woman enough to admit that she *might* have a point.

I'm sat on Dane's comfy sofa, there's an episode of *The Chase* playing on his large TV, the remnants of our dinner spread out around us, and Dane is sat between my legs.

His back is pressed up against my core and every few seconds he lolls his head back to rest against my stomach.

'Stop moving so much,' I scold him lightly, my fingers wrapped around one of his locs. We've been at it for the last couple of hours now and I'm almost finished – just one small patch at the front to neaten up, and then we'll be done.

But I don't want to be done.

I can't tell if it's Sasha's voice drowning out the usually logical one in my head or if she's just given me the blessing to act on the thoughts I've had for probably longer than I realise, but I've come to understand something.

I *do* want to fuck Dane.

I want him to push me into the cushions on his couch and sink into me in a way that makes my toes curl, my back arch, and breathy little moans fall from my mouth. I can't stop imagining it.

Every time he leans into me or brushes his hands against my leg, a warmth shoots through me and settles in the pit of my stomach in a delicious, teasing kind of way.

I'm going to kill Sasha.

I was perfectly happy living in self-imposed ignorance before. Happy to pretend like I was content with having Dane as a friend and nothing more. And then she had to go and ruin everything.

Because as much as I want to, I know that nothing can come from this. I sound like a broken record, but my rule is in place for a reason.

You've never been in a situation like this before, though. The treacherous Sasha voice in my mind makes a good point.

My rule is for one-night stands. Not friends. Not *Dane*, the man who has become an integral part of my life in four short months without me even realising.

I could break my rule.

For him.

But what happens when I break it and it goes just as it's always gone? Dane realises that I *am* broken. That having sex with me isn't going to be fun and easy and I'm more baggage, more of a burden, than he's willing to handle.

And then I lose him. Not just in a sexual way, but I lose all of this too. The friendship. The laughter. The nights spent curled up on the sofa watching him get irritated at the contestants on quiz shows when they don't know the answers to apparently simple questions.

I can't lose this just because I'm horny.

Dane shifts slightly and turns, his lips automatically splitting into my favourite lopsided smile as his gaze lands on me.

Really fucking horny.

'Everything all right?'

'Fine,' I say, clearing my throat when I realise how irritatingly high my voice sounds. 'Why wouldn't it be?'

Dane lifts a brow. 'You've just been holding my hair up for the last five minutes without doing anything.'

I glance at my hands. He's right. The loc I started on five

minutes ago is still between my fingers, thoroughly untwisted as I let my mind wander.

Definitely going to kill Sasha.

His smile splits into a knowing grin, like he can read my mind and knows exactly what turn my thoughts have taken over the last few minutes. I half-heartedly consider throwing caution to the wind and just going for it, but my phone vibrates beside me and snatches my attention away immediately.

Ever since the situation with Nan and her kitchen, I've kept my phone close to me. I know it's irrational and I can't be there all the time, but the idea of missing something important again literally makes my heart twist painfully in my chest and I refuse to feel like that again. Especially when I know that Nan can't rely on Mum or Leanne or Josh to follow up with her.

It took Mum an entire week to finally text me back. Not even a call. Leanne at least had the decency – or sense of guilt – to check in with Nan two days later but, as far as I can tell, Josh still hasn't even bothered to see what had happened.

Speaking of Leanne, her name pops up on my screen followed my several frantic messages.

LEANNE

ok ok i know what you're gna say

but this is an emergency

> can i pls borrow £200? will pay u back by the end of next week

I feel myself stiffen slightly as I read and reread her messages. Dane is still sat between my legs, but he must feel the tension in my body because he turns again, a worried frown pinching his brows together.

'What's wrong?'

LEANNE
> plsssss my rent is due and im short just a little bit
>
> promise i wont ask again

A stream of praying emojis flood my screen, followed by a handful of crying emojis, followed by:

LEANNE
> ELZZZZZZZ PLSSSSSSSSSSSS

'It's nothing,' I mutter, fingers flying to type out a response to my sister.

ELIOTT
> Is everything okay?

LEANNE

it's fine, i just didn't budget properly this month

can you borrow me or not?

i already asked mum. she said to ask you or nan

ELIOTT

Don't ask Nan.

I'll send you the money.

LEANNE

lifesaver <3

thank u, love u

Dane rises from the floor and comes to settle on the sofa next to me. In one swift movement he drapes an arm over my shoulder and pulls me into his chest.

My eyes flutter shut of their own accord and I allow myself a brief moment of peace, nestled beside him. He doesn't push me, doesn't repeat his question. He just waits patiently, his fingers softly threading through my hair until I'm ready.

'I'm fine,' I murmur, my face still buried in his chest. 'Everything is fine.'

He squeezes my arm gently. 'Baby.'

'It *is*,' I say firmly. I push myself up from his chest, not far enough to get out of his grasp, but enough that I can look into his eyes. 'It's fine. She just needs to borrow some money. I've got the money. It's *fine*.'

'Doesn't sound fine.'

'Well, it is.' My tone is sharper than I'd like, and Dane doesn't deserve that. 'Sorry,' I sigh, shifting to lean into his touch again. 'Sorry. I'm not – It's not you.'

He gives me another squeeze. 'I know.'

'It's not even the money,' I continue. 'She's my baby sister. If I can help her, I will.' I swallow down a lump in my throat I recognise as the threat of oncoming tears. 'I just worry about her. About all of them, you know? They rely on me a lot, and what happens when I can't help them?' My heart thuds furiously in my chest. I don't think I've ever voiced this aloud. It's the treacherous thought that constantly niggles at the back of mind. 'What happens when I say no and I'm suddenly not any use to them?'

Dane pulls me in even further and drops his chin on the top of my head. 'You worry too much, baby.'

'Someone has to,' I mutter.

'And who worries about you?' He pulls back just far enough so he can look me directly in the eye. My breath stutters in my throat as he brings a hand up to cradle my face in that soft, tender way he's managed to perfect over the last few months.

'I don't need anyone to worry about me.' The admission

stings my tongue as it leaves my mouth, no matter how true it is.

Dane gives me a soft, sad look as his thumb runs soothing circles around my cheek. 'I don't like that.'

I shrug, though I'm not sure how convincing my attempt at nonchalance is. 'That's just how it is.'

Dane's jaw tenses. '*Definitely* don't like that.' His thumb skitters down my cheek and runs along the rim of my lip. I fight back the urge to run my tongue along the path his thumb has just taken. 'Can you promise me something?'

I nod without thinking. 'Anything.'

'If you're going to worry, I don't want you to do it alone anymore.' Another stroke of his thumb along my bottom lip. I feel myself start to lean in. 'Tell me what's going on, and we can figure it out together.' He finally pulls away and I give into the urge and run my tongue along my lips. His gaze follows the path my tongue takes, and he swallows noticeably before continuing. 'Can you promise me that, baby?'

I don't even have to think twice about my answer. 'I can.'

Chapter Nineteen

ELIOTT

I don't think I've ever felt so awful in my entire life. Every inch of my body aches and I'm having to fight to keep my eyes open. It doesn't help that the groom-to-be hasn't said a word in ten minutes.

He's sitting on the opposite end of this bench, scrolling through his phone to avoid making eye contact with me while we wait for his fiancée to emerge from the toilets in her second outfit change of the afternoon.

I don't usually mind engagement shoots. They're typically fun and the couple tends to still be in that sickeningly in love phase that makes for a good time and great photos. But I'm not quite sure my current couple, Will and Tanya, have ever been in that phase.

Point in case, while Tanya shows up to the park we're shooting in with a full face of make-up and a small suitcase filled with outfit changes, Will has arrived in a pair of ratty old jeans, a shirt that could do with another round of ironing, and hair that doesn't look like it's ever seen a comb. He keeps an impassive look on his face the entire time I'm shooting them, only cracking a ghost of a smile when Tanya quietly begs him to.

It's awkward. And we've still got another hour – and at least one more outfit change from Tanya – to go. If this were any other day, I'd try to spark up some polite conversation with Will as we wait. But today my head is throbbing and it's taken all my control to keep myself balanced and upright on this bench.

I've definitely caught something. There were a lot of snotty noses and chesty-sounding coughs at a wedding I photographed a week ago, and I'm pretty sure I'm finally feeling the effects of the copious amounts of germs I inhaled that weekend.

Will gives me a sideways glare as I break out into yet another coughing fit. I throw him a weak smile. As shitty as I feel, I still have to be professional, I suppose.

'Have you picked a date for the wedding yet?' I ask, my voice noticeably hoarse.

He shrugs and turns his attention back to his phone. 'Nah.'

'Oh,' I say before trying again, determined to get something from this man. 'How did you propose, by the way? Were you planning it for a while?'

'Nah.'

I wait a few beats to see if he's going to elaborate, but nothing comes. Great. I glance over at the toilets, hoping to see Tanya striding back towards us in another gown, but no luck.

Fine.

If Will doesn't want to be polite, then I won't either. I don't have the brainpower to dedicate to this right now, anyway. All I want to do is curl under my blankets and sleep for an eternity – or at least forty-eight hours straight. I glance at my phone to check the time and spy a message from Dane waiting for me.

Just the sight of his name lifts my mood marginally.

DANE

still feeling crap?

ELIOTT

Awful.

Awful clients today too.

One hour left and then I can slip into a Night Nurse induced coma.

DANE

that doesn't sound safe

> **ELIOTT**
> Probably not, but I'm too bunged up to think straight.

> **DANE**
> sorry baby

> tell Sasha to take good care of you tonight

> **ELIOTT**
> I wish.

> I'm home alone tonight. Sasha and Wes have gone for a weekend staycation.

They're spending the next four nights in Cornwall to celebrate their four-year anniversary, and the last thing I want to do is dampen their spirits by letting Sasha know that I currently feel like death. And that's not an exaggeration.

> **ELIOTT**
> But it's fine. Soon as I'm done here, I'm heading home and straight to bed.

> Probably won't be much for good convo tonight, just a heads up.

I watch as the little speech bubble pops up, indicating

that Dane is typing. Then it disappears, pops up again, disappears, and then pops up one last time.

If my mind wasn't such a hazy mess of blocked sinuses right now, I'd expend more than a tiny bit of brain energy on trying to figure out what he keeps typing and then deleting. But I can't bring myself to focus on it right now.

My head is pounding, my vision is blurring, and I'm rapidly running out of tissue to wipe my apparently endlessly snotty nose.

God. When was the last time I felt this sick? I don't even remember.

'About bloody time,' Will murmurs next to me.

I glance up to see Tanya gliding across the park in an extravagant pale pink gown. She looks delighted and not at all deterred by the fact that her fiancé showed more enthusiasm when looking at the latest football score than in seeing her in her dresses.

I force what I hope is a bright grin onto my face as she approaches, even as my vision blurs some more. 'You look amazing, Tanya.'

She beams at me and then turns to Will with an expectant look on her face.

'Yeah,' he grunts, eyes still glued to his phone. I wait a beat to see if he plans on expanding on his lacklustre compliment to his fiancée, but nothing comes.

I can't tell if Tanya is bothered or not, but I don't understand it at all. I've been in the wedding industry for long enough that I've seen plenty of couples like this, and it always makes me feel strange. I barely know these women, but I can't understand why they'd settle for someone like this. My thoughts drift to Cash and Bailey and then, unexpectedly, to Dane. The idea of him treating me like this feels so unfathomable, it jolts a throaty laugh out of me.

Not that we're married, or engaged, or anything other than friends. But still.

The way Dane treats me – with kindness and respect and genuine joy when his eyes land on me and his lips spread into that soft, sweet smile? I don't understand why anyone would willingly settle for anything less.

My phone buzzes in my pocket and I summon the strength to pull it out while Will and Tanya get into their new positions.

DANE

all right baby

drive safely and let me know when you get home

Chapter Twenty

DANE

As good ideas go, I'm not sure where this one ranks in the grand scheme of things.

I check my phone for the fourth time since I arrived on Eliott's doorstep. Her car is parked outside and, according to the last message she sent me, she got home not even twenty minutes ago. In *theory*, she should still be awake. Twenty minutes is barely enough time to change into something comfortable and dive under the blankets.

But I've been ringing her doorbell for the last five minutes and she's still not come to the door.

I should go. She's probably sleeping. She *needs* to be sleeping given how awful she's currently feeling. I'm starting to doubt that this was even a good idea in the first place.

Turning up at her door unannounced when she's already told me that she feels like death? Yeah. Definitely not my best idea.

I take a step backwards just as the front door is yanked open and I find myself standing face to face with Eliott. She's wearing an oversized hoodie and a pair of ratty old sweatpants. There's a fluffy blanket draped over her shoulders and she has two wads of tissue paper stuffed up her nose. Her skin has a thin sheen of sweat stuck to it, and there are noticeable bags under her eyes.

I feel my lips curve upwards into a grin as she glares at me.

'You weren't exaggerating about the whole *death* thing,' I say as she steps aside for me to enter the house.

Still looks gorgeous, though.

'Ha, ha,' she manages to croak out, her voice as rough as sandpaper. 'What're you doing here?'

I lift the plastic bag in my hands. 'I'm here to take care of you.'

'Wh—' Eliott breaks out into a brutal coughing fit before she can voice her question, and I take the opportunity to shove her into the living room and onto the couch. She protests weakly but otherwise seems content with letting me get her settled onto the sofa.

'You just rest here,' I tell her as I pluck the blanket off her shoulders and drape it over her once she's settled on the sofa. 'Give me twenty minutes in the kitchen.'

Her eyes narrow a fraction. 'To do *what*?'

'I told you,' I say with a grin, already backing out of the kitchen. 'I'm taking care of you tonight.'

She sinks into the cushions and blinks up at me with weary eyes. 'You don't have to do this, Dane. I can take care of myself. It's just a—' Her shoulders heave as she explodes into another coughing fit. 'It's just a cold. It's not a big deal.'

I don't know what it says about her that I can tell she truly means it. She genuinely thinks that it's not worth my time to be here, taking care of her. And I don't know what it says about me that I'll do whatever I can to make sure she never feels like that ever again.

'You're not well,' I say firmly, placing the back of my palm against her forehead. She's burning up. 'Let me take care of you.'

'But—'

'I *want* to take care of you,' I say, choosing a different tack. I think this one works because her eyes widen slightly and her cheeks darken just enough for me to notice.

She gives me a small nod. 'All right.' She swallows. 'You can take care of me.'

'Good.' I flash her a grin and then make my way to her kitchen. 'I've got two things for you,' I call as I tug a thermos out of the bag and then start rifling around her cupboards until I find what I'm looking for.

Eliott looks at me with poorly concealed suspicion when I return to the living room. 'What's in there?'

I hand her the thermos and she gives it a tentative sniff.

Recognition starts to dawn in her eyes, but she's not quite there yet.

'What *is* this?'

'I'm not entirely sure,' I tell her earnestly. 'Gloria told me to make it for you. Said it helps with colds.'

Eliott pulls a face, her cute nose wrinkling as the penny finally drops. 'Oh God, I know what this is. It's her remedy. She swears by it. When I was growing up, if I so much as sneezed in her presence she'd make me drink a shot of it.'

'Does it work?'

Eliott groans as she slumps further into the sofa. 'Yes? No? Maybe? I don't know. It's disgusting, but tell her it doesn't work and she'll just say "*you're not dead, are you?*" like there's some correlation and—' She stops herself abruptly mid-sentence and looks at me, her eyes shining. 'You got this from Nan?'

I nod as I pull the lid off the thermos and start pouring the brown liquid into the two shot glasses I grabbed from the cupboard. 'I called her. You don't mind, do you?'

'No— I— *Why?*'

I let a mischievous grin take over my face. 'That's part two. First . . .' I nod to the shot glasses on the coffee table and she immediately shakes her head.

'No. Absolutely not,' she says, trying to inject some sternness into her voice. She's so bunged up, she ends up sounding more like a toddler than anything else. I ignore her and slide a shot of Gloria's remedy to her.

'Drink up.'

Her eyes slide to the remaining glass and she looks at me expectantly. It's weird. She doesn't have to say a word, but I know exactly what she's asking. I hand her a glass and then lift my own. We loop our arms around each other and catch each other's eye. Hers are tired and low, but there's a spark there when she meets mine.

I don't think I could ever get bored of looking into her eyes.

The corners of her lips lilt into a soft grin and she nods. 'Ready?'

'Ready.'

We both lean forward and bring the glasses to our mouths. In one smooth gulp, the liquid is burning its way down my throat faster than any alcoholic drink I've ever tasted. Eliott splutters as she reels back, clapping her chest as she goes. 'Ugh. Just as bad as I remembered.' She leans back into the sofa and I follow, letting her flop her head onto my shoulder.

'It was pretty rough,' I cough, my throat still scratchy from the liquid. She shivers suddenly and I reach out for the blanket to drape it over her again. As I move, I brush against some exposed skin on her arm and, once again, feel that same heat I felt on her forehead. 'Baby, you're burning up.'

She groans and burrows further into the little nook by my shoulder. 'Doesn't feel like it. I feel cold.'

She wraps an arm around my waist and rests her head just below my heart. I wonder if she can feel it. The erratic *thuds* that come from her being so close. If she can, she doesn't say anything.

'Why'd you call Nan?' Eliott asks, her voice muffled by my own sweatshirt.

I tug the blanket over her and run my arm up and down her side. 'Wanted to get the recipe for that soup you like.'

'What soup?' Her voice is tired and faraway, like she's halfway to falling asleep already.

'What did Gloria always make for you when you were younger and feeling sick?' I ask.

She doesn't answer right away and, for a second, I think she's finally fallen asleep. But then she lifts her head and her eyes are watery. 'Nan's chicken and dumpling soup?'

I nod. 'It probably won't be as good as the original, but I followed her recipe as best I could.'

'Dane.' Her voice cracks and I can't tell if it's because of her cold or something else. 'How did you—' She cuts herself off and shakes her head. 'I don't even remember telling you about that.'

'You mentioned it once,' I say with a shrug. Two years ago, but still.

A range of emotions flit across her beautiful face before she settles on a soft smile. 'Thank you.' She tucks her head back into the nook underneath my arm and I tighten my hold around her side.

'You don't have to thank me.'

'I know. But I wanted to.'

'Want me to warm up your soup?'

'Not yet,' she murmurs, her fingers tracing soft circles on the fabric of my shirt. She drapes a leg over my thighs and I instinctively bring my hands up to knead at the soft skin. 'Can we just stay like this for a little longer?'

Before I can think twice about it, I lean in and press a soft kiss against her temple. She doesn't freeze. Doesn't jerk away. Doesn't tell me off for tiptoeing over the precarious boundary lines between us. She just snuggles in closer and rests her head above my heart.

'Do you remember when you asked what are my favourite things to photograph?' Eliott asks quietly.

'I do.'

'It's moments like this,' she whispers, her fingers still flexing against the fabric of my shirt. 'The quiet moments.'

I thought I'd understood it before when we first spoke about it, but I'm looking at it with a new clarity now. Because I understand wholeheartedly what she means.

I want this moment to last forever.

★ ★ ★

'You're sure *you* made this?' Eliott asks, her spoon hovering over her near-empty bowl. 'You didn't just strong-arm Nan into doing it for you?'

'I'll take that as compliment,' I laugh, watching as she scoops up the last remaining droplets and shovels them into her mouth. 'There's more in the fridge for tomorrow. Probably about two or three more bowls' worth.'

We've spent the last hour curled up on her sofa together. Eliott's been drifting in and out of sleep and I finally managed to convince her to eat something before she heads upstairs to bed and I leave.

'Tastes just like I remember,' Eliott says with a wistful sigh. 'Nan must really like you. She normally keeps all her recipes close to her chest. Once she joked that her recipe book will be my inheritance.' She pauses and frowns. 'I think she was joking, anyway.'

The fact that Gloria apparently likes me enough to part ways with a recipe shouldn't send a jolt of joy shooting through me, but it does.

Eliott yawns suddenly, which quickly turns into yet another coughing fit, and I feel a sense of guilt. The whole point of me coming over was to take care of her and make sure she gets the rest she needs. Instead, she's spent the whole time fighting sleep in order to stay awake with me.

'Come on. You should get some rest.' I stand up abruptly and stick out my hand.

She hesitates for a fraction of a second before she grabs it and lets me pull her up. Her hand is clammy, yet another reminder of just how unwell she is right now.

'Do you need any help getting upstairs?'

She rolls her eyes. 'I told you, it's just a cold. I can make it—' Her knees give out and she stumbles forwards, collapsing into my chest.

She's weaker than she wants to admit right now. I can feel her shaking slightly beneath my touch, and her eyes look dangerously unfocused. I slip an arm around her waist and start leading her up the stairs. 'I've got you, baby.'

'This really isn't necessary,' she protests half-heartedly.

'Humour me.'

'You'll catch my cold.'

I don't know why she's still trying to deter me. We're halfway up the stairs.

'At this point, I think it's more than a cold.' We reach the upstairs landing and she points me to a room at the end of the hall. 'If you're still feeling like this tomorrow, you should really make an appointment with your doctor.'

'I will,' she promises. 'I am feeling better already, though.'

'Gonna tell Gloria it was her remedy.'

Eliott pulls a face. 'God, please don't. I'll never hear the end of it.'

She pushes open her bedroom door and coughs out a

dry laugh. 'This wasn't how I imagined I'd be bringing you back up here again.'

'Imagining me in your bed?' I ask, a teasing brow raised as she crawls under her sheets and immediately wraps her blanket around herself. 'That doesn't feel very *friendly* of you.' I mean it as a joke, but I think she's too sick to pick up on it, because she shrugs and extends a hand towards me.

'Maybe I'm tired of being friendly.'

I'm pretty certain my heart misses a beat or two. 'Eliott.'

'Please.' Her eyes are wide as she wiggles her fingers at me. Even the tissues stuffed up her nose and the thin layer of sweat coated to her forehead can't do anything to distract from the fact that Eliott is so goddamn beautiful. 'Can you just lay with me? Just for a little bit.' She drops her gaze and her hand at the same time. 'I don't really want to be alone right now.'

And what am I supposed to say to that? No?

'Five minutes,' I say as I slide under the blankets with her. She immediately curls around me, slinging an arm over my waist and intertwining her legs with mine. My body reacts almost on instinct, snaking an arm around and pulling her in as close as I can get. The vanilla and cocoa scent in her hair invades all my senses, and it takes every inch of willpower I have not to bury my face in her hair and take a deep inhale.

'You're so warm,' Eliott mumbles, burrowing further under

the blankets and into my side. She yawns loudly and her breathing peters out into something shallow and measured.

I'm not sure how long I lie there with her, listening to the soft sounds of her breathing and paying attention to the steady rise and fall of her chest on mine, but eventually I realise that it's dark outside and the street lamps are on.

I start to extract myself from underneath her, sure she's fast asleep, but she stirs suddenly and looks up at me with bleary eyes.

'Dane?' she mumbles.

'Yeah, baby?'

Her brows furrow and she leans in before I can stop her and presses a quick, chaste kiss just to the right of my lips. I freeze as her head lolls downwards again and she nuzzles into the crook of my neck. 'You're more than enough for me.'

And then she's softly snoring again like she hasn't just turned my whole world upside down with one delirious, sleep-deprived sentence.

You're more than enough for me.

Chapter Twenty-One

ELIOTT

This can't be happening. This absolutely, one hundred per cent *cannot* be happening. I bite my bottom lip and push the START button again, praying that this time I'll get a different result.

No such luck.

My car sparks to life for a few misleading seconds before letting out one last pathetic splutter as it shuts down completely.

Fuck.

My car is dead and I've got a wedding to be at in three short hours. A wedding that's at least a two-hour drive away – and that's only if I manage to beat the early morning rush hour traffic. And I have no one to blame but myself.

This is all my fault.

I knew I should've paid attention to the strange sounds coming from my engine when they first started up two weeks ago, but I'd pushed the issue to the side in favour of more pressing concerns.

Nan's leg has been acting up again and I've spent the better part of the last few weeks ferrying her back and forth between doctor and physio appointments. On top of that, Leanne's finished with university for the summer and somehow she managed to convince me to become her personal moving van to help her bring a few things back to her dad's place.

I quickly learned that we had very different definitions of '*a few things*' and I ended up doing three trips back and forth with only a vague promise from Leanne to send over some money for petrol at some point.

The past few weeks have been one long series of distractions, and now my car is paying the price. My frustration reaches its peak as I slam my hands onto the steering and take in a deep, *deep* breath. Think, Eliott. Think.

What're my options here?

I could order an Uber? No. Just the thought of how much that return journey would cost is more than enough for me to nix that idea as fast as it came. Ditto for renting a car with such late notice.

I could cancel. Let the couple know what's happened and refund them their entire fee. No, can't do that either. Not only is it wildly unprofessional, I'd never be able to live down the guilt of leaving a couple hanging on their wedding day.

What the hell am I supposed to do here?

My mind runs through a million scenarios, but nothing feels right.

Pain sears through my lip as I bite down hard enough to draw blood. I hate being in situations like this. I'm always the one who has it under control. The one who knows exactly what to do and solves everyone else's problems. I'm not used to feeling so helpless.

'Tell me what's going on, and we can figure it out together.'

Dane's voice rings in my mind as clearly as if he were sitting right next to me, and a thought jumps into my mind.

'You don't have to shoulder every burden yourself.'

I shove away the creeping feeling of failure and inadequacy and reach for my phone. I've spent so much of my life being the person everyone relies on. Choosing to lean on someone else doesn't come naturally to me. My fingers stall over Dane's name as excuses start to flood my mind.

It's too early and I'm asking for too much. Aren't I? If this were Sasha or Leanne, or literally anyone else, I'd tell them that it's perfectly fine to reach out and ask for help. So why is it so different when it comes to me? Why do I feel like such a goddamn burden?

Hasn't Dane shown me time and time again that he's someone I can rely on? That he'll hold my hand when I'm on the brink of a panic attack or spend hours in the kitchen learning how to make my favourite soup when I'm ill? That he'll be there for me without me even having to ask.

I take a deep breath and silence the self-doubt that lingers in the back of my mind.

Dane answers on the third ring. Just the sight of his yawning face filling my phone screen sets me at ease. I feel myself relax into my seat, the anxiety and stress literally rolling off of me in waves.

He blinks a few times and then concern flits across his face. 'Are you all right?'

Despite everything, I can't help but smile. I've just woken him up before the sun has even fully risen on a Saturday morning, and the first thing he asks is that.

'I'm fine,' I say quickly, trying to temper the worry I can see mounting across his features. 'I know it's early, and you were just sleeping. But—' I pause, nerves suddenly choking in my throat.

Dane sits up, his eyes suddenly more alert now. 'What's wrong, baby?'

Baby. These days, I think he calls me that more than he does *Eliott*. I definitely shouldn't like it as much as I do.

'My car's broken down,' I tell him. 'And I've got a wedding in a couple of hours and—'

His face disappears from the screen and his next words are muffled by the sound of blankets rustling. 'Give me twenty minutes. Is that all right?'

'I haven't even asked you yet,' I say, blinking in disbelief at the now-empty screen.

Dane's face pops back into view. He shrugs and lets out another tired yawn. 'You didn't have to.'

★ ★ ★

'I really do owe you one.'

Dane puts his van in park and then shoots me a decidedly unimpressed sideways glance. 'How many times are you gonna say that?'

My lips curve into a sheepish grin. In the two and a half hours it took us to arrive at the venue, I've probably uttered some form of thanks to him at least twenty times. 'Got it,' I laugh. 'No more thanking you.'

'Exactly,' Dane says, matching my grin with a wide one of his own. 'I'm here for you, baby. It's not even a question.'

But it *should* be. Shouldn't it?

I've never had anyone in my life be so willing to go above and beyond for me. I'm used to being that person for everyone, and it feels weird being on the other side of things.

'You look gorgeous, by the way.'

I've never been one to shy away from a compliment, but there's something about the way he's staring at me, the way his gaze appreciatively roves over my body, that sends a current of heat pulsing through my veins.

There's nothing particularly special about my dress. As a wedding photographer, I've had to learn how to blend in with the crowd yet still dress appropriately for the wedding without veering too much into the territory of looking like a guest. Today is a formal affair, a few notches down from full-blown black tie, and I'm wearing a simple wrap dress.

I follow Dane's line of sight, watching the way he slowly maps out every one of my curves. He lingers around my waist and the urge to lean across the space between us, crawl into his lap, and let him do every single dirty thought that's currently flitting through my mind is overwhelming to say the least.

I clear my throat and his gaze reluctantly flickers up to meet mine. 'Thanks.'

He makes a noncommittal noise of approval and then nods to something just outside my line of sight through the window. 'Looks like you're up.'

I glance over my shoulder and spot a taxi pulling into the currently deserted car park. This venue doubles up as a boutique hotel, and the bride is going to get dressed here before her guests arrive. I watch as my bride for the day climbs out of her taxi dressed in a white loungewear combo with the word BRIDE splashed across the front. Several women I assume are her bridesmaids spill out after her, all looking ridiculously excited and giddy.

I feel my own surge of excitement as I watch them wander up to the hotel entrance. It's always good when the client and the wedding party are in high spirits, their mood almost infectious.

'And you're sure you're fine to wait here?' I ask for probably the umpteenth time.

'It's too late to change my mind now,' Dane drawls before reaching forward and running a thumb along my jawline. I lean into the touch without thinking about it. 'But, *yes*. I'm more than sure. Like I said—'

'You're here for me?'

His smile turns soft. 'Exactly. Always.'

Always.

For the first time since I slid into his van this morning, there's no doubt in my mind that he really means what he's saying right now.

Dane will *always* put me first.

My heart clenches and a wave of emotions threatens to drown me. I tear my gaze away from him before I do something stupid like burst into tears.

'Cool,' I choke out, my voice noticeably thick. In my periphery I see him frown. 'I'll come back during my break; maybe try to steal an extra plate for you to eat if I can. If you get bored, or change your mind—'

'I'm not going to change my mind, baby.'

'Right.' I risk one last glance up at him and offer him a watery smile. 'I'll see you in a bit.'

He nods, a small frown pinching his brows together. 'See you.'

★ ★ ★

The wedding serves as the perfect distraction to the maelstrom of thoughts swirling in my mind. For the next four hours, I let myself forget all about Dane and the way he's currently making me feel.

I usually look forward to the reception dinner when I get a break for an hour or so and can camp out in my car and decompress for a little.

But Dane is out there waiting for me tonight and just the thought of him has me gulping for air.

Because I've started to realise that Sasha was only half right.

I *do* want to fuck him.

But I think I also want something more. And that's just not going to happen. We've got a good thing going on with our friendship and besides, Dane just isn't the kind of person who does serious.

He doesn't do long term.

He definitely doesn't do love.

And I'm pretty sure that's where I'm heading.

Fucking hell.

I think I'm falling in love with Dane. Hell, I might be there already.

All the emotions I've been keeping at bay while I've been working suddenly come flooding back, hitting me like a wave as I shoulder open the door and step out into the car park.

Dane's van is exactly where I left it, but there's no sign

of him sitting in the front seat. Instead, the back doors are open and I can see his legs swinging over the edge.

He grins, wide and bright, as I approach and despite everything, I can't help but smile right back.

'How is it so far?' he asks, shuffling over slightly so I've got some space to slot beside him.

'Pretty good,' I say. 'The bride and groom are both lovely and, as far as I can tell, there's not been any drama.'

'Is there usually drama?'

'Sometimes,' I say with a shrug. 'A drunk uncle. Someone turning up in something wildly inappropriate. The rings going missing. You'd be surprised at some of the crazy shit I've seen.'

'And it doesn't turn you off?' he asks, looking genuinely curious. 'Getting married, I mean? Seeing everything you see. Seeing first hand all the stress that goes into planning a wedding? You'd still do it?'

'I would,' I say without thinking. 'With the right person.'

Dane hums.

'I probably wouldn't have a huge wedding, though. Something small and cosy. Just a couple of friends and immediate family, you know?'

He hums again, his expression turning thoughtful. 'I could do small and cosy,' he murmurs. Judging from the unexpectedly startled look on his face, I don't think he means to say it aloud.

'Yeah?' I ask.

'Yeah,' he says firmly, staring at me with an intensity that makes me want to turn away. I don't, though. I hold his gaze as he licks his lips and says, voice slightly hoarse. 'I think I could.'

He still looks vaguely startled, as if he's surprising himself with the words coming out of his mouth. He shuffles a little closer to me and bumps his arm against mine. 'With the right person.'

Am I the right person? The question lodges itself in my throat, unspoken.

I shake my head. This is too much. We're veering dangerously close to talking about something I don't think I'm quite ready for.

'But that's not something I have to worry about anytime soon,' I say airily. Dane lifts a questioning brow. 'Getting married,' I elaborate. 'Or more, finding someone to marry, I guess. I doubt I'm going to find The One with my rule still in place.'

Dane huffs out an exasperated breath. 'Right. Your *rule.*'

I'm not sure why, but he sounds almost irritated.

'Why do you even still have it?'

'Because I'm tired of being treated like a game,' I tell him honestly. 'Or like a challenge for people. Even you. As soon as I told you that I can't come, you wanted to try again just to prove that you could.' I force myself to meet his gaze. 'And it sucks. It fucking sucks.'

Dane's eyes go wide before he hums and cocks his head to the side. 'Then I'm definitely doing something wrong.'

Before I have the chance to ask for clarification, he closes the miniscule gap between us and threads his fingers in my hair. He twists his fingers around my curls and tilts my head upwards. 'Because what part of this feels like a game to you, baby?'

I open my mouth, but nothing comes out.

He brings his head down to meet mine. 'The only challenge here is me trying to stop myself from staring at you non-stop whenever I get the chance.' He brushes his lips against mine. Not quite a kiss. More like a shadow against my skin. 'I could never – *never* – get bored of you, baby.'

I swallow around a thick lump in my throat. 'Dane.'

'Having you in my life has been the best thing to ever happen to me,' he murmurs. 'And I'll take you in whatever form you want.'

He uses his free hand to stroke my cheek in that gentle way he's perfected over the last six months. 'We can just be friends. Or something more. As long as I get to have you in my life.'

My heart stutters. 'I'm not going anywhere.'

His lips lift into a soft smile. One that's just for me. 'Good.'

And then he's kissing me.

Slowly. Sweetly.

His lips slant perfectly against mine and I bring my hands up to fist his shirt to give myself some balance.

This is nothing like our first kiss two years ago. There's something else here this time. Something more than just a spark of attraction between two strangers.

He drops a hand to my waist and pulls me deftly across him with more speed and strength that I'm expecting. He doesn't break the kiss, though. Just holds me firmly at the waist while my dress rides up as I straddle him.

I can feel his heartbeat through the fabric of his shirt, a steadily increasing thrum thudding against my palm.

'*El-i-ott.*' He groans my name without breaking the kiss, and the vibrations send a delicious tickle down my spine. 'You. Are. *Everything.*' His hands trail down my body and each word is punctuated with a squeeze of my thighs. '*Everything* to me.'

I moan. I can't tell whether it's from his kiss, his touch, or what he's saying, but I don't care. I'm in sensory overload right now, and I don't want him to stop.

I grind against him and a shudder wracks through me as the fabric of my panties brushes against his dick.

He's already so hard. I can feel him through the thick material of his sweatpants, and I want more.

I want so much more.

I *need* more.

I don't think I've ever felt like this before. Don't think I've ever *wanted* anyone like this before.

His hands slip beneath the hem of my dress to grab at my ass and pull me in even closer. There's not so much as a sliver of space between us, but it's still too much.

'*Fucking*—' He grunts as I drop a hand on top of his and guide him towards my pussy. '*Baby.*' Even without dipping beneath the fabric of my panties, his touch sends shockwaves of pleasure shooting through me.

'Dane.'

He presses his thumb against my clothed clit and I arch my back, squashing my tits even more against his chest.

'You're going to be the end of me,' Dane mutters, letting his head tilt forward to rest against my tits. 'You know that, right?'

I open my mouth to respond, but he chooses that moment to bite down on the soft skin just above my nipples, and the sound that comes out is more like a whimper than anything else.

'Gorgeous.' He softly kisses the spot he just bit. 'Fucking.' Another kiss. '*Gorgeous.*'

'Dane, I—'

A shrill beeping sound jolts us both back to reality.

'Shit,' I mutter, reaching for my phone to turn off the alarm I'd set earlier. 'My break's over.'

Dane groans as he lets his head slump against my shoulder. 'Are you kidding me?'

I can't help but laugh as I peel myself off him. 'Unfortunately not.'

He looks up at me through hooded eyes and I have to admit, I like this look on Dane. His chest is still heaving, his lips are wet and slightly swollen, and his dick is still happily standing to attention in his sweatpants.

I did that.

Dane and I aren't destined for love, that much is for certain. But maybe this can be enough for me.

Maybe.

Chapter Twenty-Two

DANE

Eliott is going to be the end of me. I'm sure of it. You can practically put it on my tombstone at this point.

Here lies Dane Clarke. Cause of death: Eliott Rayne.

Because it's been two weeks since I drove her to that wedding and, despite the turn our 'platonic' relationship has taken, we've not got anywhere close to replicating what happened in the back of my van.

Every time I close my eyes, I'm transported back to that moment. Even now, as I'm sitting on Cash and Bailey's sofa waiting for the groom-to-be to finish shoving last-minute items into his suitcase, I'm still thinking about Eliott.

The way she sounded. The way she felt. The way she made *me* feel. Better than anything I've ever felt in my life.

It's not like we haven't tried to pick up where we left off. When she finished the job and came back out to the van that evening, we both briefly entertained the idea of resuming things. But then all the guests started piling out of the venue and we both agreed that it probably wasn't the right time or place.

I dropped her home, and she invited me in, an invitation I was more than happy to accept. But then Sasha came bounding out of the front door and we both knew that any hope of privacy was dashed.

Our work schedules over the next two weeks just didn't line up either.

'*It's wedding season,*' Eliott told me wryly when, for the fifth night in a row, she had to spend the evening photographing another happy couple instead of curling up beside me in bed.

And now this is the first free weekend she's had in weeks, but I'm about to head off on a four-day trip to Amsterdam for Cash's stag do. It's something I should be wildly excited about, but I can't help the itch of frustration simmering beneath the surface.

I glance up as Finn walks into the room, tugging a suitcase that looks like it cost more than three of my monthly mortgage payments behind him. I can't help but snort. I make good money with my business, but it's definitely not Finn Hawthorne kind of money.

'Can you send over the link for the train tickets again?'

'Sure.'

I forward over the booking confirmation email for our

train tickets from London to Amsterdam later this afternoon. Cash, Finn, myself, and two of our other friends, Leo and James, make up the groomsmen, and we're celebrating with four days in Amsterdam before we head on over to Italy for the wedding.

'Thanks,' Finn says as he drops into the seat opposite me and immediately begins tapping away on his phone. It wasn't a surprise when Cash told me he wanted to ask Finn to be one of his groomsmen. They've got closer since Amber and Finn started dating and Cash and Bailey have been on more double dates with the two of them than I can keep up with.

They flew in last week so Amber could host Bailey's hen party and wedding shower, and now it's our turn for some fun.

'All right,' Finn says suddenly, looking up from his phone to grin mischievously at me. 'I've upgraded us to first-class.'

I snort again. This is what I mean by *Finn Hawthorne kind of money*, but I'm not complaining.

'Nice,' Cash cheers as he strolls into the room, tugging his definitely overpacked suitcase behind him. 'Thanks, man. You didn't have to do that.'

Finn shrugs noncommittally. 'It's no big deal. Think of it as another part of our wedding gift to you guys.'

'Woah,' I shoot Finn a look of faux concern. 'Are you trying to upstage the best man?'

'Never,' Finn laughs, and I can't help but appreciate how

easy he is to get along with. 'You're the one who planned this whole trip. I can't take any credit for that.'

He's got a point there. I've spent the last six months meticulously planning this trip for Cash, and I'm pretty proud of the itinerary I've put together. We've got a canal cruise, a brewery tour, a pedalo treasure hunt, a list of coffee shops to check out over the four days, and that's all on top of the sprawling Airbnb I managed to find at a decent discount for us to stay in.

Cash is going to love it and I feel my excitement starting to build again.

My phone vibrates and I know who it is without even having to look.

ELIOTT
Hey. Have you left yet?

Have a safe trip. Take lots of pics.

And I'll see you in France :)

That's right. Eliott's joining Bailey and Amber on the train ride from London to Italy, and we'll meet up with them in France to head to our final destination.

'What's so funny?'

I jerk forwards as Bailey and Amber suddenly appear behind me, both nosily trying to squint down at my phone screen. I shrug them off and shove my phone into my pocket. 'Funny?'

'Yeah.' Bailey grins as she plops herself down onto the armrest of the sofa. 'You were smiling.'

Amber sits on Finn's lap and his hand immediately comes up to rest on her lower stomach. 'Go on, Dane. Share the joke.'

I scowl at the both of them, but their grins just widen like they know some huge secret and they don't plan on sharing. I stand up abruptly before they have the chance to continue. 'We should get going. If we miss our train, that's the whole trip ruined.'

That kicks off another five minutes of Bailey and Cash and Amber and Finn saying their goodbyes to each other. It's cute, I suppose. In that annoying way that couples who are so overwhelmingly in love with each other are.

Could I ever be like that with anyone? If you'd asked me six months ago, the answer would have been a definite *no*. But now? Now I'm not so sure.

I can almost picture myself kissing Eliott goodbye. Stroking her cheek and whispering something special in her ear, something just for her, before we pull apart.

That's what they're all doing now.

Finn says something to Amber that makes her smile, before she gives him a small nod and tries to pull away. He doesn't let her, though. His hand, still on her stomach, lingers for a little while longer before he reluctantly lets it drop.

One More Shot

I reach for my phone and pull open my chat history with Eliott.

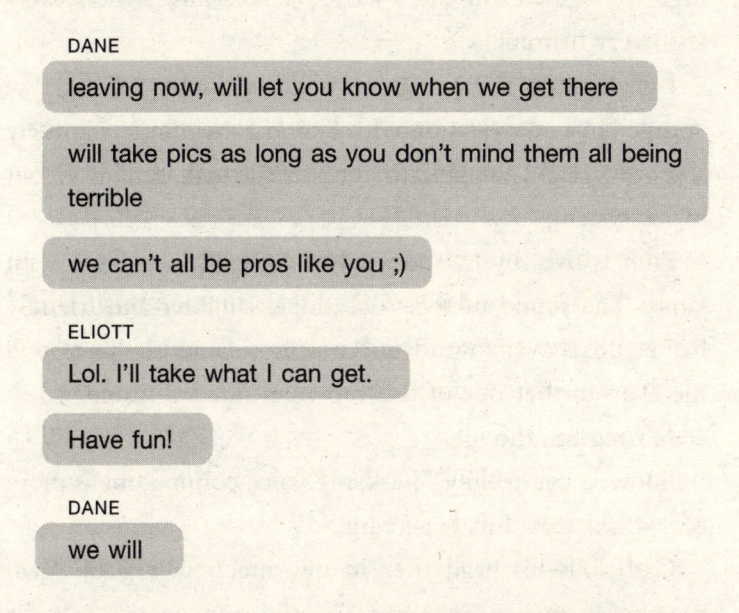

> **DANE**
> leaving now, will let you know when we get there
>
> will take pics as long as you don't mind them all being terrible
>
> we can't all be pros like you ;)
>
> **ELIOTT**
> Lol. I'll take what I can get.
>
> Have fun!
>
> **DANE**
> we will

I hesitate for a second and then my fingers are flying over the keyboard before I can put too much thought into it.

> **DANE**
> miss you
>
> **ELIOTT**
> Miss you too.

★ ★ ★

The brownie I halved with Cash earlier today is just about out of my system. My limbs no longer feel heavy and the urge to vegetate on this sofa for all eternity is noticeably less overwhelming.

I glance over to my right. Cash is still sunken in his seat, engaged in a conversation with Leo. His eyelids are definitely less heavy and I imagine the brownie is making its way out of his system, too.

Finn is over by the pool table, engaged in a game with James. The sound of their occasional laughter and friendly banter floats over towards me on the sofa and helps to pull me even further out of this brownie-induced slump.

No regrets, though.

'How're you feeling?' I ask, my voice coming out as more of a drawl than I'm expecting.

Cash lolls his head over in my direction, a goofy grin tugging at his lips. 'Not bad. You still want to try to make our reservation tonight?'

I groan as I remember that we've got a reservation at a semi-fancy restaurant in Amsterdam's centre this evening. I wouldn't say that I'm high anymore, but the idea of leaving this incredibly comfy spot on the sofa isn't an appealing one.

Cash laughs. 'Yeah, I feel you. You want to stay in tonight? Could order some pizza and play some games?'

I sink further into the sofa and match Cash's grin with one of my own. 'Sounds perfect.'

One More Shot

Two hours later and the five of us are scattered around the coffee table surrounded by empty, greasy pizza boxes and several open bottles of wine.

'Okay, okay,' James slurs. 'I've got one. Never have I ever . . . had a one-night stand.'

Everyone, bar James, takes a long sip from their drink. He's been with his wife since we were in school and was the first one in our friendship group to get married.

'Boring,' Leo laughs. He's been with his fiancé for five years now, and they're due to get married next winter.

It hits me with a jolt that out of the five of us, I'm the last hold-out.

James is married. Leo's engaged. Cash will be married to my sister in just a few days. Even Finn. He and Amber might not be married yet, but from the way he looks at her and how he's been checking in with her every couple of hours, it's easy to tell that they're not far behind.

'You go then,' James says, rolling his eyes.

'Never have I ever . . .' Leo trails off and wiggles his brows. 'Never have I ever had sex in a public place.'

There's a brief pause and then—

'Define *public*,' Finn says slowly, reaching for his glass.

'You can decide,' Leo says with a shrug before downing his own drink.

Finn hesitates for a second, the tips of his ears going pink, and then takes a small sip. James follows suit and Cash . . .

Cash shoots me a guilty glance before he brings his glass up to his lips.

Oh God.

'I'm gonna get some air,' I say quickly.

The intricacies of Cash's relationship with Bailey are high up on the list of things I absolutely don't need to know *anything* about, so I take the opportunity to slip outside. Thankfully, no one protests my sudden absence.

We're only about twenty minutes from the city, but you'd never believe it. Sprawling fields stretch in every direction and the only thing I can hear is the faint sound of laughter from the guys inside, mixed with the gentle breeze.

It's peaceful.

Beautiful.

And I wish Eliott were here.

The thought comes to me without any hesitation, but it doesn't surprise me in the slightest. It feels right knowing that Eliott's become the person I want to share moments like this with. She's the only person I want around right now.

I don't have to think twice about calling her, and her smiling face quickly fills my screen as I sink into a comfortable lawn chair.

'Hey, gorgeous.'

Her smile widens, illuminating her whole face. 'Hey.'

It's late, and she's dressed for bed, wearing an old t-shirt and her hair wrapped with a purple silk scarf. I've never been the possessive type but I feel a little jolt of pleasure shoot through me, seeing her so relaxed and comfortable in front of me.

Just me.

Nobody else gets to see her like this.

I like it more than I probably should.

'I wasn't expecting to hear from you tonight,' she says. Her smile dims just a little and makes way for a look of concern. 'Is everything all right?'

Nothing was ever wrong, but I still say, 'Now it is.'

She rolls her eyes. 'You can be so cheesy when you want to, you know that, right?'

'They're playing a drinking game,' I tell her with a laugh. 'Figured I probably didn't want to hear some of the answers. I left right after "*never have I ever had sex in a public place*" and I realised Cash was looking at me guiltily.'

Eliott cackles. 'Yeah, I can see why you'd leave.' Her expression suddenly turns curious. 'Have you, though?'

'Believe it or not . . . No.'

The closest I've got was in the van with Eliott two weeks ago.

'I don't believe it actually.'

A quiet laugh ripples through me. 'It's true.'

She snorts and shakes her head. 'Wow, don't let anyone hear this. Your reputation will never recover. You're practically virginal.'

'I don't need my reputation to recover,' I say with a

nonchalant shrug. Not anymore, anyway. There's only one person whose opinion I care about these days.

Eliott grins as she leans against her headboard. 'Never took you for the shy type.'

Shy is definitely not a word I've ever used to describe myself. 'It just never happened,' I say with a shrug. 'Maybe I've just been waiting for the right person.'

I pause for a moment.

The sun is cresting over a nearby hill and the laughter inside the house has dulled. Someone's put on some mellow music.

'I wish you were here with me right now, baby.'

Her expression softens. 'What if I was?'

Four words.

Four simple words.

And they go straight to my dick.

'Eliott . . .' My voice is a low rasp.

She shifts again in her bed. 'If I was there,' she continues, either oblivious to the torture she's currently putting me through, or just perfectly fine with it. 'Would I be the right person?'

I swallow. 'You're the only person.'

She bites her lip, her gaze lowering for a second, almost out of reflex. 'So tell me.'

My words choke in my throat. 'Eliott . . .'

She drags a hand slowly down her chest, stopping to cup

her breast. I watch as she palms at the soft skin through her shirt.

My dick twitches.

'Tell me,' she says again, her voice a quiet demand, and it's one I can't ignore.

I follow her lead and dip my free hand below the waistband of my sweats. My fingers wrap around my dick and I give myself a gentle squeeze, imagining it's her soft fingers doing the work.

'I don't hear you telling me,' Eliott says with a teasing grin. 'Come on, baby. Use your words.'

Like I said, Eliott is going to be the end of me.

A low moan slips from my lips as I rub my thumb over my head. 'If you were here, I wouldn't be able to keep my hands off you.' I let my head loll back and my eyes flutter shut, imagining Eliott climbing on top of me, her pussy sliding against my dick. 'I want to feel you. *Every* part of you. Your tits—'

My eyes snap open just in time to watch as she squeezes one of her breasts.

'You like it when I play with your tits, baby?'

She nods.

'When I suck your perfect nipples?'

'*God* . . .'

'Suck your fingers for me, baby.'

She doesn't hesitate. My dick twitches impatiently as she

takes her free hand and runs her tongue along two of her fingers. She doesn't break eye contact with me as she does it, and I let out another, deeper moan.

'Imagine that's my tongue.'

The sounds of her moans intermix with mine as she brings her wet fingers back to her breast and starts playing with her nipple.

'*Dane . . .*'

'I want to taste you. I *need* to taste you.' Need to feel her thighs against my cheeks, squeezing every last breath out of me as my tongue runs along her dripping lips. 'You want that, baby? You want me to fuck you with my tongue?'

'*Jesus fuck. Ye*— No.' She shakes her head forcefully. '*No.*'

I raise a brow. 'No?'

She meets my eye again. 'I want *you*. I *need* you to fuck me with your *dick*.'

I grin and curl my fingers tighter around myself. 'But I want to take my time with you.'

I want to savour every moment. To spend so much time slowly working my way down Eliott's body that every inch of it becomes ingrained in my mind.

She rolls her eyes, but her lips twitch slightly. 'Save that for round two.'

My brow floats even further into my hairline. 'Round two?'

'What?' she says with a smirk. 'Worried you can't keep up?'

'Worried I'll never want to stop.'

She lets out a breathy moan before her camera drops to the side, buried beneath her sheets. I can hear the muffled sounds of her moving around, opening and closing a drawer, and then climbing back into bed.

When she brings the camera back up to her face again, her cheeks are slightly flushed. 'Can you just—' She swallows. 'Just keeping talking to me. Okay?'

'I can do that.' I watch as she leans back into her pillows and her eyes flutter shut. Soft little pants spill from her lips as her chest rises and falls, and I can hear a light buzzing noise in the background.

It doesn't take me long to connect the dots.

She's using a toy.

'You look so beautiful right now, baby,' I tell her, my voice hoarse as I start to slowly pump up and down my shaft. 'Such a good girl using your toy for me.'

She whimpers and squeezes her eyes shut a little tighter.

'Tell me how it feels.'

'*Good*,' she gasps out. 'So fucking good.'

'Will you bring it to Italy?' I ask.

She nods and bites down on her bottom lip.

'Will you let me use it on you?' I rub my thumb over my head and a jolt of intense pleasure shoots through me. 'Will you let me slide into you and fill you up while I press your toy against your clit?'

'Stop *teas*—'

'Yes or no, baby? Use your words.'

Her eyes snap open for a second, just long enough to shoot me a glare. '*Yes*,' she grits out. 'Yes, I want you to use it on me.'

I swear the image of Eliott right now – chest heaving while she plays with herself, getting herself off on the thought of me sliding into her – is almost enough to send me over the edge.

And then her eyes flutter shut one last time, her entire body stiffens, and her mouth falls open as my name comes spilling from her lips. '*Dane.*'

Yeah, that'll do it.

I squeeze my eyes tightly shut and imagine burying myself deep inside what has to be the most exquisite pussy I'll ever have the pleasure of tasting. '*Eliott.*' One more pump and it's all over. I have to bite down on my lip to stop my groan of pleasure from being too loud and alerting the others inside as to what's going on out here. 'Fucking hell, *baby*. That was—'

I lean back in my chair and try to catch my breath.

'Yeah,' Eliott pants, the rise and fall of her chest becoming softer as she regains control once more. 'Same.'

I'm not sure how long we sit there, just listening to the sound of each other breathing as we bask in our post-orgasm glow, but the sound of the garden door sliding open snaps me back to reality.

One More Shot

'. . . swear he came out here,' I hear Cash mumble. 'Shit.'

Eliott looks on with barely concealed amusement as I fumble to get myself decent before anyone finds me.

'I have to go,' I mutter reluctantly as Cash's shadow looms just around the corner. 'But I'll see you soon. Just two more days.'

The smile Eliott shoots me is one I haven't seen before. It feels like a smile reserved just for me. 'Two days.'

I can't wait.

Chapter Twenty-Three

ELIOTT

'And when will you be back?'

I resist the urge to roll my eyes as I continue tugging Nan's laundry off the line. We've had this conversation about ten times over the last couple of weeks, but Nan's acting like it's the first time she's heard any of this.

'Like I said,' I grit out, trying and failing to keep the frustration out of my tone. 'I'll be back on Sunday evening. But I can pass by on my way home if you want?'

She's perched on the top step of her newly refurbished patio, watching as I methodically move down the washing line and fold up her sheets. 'Don't go out of your way,' Nan says. 'But if you have the time . . .'

She trails off and I shoot her a grin over my shoulder. 'You know, you can just admit that you're going to miss me. The world won't end or anything.'

Nan purses her lips, but there's an unmistakable twinkle

in her eye. 'It's four days. I think I can manage that much alone.'

It's not that I think she can't manage by herself. It's just that I can't help but worry about her. All it takes is one accident, one slip, one nasty fall . . . And who'll be here to help her? I already know that I can't rely on Mum, Leanne or Josh to check in on her with any kind of regularity, so I've asked Nan's neighbours if they wouldn't mind keeping a subtle eye on her while I'm away.

'You can't control everything.'

Nan is looking at me with a surprisingly soft expression on her face.

'Huh?'

The expression drops in favour of a scowl. 'Don't *huh* me,' she sniffs. 'I said you can't control everything.'

I rest the washing basket against my hip and make my way back across the lawn. 'What's that supposed to mean?'

Nan shrugs. 'I know you like to be the one in control. The one in charge.'

I let out a strangled sounding noise that's halfway between a shriek and a laugh. 'You think I *like* this?'

For real?

She thinks I like having to always be the one to piece everyone back together?

That I like having to spend most of my brainpower worrying about everyone but myself?

That constantly feeling like I'm the worst person in the world, like I'm nothing but a selfish witch whenever I try to take any time for myself, is something I genuinely *enjoy*?

Another shriek-slash-laugh tumbles out of my lips. '*Nan*. You can't be serious.'

Her scowl deepens, and she opens her mouth to respond, but whatever she says is drowned out by the sound of a door slamming, followed by a high pitched:

'*Naaaaaaaaaaaaaaaaaaaaaan*?!'

Three seconds later, and Leanne comes striding into the kitchen. 'Nan, are you— *Oh?*'

She stares at me dumbfounded for a beat or two, like my presence at Nan's house is a surprise to her for some reason. 'Hey Elz, what're you doing here?'

I'm *always* here. The petty response is on the tip of my tongue, but I catch myself before I can spit it out. Leanne hasn't done anything to deserve my ire.

Not yet anyway.

'Just helping Nan out with a few things before I leave.'

'You're leaving?' Leanne asks. She gives Nan a quick hug and steps aside and lets me tug the laundry basket into the kitchen. 'Where're you going?'

'A wedding,' I say. Pretty sure I've told her this before. 'In Italy. Remember?'

'Oh. Yeah. That's cool.'

She sounds like she's already bored of me, her attention

a million miles away. I glance over my shoulder and see that she's pulled her phone from her purse and is quickly tapping away.

'What about you?' I ask.

'Hm?' She looks up for a brief second before turning her attention back to her phone. 'What was that?'

'What're you doing here?' I can practically feel my patience ebbing away. 'Nan didn't mention you were passing by.'

'Oh.' She looks up again and I wonder if I'm imagining the slightly guilty look on her face. 'Right. I was in the area and just wanted to say hi. Am I not allowed to say hi to my grandmother?' She flips her hair and rolls her eyes. 'God, Elz. Sometimes you act like you're the only one who's allowed a relationship with Nan.'

Seriously? What is in the air today?

Nan saves Leanne from a sharp response by shuffling into the kitchen. 'Let me grab my purse, darling. I'll just be a minute.'

Realisation dawns on me.

Leanne dropping in unexpectedly. The guilty look on her face when I asked why she was even here in the first place.

I wait for Nan to leave the kitchen and then let the laundry basket drop to the floor with a loud bang. 'Tell me you're not borrowing money from Nan.'

She rolls her eyes. 'I'm not borrowing anything from her.'

I let out a tiny sigh of relief. 'Good, because—'

'It's a gift,' she continues smugly. 'A "congratulations for finishing your second year of uni" gift.'

'You barely even passed.'

Another roll of her eyes. 'That's not the point. It's a milestone for me and Nan wants to celebrate.'

'By giving you money?'

Leanne shrugs. 'I guess.'

'You're unbelievable.' Every ounce of patience I usually have for my sister is gone. 'This is the first time you've seen Nan in how long, and you're just here for some money?'

Leanne lets out a snort and leans against the countertop. 'Okay, here we go. Do your thing.'

'My *thing*?'

'The whole "I'm Eliott and I'm better than everyone else" speech.' Her lips twist into a sneer that feels uncharacteristic. 'You're not my mother, Eliott. You know that, right?'

'I'm not trying to be!' I snap out. 'For fuck's sake, Leanne, do you think I like this? Do you think I like being the one who deals with everyone's shit? The one who has to constantly bail you out because you either can't or won't get your own shit together? The one who always has to be perfect, because if I'm not, then the rest of you will fall apart? Seriously? You think I like it?'

'You're acting like we aren't there for you too!'

'When?' I hiss out, tears blurring my vision just a bit.

'When have you ever been there for me, Leanne? When has anyone?'

We stand there in a charged silence for at least twenty seconds. I can practically see the gears working overtime in her mind, trying to comb through her memories to find something, anything, she can use against me.

It's obvious that she's come up blank because she suddenly shakes her head and scoffs, 'God, you can be such a fucking martyr sometimes.'

'And you can be such an ungrateful little—'

Nan clears her throat suddenly, stopping me from saying something I know I'll eventually regret. She's standing in the doorway holding her purse, a pained expression on her face.

'Darling,' she clears her throat and then hands a wad of notes to Leanne. 'This is for you. Don't spend it all on sweets.'

'Nan!' Leanne squeals. She crosses the small gap between them and pulls Nan into a tight hug. 'Thank you, thank you, *thank* you.'

'Are you staying for dinner?' Nan asks.

Leanne glances at me for a brief second before she shakes her head. 'Not today, but maybe we can do something soon? I'll check my diary and get back to you.'

Nan gives her a stiff smile. 'All right, darling.'

'I've got to meet a friend now, but I'll message you soon.'

Leanne gives Nan a brief peck on the cheek and then shoots me a withering glance over her shoulder. 'See you around, Eliott.'

I grit my teeth together so tightly, I'm surprised I don't crack anything.

Nan waits until Leanne's closed the front door behind her. 'You don't really feel like that, do you?'

I run a tired hand through my hair and sigh. 'We were just having a stupid fight. Sister stuff. It's nothing serious. You don't have to worry about it.'

Nan strides across the kitchen and grasps my hands in hers. Her eyes are watery and the realisation makes my heart stop for a second. 'What you said,' she croaks out. 'About nobody being there for you . . . Is that how you really feel?'

'Nan—' My voice breaks. Suddenly I feel like I'm nine years old. 'I don't—'

'Tell me the truth.'

I don't want to. I've kept this truth to myself for the entirety of my life and Nan, of all people, doesn't need to hear it.

'Please,' Nan says as one lone tear starts to trail down her cheek. 'Just tell me.'

Something inside me breaks.

'I'm just so tired,' I whisper. 'I'm so tired of doing *everything* for *everyone*. I'm tired of nobody else even thinking about me, and if *I* need help. Everyone just assumes I'll be there to save the day. It doesn't matter what I've got going on or what my plans are, you all lean on me *so much*.'

Tears streak down my cheeks and my words are broken up by hysterical little hiccups, but I can't stop now. It's like the floodgates have been opened.

'And I end up hating myself because what kind of terrible person must I be to resent having to help my family?'

Nan's hands come up to cup my face. 'You are *not* a terrible person, Eliott. My little love.'

'Nan—' I manage to get out a loud sob when I hear the nickname she used to call me as a child.

'You're the most marvellous, most wonderful young woman I've ever had the pleasure of knowing. And I ask you for too much. I know I do.'

I try to shake my head, but she holds me firmly in place.

'I should've known that it's been taking its toll on you. Having to do all this for me. Having to keep an eye on Leanne and manage your mother and your brother all the time. It's too much for anyone.'

'But I *want* to help you, Nan,' I sniff out. 'Because if you can't rely on me—'

'Who can I rely on?' Nan finishes off wryly. She knows just as well as me how unreliable the others are. 'I don't know, my little love. But that's not your burden to shoulder alone. It never should've been. But you were always so smart.

So quick. So resilient.' She gives me a watery smile. 'Even as a child, I knew I never had to worry about you.'

'I jumped on that,' I say. 'I liked that I never caused anyone any trouble. That all the grown-ups could rely on me.'

'Maybe we've relied on you too much,' Nan says softly, her thumbs rubbing my tear-streaked cheeks. 'We've been leaning on you for so long, we've forgotten how to stand ourselves.'

'If I'm not there for you all, I get scared that you won't need me anymore.'

The calls, the messages, they'll all stop coming once they realise I'm not useful to them any longer.

'I will *always* need you, my little love,' Nan says. 'But not like this. You look like you're one step away from a nervous breakdown.'

Despite everything, I can't help but laugh. 'It feels that way sometimes.'

'I want you to stop thinking about everyone else, just for a minute and answer me this: what good are you to *yourself* if this is how you're feeling all the time? When do you get the chance to enjoy your life when every second of the day you're worrying about me or Leanne or someone else?'

I let out another dry laugh. 'You sound like Dane.'

Nan gives me a knowing smirk. 'Good. He's a smart boy. I like him.'

I like him too.

'Promise me, my little love,' Nan says, her voice suddenly serious. 'Find your balance, because this is no way to live your life. I'm not going anywhere. Leanne too, once she matures a bit. We don't love you for the things you do for us, Eliott. We love *you* for *you*. And I'm sorry I haven't shown you that recently.' She squeezes my cheeks tightly and gives me a wide smile. 'So promise me you'll start to put yourself first.'

My smile mirrors hers. 'I promise.'

Chapter Twenty-Four

ELIOTT

> **DANE**
> leaving the airbnb now
>
> **ELIOTT**
> Nice. I'm just finishing packing and then I'll head to the station.
>
> **DANE**
> :)
>
> cool
>
> cant wait to see you

My stomach does a weird little flip as I read and then reread Dane's last message to me.

Can't wait to see you.

Anticipation thrums through my entire body like an

electrical current. There's an unspoken expectation of what's going to happen between us on this trip and, for the first time, the thought of it isn't making me sick with nerves.

Dane and I are going to fuck.

I'm not putting any expectations on it. This will be nothing like our first attempt, when I put too much pressure on both myself and him to perform.

To give me an orgasm.

My first.

This time I'm just going to go along with the ride and enjoy the rollercoaster that is Dane Clarke. Orgasm or no orgasm, we can still have fun.

I keep telling myself that as I grab my toy and stuff it into my suitcase, tactically burying it beneath a mound of clothes.

Sasha's splayed across my bed, her long legs dangling off the edge as she watches me pack. A smug grin splits her face in two. 'Feel free to admit I was right, by the way.'

'Right about what?'

'Dane,' she says simply. 'You guys are definitely going to fuck on this trip.' She slides off the bed suddenly and comes to sit beside me on the floor. 'Took you two and a half years, but you two are right back at square one.'

She's not wrong, but it's going to be different this time. It has to be.

'Maybe we will, maybe we won't,' I shrug.

'Holy shit.' Sasha leans back onto her haunches. 'You like him.'

'Wasn't that already known?'

'No, no, no.' She wags a finger in my face. 'I don't know what you were thinking about just now, but you got this look on your face. And it wasn't your normal "*Dane is hot and I'm horny*" look—'

'I don't—'

'It went all soft.' She leans in and gives my thigh a squeeze. 'Like Wes's face whenever he looks at me. Eliott? You. Like. Him.'

I know what she's implying. There's an unspoken weight in her words and the implication is as clear as day.

You. Love. Him.

I groan and bury my face in my hands. 'I think I do.'

Sasha frowns. 'That's a good thing, no?'

'It's . . .' I trail off and settle for giving her a sad little shrug. 'It's definitely something.'

Sasha sits upright. Any trace of teasing or smugness on her face is gone. 'I don't get it. You like Dane. Dane *definitely* likes you. What's the problem?'

'He's not a long-term kind of guy,' I explain bitterly. 'He doesn't do relationships or love, or anything like that.'

'People can change, babe.' She gives me a gentle nudge with her knee. 'For the right person.'

Why does that sound familiar?

I shake off the creeping sense of déjà vu and force a nonchalant smile. 'That person probably isn't me.'

Sasha's jaw ticks for a moment. There's something on the tip of her tongue, something she desperately wants to get out, but she changes her mind at the last second. 'Whatever you say, babe,' she says, barely concealing a small smile. 'Whatever you say.'

★ ★ ★

I spot Bailey and Amber almost as soon as I roll my suitcase into St Pancras station. They're standing by our departure gate with several of their own suitcases stacked up beside them, both wearing comfortable oversized sweatshirts that have #Team-Bride written across the front.

Bailey's face, already bright and grinning, lights up as soon as she notices me.

'*Eliott!*' she cries, once again giving me the *old friend* treatment instead of treating me like someone she barely knows. She pulls me into a quick, but no less tight, hug. 'Oh my god. It feels real now. *Really* real.'

I can't help but laugh a little. 'Glad I could help.'

'It's just us getting the train,' Bailey explains as we swipe our tickets against the barriers and start making our way to our seats. 'Everyone else is flying in. Except the guys. We're meeting Cash and them in Paris, and then we'll get the train together the rest of the way.'

'Cool,' I say, hoping I sound neutral. Like I don't know what the plan is already, and that Dane hasn't been casually updating me on their journey for the last three hours.

I get a pleasant surprise when we search for our seats and discover that Finn's upgrade didn't just extend to the guys. We're all seated in first-class and Bailey and Amber have a cushy four-person seater while I've got a row all to myself a few seats down.

'Come sit with us,' Amber says when she spots me trying to shuffle down the aisle. 'I mean, don't feel like you *have* to, but we've got the extra seats spare.'

'Yeah, come on,' Bailey says. She's already planted in her seat and is digging a bottle of Prosecco out of her bag. 'You can help me with this since—' She cuts herself off abruptly and shoots Amber an apologetic grimace.

A silent conversation plays out between the two of them, spoken only in tiny gestures and the occasional raise of the brow. It ends with Amber shrugging lightly and Bailey exhaling a small sigh of relief before she turns her attention back to me.

'Your choice,' she says. 'Just know that you are very, *very* welcome.'

I'd typically decline an offer like this – I'm here on business.

Bailey is my client, and it's important I keep up at least some pretence of professionalism. But I like Bailey. Amber too. They remind me of Sasha and myself and it's easy to forget that she's paying me to be here and we're not actually longtime friends.

'Are you sure?' I ask.

'One thousand per cent,' Bailey laughs. She fishes out two plastic wine glasses from her bag and wastes no time in pouring me a healthy amount of Prosecco. 'Let's go!'

I slide into the empty seat next to Amber and reach for my glass.

'Did Dane end up using his plus one?' Amber asks suddenly.

I choke on my drink and glance up at the exact same time Bailey's gaze comes up to meet mine. She holds it for a second or two and I have to wonder if I'm imagining the way her lips twitch ever so slightly.

'No,' she says after what feels like an eternity. 'He didn't bother in the end.'

Amber hums contemplatively. 'How very un-Dane like.'

Bailey drops her mouth into her palm, hiding an obvious laugh. 'Hm. I guess.'

Does she know? It *seems* like she knows, but maybe I'm being paranoid.

'How long have you and Finn been together?' I ask suddenly, desperate to get the conversation off Dane.

Amber smiles softly at the mention of her boyfriend. 'Coming up to three years now.'

'How'd you guys meet?'

She laughs and her hand comes up to rest idly on her stomach. 'It's a long story.'

'He was her *client*,' Bailey purrs, seemingly delighted to tell this story. 'And it was love at first sight.'

Amber snorts. 'It absolutely was not.'

'For Finn it was,' Bailey says with a sage nod. 'He just didn't know it at the time.'

'What about you?' Amber turns to me. 'Are you seeing anyone?'

There it is again. An almost imperceptible twitch of Bailey's lips.

'No,' I say. 'Not officially, anyway.'

'Ah,' Amber nods in understanding. 'It's one of those.'

'One of what?'

'When you both know there's something there, but you're too afraid to say it out loud in case it ruins everything?'

I blink over at her. 'I— I guess?'

Her smile turns sympathetic. 'It'll work out.'

'I'm not so sure,' I say. 'But I'm fine. I'm okay with that.'

Bailey shakes her head. 'Take it from someone who didn't realise what was in front of her until it almost blew up in her face. It *will* work out. You just have to want it to.'

The train jerks forward suddenly and we start peeling out

of the station. As I watch the landscape around us turn into a nondescript blur, I realise something.

I do want it to work out.

I really, really do.

Chapter Twenty-Five

DANE

Every fibre of my being wants to race across this platform and pull Eliott into a bone-crushing hug.

I want to bury my face in her hair, wrap my arms around her soft curves and bask in my own personal slice of heaven that is Eliott Rayne.

Somehow, I manage to restrain myself. But only just. Instead, I let Cash and Finn take the lead while I hang back with James and Leo. Cash reaches them first and pulls Bailey into the kind of embrace you give someone if you haven't seen them in years, not four days.

I get it though. Because I'm itching to do exactly the same thing to Eliott right now. I want to pull her into the kind of hug that'll sweep her off her feet and let her know just how much she means to me. Instead, I have to settle for giving her a friendly wave. Like there's absolutely nothing between us and we didn't spend an evening mutually masturbating on FaceTime together two nights ago.

'This is Eliott,' Bailey says once Cash has her back down on solid ground again. 'Not sure if you guys all remember her from the engagement party?'

Finn, Leo and James all say their greetings to Eliott before Bailey turns to me. She's got a sly look on her face that I don't trust for one second.

'And Dane? You remember Eliott, right?'

Cash coughs into his elbow in a terrible attempt at disguising a snort of laughter. I ignore it in favour of shooting Eliott an easy grin. 'How could I forget such a gorgeous face?'

Everyone rolls their eyes. They're all used to my flirting and probably don't see it as anything more than a quick one-liner being thrown at a pretty girl.

But Eliott knows that it's more than that and she gives me that smile again. The soft one that's just for me.

'Hey, Dane. It's good to see you again.'

I can hear the unspoken '*I missed you*' underlying her words and I give her a nod, hoping she can hear my unspoken message, too.

Me too.

We have the entire first-class carriage on the train to ourselves. James and Leo each snag a row to themselves and both conk out before the train even pulls out of the station, while the two happy couples sidle into a four-person booth together.

On any other occasion, this might irritate me, being left out like this, but not today. Instead of claiming the empty row next to their booth as my own, I follow Eliott down towards the other end of the carriage and drop down into the empty seat next to her.

'You don't want to sit with your friends?' Eliott asks as I shove my bag under the seat in front of us.

I drape an arm over her shoulders and pull her into me as close as she can get. 'I promise you, baby, I'm exactly where I want to be right now.'

She sighs as she nuzzles into my side. 'Me too.'

From up the carriage, Cash catches my eye. I expect him to say something, to alert the others as to what's going on over in my corner of the carriage, but he doesn't. He just smiles and gives me a small nod before he turns his attention back to his future wife.

I half expect Eliott to pull away once the train starts moving, but she doesn't. She stays curled up by my side like that's where she's meant to be; where she belongs. At some point in the journey we both fall asleep and, if I'm honest, it's the best sleep I've had in weeks.

★ ★ ★

'Just look at this *view!*' Bailey squeals as she throws open the doors to the balcony. 'It's even better than in all the photos.'

Cash and Bailey definitely undersold this place. They've been describing it as a villa for the last few months, but it's more like a castle embedded in the mountains than anything else. The host has been giving us a guided tour for the last thirty minutes, and I don't think we've seen even half of the property.

Even Finn, who bought Amber a multimillion-dollar lake house in New York like it was nothing, looks impressed.

'We'll be conducting the ceremony down there,' the host says, following Bailey out onto the balcony to point towards the fairy tale-esque terrace below us. 'My staff are still setting up below but we should be finished within an hour or so for you to check through.'

I peek below and get a glimpse of a small army of staff setting white chairs up and draping the trees and bushes with lanterns. An unexpected wave of emotion hits me and I can't help but grin as I turn my attention back to the rest of the group. Tomorrow, I get to stand up there with my little sister and my best friend and watch them get married.

I'm happy. *Genuinely* happy.

A cloud of dark brown curls suddenly appears in the corner of my vision. My grin widens and that feeling of happiness expands in my chest, morphing into something else entirely. It's an emotion I don't think I've ever felt before, and I can't quite put my finger on it.

Eliott's down there, amongst the staff setting up, getting some test shots in preparation for the big day tomorrow. Even from here I can see the smile on her face and I just know there's a glimmer of excitement sparking behind her beautiful brown eyes as she works.

I can't wait to see if I can coax out that same level of excitement and joy from her later tonight.

Everyone who is part of the wedding party is staying here over the weekend, but Eliott's got a room at a boutique hotel in the town below us. If I'm being honest, I'd much rather her join me in my suite so we can take advantage of the comfortable king-sized bed in my room, but I doubt she'll go for that idea.

She looks up suddenly and meets my eye. Her expression softens slightly and that emotion from earlier, the one I can feel in the very core of my chest, swells within me some more.

I could stand here and watch Eliott work all evening, but our host pulls us away to continue the rest of the tour and I reluctantly follow.

The rest of the tour takes about another half hour, but I'm barely listening as we traipse after our host. I don't think it's possible for me to care any less about the antique bay windows in the main foyer that have Amber gasping and reaching for her phone to snap photos, or about the spot in the second terrace around the back of the villa that apparently is the best spot for golden hour photos that Bailey makes note of.

My disinterest must be obvious because Cash suddenly pulls back from the rest of the group and nudges his shoulder against mine.

'Somewhere else you'd rather be right now?' he asks with a knowing smirk.

'Nah,' I lie. 'Just a little tired after all this travelling.' We've been up since about four and have crossed three borders today. I'm actually surprised everyone else isn't dead on their feet.

'I think the plan is to have an early night,' Cash says. 'Everyone in bed by ten since we'll be up early tomorrow.'

I pretend to frown. 'Tomorrow? Why? Is something happening?'

'Hilarious,' Cash deadpans. 'Seriously though, are you good? You seem . . . distracted.' That smirk is back again in full force, like he knows something, but he's not willing to say it aloud just yet. He's waiting for me to take the first step.

'I'm not—'

Eliott chooses that moment to waltz in through the secondary terrace doors and I suddenly understand exactly what our host was talking about when she mentioned golden hour.

The world seems to slow down and the sounds of everyone talking and laughing around me fade away until the only thing I can hear is the steady thrum of my heartbeat.

Eliott is bathed in a warm glow and the sunlight is practically dancing across her skin.

Her gaze scans the room and quickly finds my own. Eliott's eyes — always beautiful, always expressive — catch the last rays of the sun before the doors swing closed behind her, making them sparkle with an intensity that quite literally takes my breath away.

She looks like a goddess.

Ethereal.

Her full lips curve into a shy grin of acknowledgment before she turns and waves down Bailey and Cash.

'I think I've got everything I need, so I'll head over to my hotel now.'

I cross the room without even thinking about it, my legs moving on autopilot.

'Are you sure?' Bailey asks. 'We're not doing anything crazy tonight, but we'll probably hang out around the fire pit for a while and have something to eat. If you want to join us, you're more than welcome to.'

'That's so kind of you,' Eliott starts. It's only for a brief second, but her gaze flickers over to me before returning to Bailey and Cash. 'But I'm pretty tired, so I'll just head back and get an early night.'

Bailey's lip twitches and Cash ducks his head suddenly as if he's hiding a laugh.

'Totally understand.' Bailey turns and raises a brow at me. 'What about you, Dane? You coming to hang by the fire pit?'

'Sure,' I say with an easy shrug. 'I'll meet you guys out there.'

Bailey's lip twitch turns into a full-on grin. 'Are you going somewhere first?'

I feel my cheeks start to warm. She knows exactly what she's doing and I've fallen straight into her trap. I shrug again, trying to keep my expression as casual as possible. 'Thought I'd help Eliott carry her stuff back to her hotel.'

'We can get a taxi for her,' Cash says. The grin on his face is almost identical to Bailey's.

Those two really are meant for each other.

'Waste of money,' I say dismissively. 'And I wanted to get some air, anyway.'

It's an incredibly lame excuse and I expect them both to pick it apart immediately. But they don't. Instead, their grins soften slightly into something a little less shit-eating and a little more genuine.

'Cool,' Cash says. 'We'll catch you later tonight, then.'

'Yeah.'

Cash pulls Bailey into his side and drags her away over to where the rest of the group has started spilling out onto the terrace.

'See you tomorrow, Eliott,' Bailey sings as she allows Cash

to guide her away. She turns around just before they reach the door and wiggles her brows. 'Have *fun*.'

And then they're disappearing through the doors and it's just me and Eliott alone in the room.

A grin splits my face in two.

'You know,' Eliott says, quirking her brow as she turns to look up at me. 'We probably should've taken the taxi offer. It's a long walk and my bags are heavy.'

'That just means more time with you,' I say. I mimic Cash's earlier action and pull Eliott into my side. She slots in perfectly and I realise that I'll never get tired of this. Just the feel of Eliott by my side is a high I never want to come down from. 'And I'm definitely not complaining about that.'

She hums and the sun catches her eye again as she looks up at me. 'Me neither.'

Everyone else is only one bathroom break away from stepping through the doors and spotting us, but I don't care. I lift a finger and tilt her chin upwards, enjoying the way she lets me guide her without any hesitation.

I lean down, my lips brushing against her forehead. It's the softest of touches, one I've done several times before, but this time it sparks something inside me.

It's that feeling from before. The one I felt in the deepest caverns of my chest that quickly becomes all-consuming.

Eliott lets out a soft whimper as fingers come up to fist my shirt. 'We should go,' she whispers against my lips.

We should.

But we don't. Not yet.

I close the minuscule gap between us and press my lips against hers, enjoying the way she lets out a pleased sigh as she sinks into my touch.

Kissing Eliott is very quickly becoming my favourite activity. Everything about it sets each one of my senses on fire in the best kind of way. The sounds she makes. The way her tongue slides against mine. The feel of her curves pressed against me.

It's simultaneously too much and not enough.

I want more.

I *need* more.

'Let's go,' I mutter before I reluctantly pull away.

She huffs out a sigh of frustration I understand only too well. 'Yeah.'

'Don't worry, baby,' I say with a teasing grin as I tug her towards the door. 'There's still more to come.'

Her next four words send blood rushing straight to my dick and, judging from the satisfied smirk on her face, she knows it too.

She licks her lips and pins me in place with a sultry stare. 'I'm counting on it.'

Chapter Twenty-Six

ELIOTT

The sense of déjà vu is almost overwhelming.

We've been here before. Frantically clawing at each other's clothes as we stumble around in the darkness.

It feels different this time, though.

We're not two horny strangers with nothing but a mutual physical attraction between us to keep us going.

There's something more this time.

The air between us is thick with anticipation, charged with a potent mix of desire and something much deeper. It's more than just passion or us trying to satisfy a craving.

I feel it in the way Dane holds me, soft and gentle, as he lowers me down onto the bed with him. It's in the way he whispers my name almost reverently as he starts to pepper slow, tender kisses down my body. It's in the way I arch into his touch, my body reacting to his every caress like it's the first time I've ever experienced anything like this.

Hell, it might as well be.

'Gorgeous,' Dane murmurs as I finish discarding the last piece of clothing I have on. His eyes are dark and heavy and I feel my entire body flush as his heated gaze takes its time roving over me. 'Have I ever told you that?'

'You might've mentioned it once or twi— *Ah*.' My words and any hope of coherent thought are drowned out by the whimper he coaxes out of me as he leans forward and catches my nipple in his mouth. 'Not fair.'

I shudder as his chuckle reverberates through me, but he doesn't stop. In fact, every moan that falls from my lips seems to spur him on. I feel his lips curve into a grin as he brings up his free hand to palm at my other breast while his tongue rolls torturous circles around my nipple.

I wiggle beneath him impatiently, desperate for more. He takes the hint and satisfaction surges through me as his free hand skitters down my body and gives my pussy one firm but gentle stroke.

'God.'

I've never been this vocal before in bed, but Dane somehow knows exactly what to do to have me keening beneath him.

How?

How can it possibly be this good?

I see stars as he slips a finger between my lips, his thumb pressed firmly against my clit.

I suddenly feel it — that telltale building of pleasure in the pit of my stomach.

That feeling of déjà vu is back again. Suddenly it's two and a half years ago and I'm back in my bedroom, pinning all my hopes on Dane for an orgasm.

'Relax, baby.' Dane slides his finger out of me and I immediately miss his touch. He comes to sit beside me on the bed and pulls me onto his lap as he goes. I probably enjoy that a little too much. The way he can effortlessly lift me up like I'm a doll.

I wrap my arms around his neck, pulling myself forward until my breasts are flush against his chest. 'I am relaxed.'

'You're not.' He starts rubbing soothing circles into my thighs. 'You're overthinking things. *Relax.*'

I do what he says and try to force my brain to switch off. I allow myself to lean into the abundance of pleasant sensations currently coursing through me as Dane's fingers dance back down towards my pussy.

'I wish you could see yourself right now,' Dane says, his voice nothing more than a hoarse whisper by this point. 'You're so beautiful, baby.' He slips in another finger and curls them both inside me. My entire body shakes, but Dane holds me firmly in place with his other hand. 'Did you pack your toy?'

I freeze and my throat suddenly feels dry. 'Huh?'

Dane looks at me in amusement. He shifts slightly and slides his fingers out of me. The movement jostles me a little and I get another taste of delicious friction as his dick slides against my clit.

'Did you bring your toy?' he asks again.

'Why?'

He raises a brow. 'So we can use it. Like I said. Remember?'

I nod furiously. It'll be a long time before I ever forget that particular phone call. 'I guess I just thought you meant we'd use it after.'

His expression turns serious. There's no trace of any humour in it now. 'After what?'

The urge to reach for a blanket to cover myself up right now is all-consuming. Every inch of me feels hot and not in a good way. 'After you finish,' I manage to force out. 'Then we'd do me.'

He sits upright fully but grabs my thighs and keeps me in place so I'm still sitting flush against him. 'Eliott, baby. No.'

My heart stops.

This is it. The moment I've been dreading. Dane's finally realised that sex with me isn't going to be as fun as he thinks. That the idea of getting me off is too much work for him to bother with. I try to slide off him, but he brings both hands up to my face and cups my cheeks.

I'm straddling him, completely naked, but the way he's holding my face right now is more intimate than anything we've done tonight.

'You're not an afterthought, baby,' he murmurs. The sound

of his voice – soft, hazy, filled with something I can't quite place – is enough to kick-start my heart again. 'Not with me. Never with me.' He leans in and steals a kiss. 'Do you understand?'

I nod, not quite trusting my voice, and he gives me a satisfied smile.

'Good. Are you ready to get your toy now?'

I hesitate. 'It's not cheating?'

Dane snorts. 'Cheating how?'

I shrug. I don't want to do this right now. Don't want to relive the far too many memories I have of being in this exact position. Of men sneering at the thought of using a toy, unwilling to take the apparent blow to their ego.

Dane's expression softens like he's read my mind. He brings a hand up to my face again and runs his thumb along my jaw. 'Good sex is whatever *you* want it to be, Eliott. It's all on your terms. If you need some help to get you there, then that's what we'll do. No such thing as cheating.'

God. This man.

This *fucking man*.

I surge forward and capture his lips with mine. Dane lets his hands drop down to my waist and we immediately pick up where we left off.

He sets a slow pace, guiding my hips back and forth so I can slide along his dick. My pussy clenches with each movement.

I don't think I've ever wanted anyone like this before.

'Toy,' Dane groans against my lips as I wiggle my hips in a figure eight formation. 'Get your toy. *Please*.'

I roll off him and reach for my suitcase. I can feel Dane's eyes on me the entire time and when I turn back to face him again, there's a fiery intensity burning in his gaze. He doesn't blanch at the sight of my toy. Doesn't frown or gingerly touch it like it's something to be ashamed of. He just reaches for it as I settle myself back on his lap.

'We don't—'

'We *do*,' Dane cuts me off before I can even finish talking. 'Let me make you happy, baby.'

'You already do.'

His smile lights up his whole face. 'Then I'm not planning on stopping any time soon.'

He pulls me in for another searing kiss as his fingers fumble around with my toy. Before I know it, a soft buzzing noise starts to mix in with sounds of our moans and then Dane is pressing my toy against my clit.

'*Fuck*.' My head rolls back between my shoulder blades and I have to fight to keep upright. It's difficult, because every single one of my bones suddenly feels like it's turned into jelly.

'You're good, baby.' Dane's voice cuts through my increasingly hazy thoughts. 'You're doing *so* good.'

My pussy clenches as he changes the setting on my toy

and it begins sucking at my clit in my favourite rhythmic pattern.

'I can't— I can't—'

Dane surges forward, flipping our position and pushing me back into the mattress. He keeps the toy pressed firmly against my clit with one hand and uses the other one to wrap my legs, one by one, around his waist.

'You *can*, baby,' he assures me, leaning forward to press soft, tender kisses along my neck. 'Does it feel good?'

'So good.'

I feel him grin against my neck. 'That's my girl.'

His girl.

I let out a mewl of displeasure when he pulls away suddenly, taking the toy with him as he goes. My eyes snap open and I hadn't even realised I'd shut them.

Dane chuckles as he leans over the side of the bed and starts fumbling around for the bag he'd dropped there earlier. He pulls out a condom from the front pocket and tears it open.

His dick looks almost painfully hard, and I can't stop myself from reaching over to touch it. He freezes, condom in hand, and lets out a shuddery moan as my thumb rubs along his head, spreading pre-cum as I run my fingers down his length.

'*Eliott.*' The way he says my name is almost like a warning.

I don't even pretend to heed it.

The sound that comes out of his mouth when I wrap

my fingers around his dick and squeeze is more of a muffled roar than a moan. His entire body shakes, and I take that as an invitation to keep going. I slowly pump up and down his length, enjoying the way his eyes roll back and how he pulls his bottom lip between his teeth to bite down. He's been in control from the very moment we stepped into my room, but it's time for that to change.

'Sit back,' I murmur. His dick twitches in my hand at the order and I file that little nugget of information away for later use.

Dane likes it when I tell him what to do.

He follows my instruction without any hesitation and settles himself against the headboard, his long legs splayed out wide in front of him. Just the sight of him sends another shockwave of pleasure rippling through me. I press my finger against his mouth and pull his bottom lip downwards.

'Open up.'

Another immediate response. He lets his mouth drop open and I slide a finger inside, relishing the way his tongue wraps itself around my digit.

He lets out a small groan when I pull my finger out and start slowly tracing it down his body. I take my time as I go, ignoring each little impatient twitch of his dick as I run my soaked finger over his nipples, down his chest, and along the neat line of hair that starts at his belly button and goes down, down, down.

'Have you always been such a tease?' Dane grits out. His fingers are gripping the surrounding sheets so tightly, his knuckles have started to pale.

'You don't like it?' I pretend to pout as I shuffle back slightly and drop to my knees. 'That's a shame.' I lean forward and let my lips ghost against the tip of his dick. 'Because we were just about to have some fun.' I run my tongue along his head and then everything seems to happen all at once.

Dane's hands come up to fist my hair tightly. Not painfully, never painfully, but hard enough for me to know that I'm no longer the one holding the reins here.

'*Eliott*,' he rasps out as he guides me back into a seated position. 'You're going to be the fucking death of me.' He lays me back down onto the bed and comes to hover over me. 'But I'm not complaining.'

He captures my lips in another scorching kiss before finally sliding on the condom. 'Do you trust me, baby?'

I nod without even having to think about it and he treats me to my favourite lopsided grin in return.

'Good.' And then he's pressing my toy back up against my clit and my eyes are rolling to the back of my head.

My entire body shakes, stars start to swarm behind my eyelids. I'm close.

I'm *so close*.

My toys have always been able to get me there, but it's

never felt this good before. Never felt so all-consuming. So addictive. So *right*.

'That's it.' Dane's voice cuts through the thick maze of thoughts rushing through my mind. 'Come on, baby.' He changes the pulsating setting on my toy to something a little faster and stronger. 'Come for me.'

My mouth falls open in a soundless scream as fireworks erupt in my vision and my entire body turns into a live wire. Every touch, every kiss, every breath sends shockwave after shockwave surging through me and then—

'*Dane.*' His name comes out as a choked sob as he slides into me, pushing against the still spasming walls of my pussy.

'*Eliott . . . fucking . . . God. Eliott.*'

My walls clench around him with each well-timed stroke. His fingers dig into the skin around my waist, pulling me in closer like he can't get enough of me, and the realisation sends yet another burst of pleasure shooting through me.

This is sex.

Everything I've experienced up till now has been a sham and I don't know how I'm going to go back to living that kind of life now that I've had a taste of this.

'Perfect,' Dane groans, his strokes becoming more frenzied with each passing second. 'Just – *perfect.*'

I lift my arms and wrap them around his neck, pulling him in close. 'Dane?'

'Yeah, baby?'

I press my lips against the shell of his ear and whisper the same three words that had me coming undone just a few minutes ago. 'Come for me.'

He freezes for one long second, and then his entire body shudders as he thrusts into me hard and deep. '*Eliott—*'

I swallow my name on his tongue as he finishes and plant soft, chaste kisses down his neck as we both lay there, catching our breath.

'Like I said,' he pants, breaking the silence after a minute or two. 'You're going to be the death of me.'

I laugh as he rolls off me, scooping me up into a sweaty hug as he goes. 'No complaints though?'

He tilts my chin upwards and presses a soft kiss against my lips. 'No complaints.'

* * *

The wrong kind of buzzing noise wakes me up the next morning. It's loud and urgent and doesn't come with the waves of pleasure I've started to associate with a noise like that.

I groan and pull the blankets up over my head. 'Someone really wants to talk with you.'

Beside me, wrapped up in my blankets like it's a toga, Dane huffs out an equally unimpressed groan. 'Don't care.'

He shifts in the bed and drapes an arm over my side,

tucking me into him. That's how we fell asleep last night – with Dane curled protectively around me, hot and sweaty after two and a half more rounds of toe-curling sex – and there's nowhere I'd rather be right now.

A very large part of me is more than content to stay in this spot until we get at *least* one more round under our belts, but the rational side of me wins this particular war.

Dane's phone angrily vibrates again and I emerge from the blanket nest we've created and reach for my own phone.

No missed calls or messages, so it's probably nothing *urgent* but . . .

'It's 8am,' I yawn. 'We should probably start getting ready.'

Dane lets out a grunt of disapproval as his arm comes to wrap a little tighter around my waist, firmly holding me in place. 'Ten more minutes.'

'You said that thirty minutes ago.'

Another grunt.

I snort and start to slowly extract myself from his grip. If Dane has his way we'll never leave the bed and, as tempting as that sounds, I've still got a job to do.

'Come on,' I say, sliding out of the bed. 'And check your phone. It might be important.'

Another grunt, though this one is at least accompanied by a yawn and a stretch as Dane reluctantly sits upright and reaches for his phone. He blinks blearily at the screen and then lets out a sharp bark of laughter.

'What is it?' I crawl back into the bed and peer over his shoulder at his phone. There's a notification for several missed calls – all from Cash – and a stream of unread messages, also all from Cash.

> **CASH**
>
> Open your door I can't sleep.
>
> Dane?
>
> What kind of best man leaves his groom hanging like this?
>
> Wait did you even come back last night?
>
> No. You didn't. Your welcome basket is still outside your door.
>
> So you and Eliott . . .
>
> Nice. But now I do owe Amber £20. You couldn't wait until after the wedding??
>
> Wait.
>
> If you two were just gonna buddy up you should've let us know. Saved us a bit of money on the hotel room.
>
> Tell Eliott I said hi.
>
> And ask her if I could please have my best man back

> now because we're running on a schedule and I didn't account for Dane being halfway across town on the MORNING OF MY WEDDING.

'Sounds like your groom needs you,' I laugh as I roll back out of bed and start padding towards the bathroom. 'You should probably go and meet up with him before he has an aneurysm.'

'Yeah, yeah,' Dane chuckles, thumbs already moving at lightning speed to type out a reply.

'Think he's getting cold feet?' I call from the bathroom.

'No way,' Dane scoffs. I can hear the sound of him rustling around for his clothes. 'Those two were made for each other. He's just excited. Probably wants to go over his speech a couple times too.'

The bathroom door creaks open and Dane's still-sleepy face appears in the crack. 'Do you need any help carrying anything back to the villa?'

'I'm good.' It had been a flimsy excuse last night, and it's even flimsier in the warm light of day. 'You go. I'll see you in a couple hours.'

I take a step towards the shower, but Dane is quicker. His hand wraps around my wrist and tugs me towards him, and then his lips are on mine before I even have the chance to think about protesting.

Not that I want to.

I could easily get used to this.

Waking up with Dane curled around me, his dick pressing into the curve of my lower back. Soft kisses stolen beneath the blankets. Warm, wandering hands reverently exploring every inch of my body.

I could *definitely* get used to this.

And that's dangerous.

Because it's only a matter of time before this all comes crashing down on me and Dane does what Dane always does and moves on to the next woman.

It's stupid of me, but I ignore the warning bells ringing in my mind and let myself cling onto this version of Dane. The one who apparently doesn't care about my morning breath as he swipes his tongue along my bottom lip to deepen our kiss.

The one holding my face so gently, you'd swear I was the most precious thing in the world to him.

Like he loves me the way I'm pretty sure I love him.

Chapter Twenty-Seven

DANE

There's something about seeing your best friend put on the tuxedo he's about to marry your sister in that makes time stand still.

My unused bedroom has been turned into the unofficial groom's suite for the day and myself and the other three groomsmen all crowd around Cash as he puts the finishing touches on his outfit. As I watch him adjust his tie in front of the mirror, my mind starts to flood with memories of the last two and a half decades of our lives.

Cash is in every single one of my core memories, grinning by my side; a shoulder to cry on when I've needed him, an endlessly supportive hand ready to pull me up. He's been a brother in everything but name for the last twenty years and, after today, he'll officially become family.

Cash straightens his bow tie and the weight of the moment settles around the room.

'Looking good, man,' Finn says with a wide grin.

'Groom of the year,' James says, lifting his champagne glass in toast.

Everyone murmurs in agreement, and I clear my throat. I hadn't been expecting the wave of emotion I'm currently feeling, but I lean into it and clap Cash on the shoulder, pulling him in for a one-armed hug.

'I'm so proud of you, man,' I say, my vision blurring ever so slightly as I stare at our reflections in the mirror. 'There's no one I'd trust more with my sister's heart than you. You're an inspiration to everyone in this room.'

I pause and swallow a sudden lump in my throat as I think about the ways Cash makes it his sole mission on Earth to love on my sister. She's never shed so much as a single tear when it comes to Cash and I know, without a shadow of a doubt, that he'll dedicate the rest of his life to making her even happier than he already does. And what more could you want for your little sister?

'You give me hope,' I continue with a slightly watery smile. 'One day, maybe I'll finally find love like this. But until then . . .' I reach for my glass of champagne and hold it high in the air. 'To Cash and Bailey.'

'To Cash and Bailey,' Finn, James and Leo all echo in agreement, raising their own glasses in support.

Cash doesn't say a word. For some reason, the smile on his face has been wiped in favour of an odd frown.

He's looking at me like I've suddenly sprouted another head.

'You can't be serious,' Cash says, his voice a droll deadpan. He shakes his head and then runs a stressed hand through his hair. 'Dane. Come on now, man.'

I frown. 'What? You didn't like my speech?'

Well, that doesn't bode well for my best man's speech at the reception later.

Cash huffs out a frustrated puff of air through his nostrils. 'You *are* serious. You're actually serious.'

I glance over at the others and, to my relief, can tell that they're just as confused as I am.

'Talking about how I'm an inspiration and I give you hope that you'll finally find love one day?' Cash rolls his eyes. 'Come *on*.'

I'm still not getting it and the confusion must be evident on my face because Cash suddenly puts both hands on my shoulders, looks me square in the eye, and gives me a shake. 'Dane. You. Are. In. *Love*.'

I blink at my best friend in disbelief. 'What?'

'You're in love, Dane,' Cash says with an exasperated laugh. 'With Eliott. You love Eliott and I'd say you've probably been in love with her for a while now.'

The room around me starts to spin slightly. '*What?*'

Cash groans and pulls away. 'It's my wedding day. I can't do this. Finn, you're up.'

Finn gives me a sheepish grin. 'Yeah, I guess I kind of just assumed you and Eliott were together?'

Beside him, both James and Leo nod in agreement.

'I didn't realise that you weren't until Amber and Cash made that bet on the train.'

My eyes slide over to Cash, who at least has the decency to look somewhat apologetic.

'We were wondering how long it would take you guys to make things official. I said it'd be after the wedding. Amber said she gave you guys twelve hours.'

'Amber won,' Finn clarifies cheerfully.

'Yeah,' I mutter as I slide down into the nearest armchair. The world around me is still spinning, still slightly out of focus. 'I got that.'

'Listen,' Cash crouches beside me and gives me a sympathetic grin. 'I didn't say this to give you a nervous breakdown.'

'Really?'

'Really,' Cash laughs. 'I thought you knew and you guys just weren't ready to say anything yet.'

'But I don't— I *can't*—'

Love is not for me. I know this better than anyone else in the world. I'm just not built for it. I'm not Cash. I'm not Finn. I'm *me*.

Dane Clarke.

The guy who is never enough.

And Eliott deserves more than enough. More than I can give her.

Right?

Cash gives my thigh a sympathetic squeeze. 'I know you've been hurt before,' he says, dropping his voice to a low murmur that only I can hear. 'And you've put up walls to stop it from happening again. But I think those walls have been up so long, you can't recognise real love when you feel it anymore.'

I lean back into the armchair and try to sort through my thoughts. Do I love Eliott?

Really, genuinely love her?

I care about her. I know that for sure. I want to be the reason she wakes up with a smile every morning. I want to be the person she can rely on without even having to think twice about it. I want to be the constant in her life – the one thing she never has to worry about because she knows I'll always be there.

Is that love?

Almost as if on cue, there's a sharp knock on the door and Eliott's voice suddenly floats through the wood. 'Are you guys decent? I'm here to take your "getting ready" photos.'

Just the sound of her voice realigns my entire world. The walls stop spinning and everything comes back into perfect focus.

Cash gives me a knowing smirk before he turns his head and calls out, 'Come on in, Eliott. We're good.'

My heart stops, then starts and then stops again as the door is pushed open and Eliott comes striding in.

Do I love Eliott? I ask myself the question again as I take in the sight of her. She's wearing a flowy green dress that pinches at her waistline, showing off the beautiful curves I spent the previous night tracing with my fingers. She looks absolutely gorgeous. That goes without saying.

But do I love her?

The smile she's wearing softens slightly as her brown eyes scan the room and eventually land on me. All the moisture in my mouth evaporates and I choke on any hope of a greeting I had on the tip of my tongue.

Yes.

The answer comes to me with unwavering clarity.

I do love her.

Now I've admitted it to myself, it seems so obvious. How could I not love someone as brilliant, as sweet, and as caring as Eliott? Someone who gives her all to the people she cares about without asking anything in return.

She might not ask for it, but I want to give it to her, anyway.

I want to give her the world if she'll let me.

I love this woman with every fibre of my being, and the thought terrifies me.

Because I've been here before and I know how this ends. And it can't end like that this time. Not again. Not with Eliott.

A memory floats to the forefront of my mind.

Eliott, sick in bed and curled around me for extra warmth. I remember that day perfectly. The way she leaned on me and let me take care of her when she needed it. How she felt pressed up against me as we cuddled in her bed. And how she made my heart stop when she lifted her head and murmured, still slightly delirious, *'You're more than enough for me.'*

Did she mean that or was it a sickness-induced bout of insanity?

I'm running on autopilot as Eliott stages us for photos. I can barely remember a word anyone says as I let them shuffle me this way and that, forcing a grin onto my face for the camera.

Part of me wishes that Cash had never said anything at all. That he just let me live in my self-imposed delusion for the rest of my days.

But another steadily growing part of me is grateful he said anything, because now I'm allowing myself the opportunity to imagine a world where me and Eliott have the chance to grow into something amazing.

And I'm starting to like the idea of living in that world.

Chapter Twenty-Eight

ELIOTT

The excitement in the bridal suite is infectious.

Bailey is sitting on the bed, holding back tears as her mother zips up her wedding dress for her. She's not the only one with tears threatening to destroy three hours' worth of make-up.

Amber's standing off to the side, her shoulders shaking every few seconds as she tries to choke back her sobs. Bailey's other bridesmaid, a young woman named Bea who arrived on the first flight in this morning, is using a beauty blender to dab at her own tears.

I don't blame them.

Bailey looks stunning, like she stepped right off the pages of a fairy tale. Her hair floats around her in a beautiful, voluminous cloud of black curls and her dress, a flowing white gown that looks like a shimmery wave when she walks, fits her like a glove.

'You look *phenomenal*,' Amber cries, giving up any pretence of holding back her tears.

'Beautiful,' Bea sniffs, still dabbing away with the blender.

I cling to the outer edges of the room and snap photos as I go, documenting every watery smile, every choked laugh, every tight hug. I capture it all and my heart swells with each press of the shutter button.

Bailey's mother and Bea both leave after a few minutes to run downstairs and help with a handful of last-minute preparation tasks, leaving me alone in the room with Bailey and Amber.

'I'm so happy you two found each other,' Amber says, still blinking back tears. 'That you've found the person who loves you the way you deserve to be loved.'

'And you,' Bailey says, pulling Amber into a tight hug. 'Every time Finn even looks at you, I just melt.'

Amber uses a finger to wipe away one of Bailey's tears. 'Today isn't about me.'

'But I'm not wrong.'

'You're not,' Amber laughs. 'We both got lucky, I guess.' She takes a step back and runs her hand along the front of her pale pink bridesmaid dress. Bailey's hand follows the same path and they both stop just above the slight, barely noticeable bump of Amber's stomach.

I snap a shot of this intimate moment, blinking back tears of my own. I'm not usually this affected by displays of love, but there's something about Bailey and Amber's friendship that tugs at my heartstrings.

It's beautiful and pure and I can't help but want the best for these two women I barely even know.

'*God,*' Bailey sniffs, wiping away the last remnants of her tears. 'If we don't stop soon, we'll have to call the make-up artist to come back and fix all of this.'

'You look beautiful,' Amber says firmly. 'Perfect. If Cash doesn't burst into tears the second you step onto that aisle, I want a redo.'

They both burst into contagious giggles, spreading a warmth that seems to fill the entire room.

I can't help but wonder if this will be me and Sasha one day. It's only a matter of time before Sasha and Wes tie the knot, and then will it be the two of us standing together in her bridal suite, blinking back tears as we talk about the turn our lives have taken?

Sasha has Wes, and I – who do I have?

Dane?

Will I still have Dane?

Do I even have him *now*?

Five years from now, will Dane be my person in the same way Bailey and Amber have Cash and Finn? Or will the last six months become nothing more than a blip in my life?

I really hope not. I don't want this to be just a brief fling that we both move on from once we're back in the UK. There's something *more* between us. More than just sex, more than just a fiery physical attraction.

But he has to want it as much as I do for anything real to happen between us.

And I'm not sure that he does.

I don't think he even believes that he's capable of wanting more. Of *deserving* more.

'Hey, Eliott?' Bailey's voice snaps me out of my thoughts.

I blink back to reality and find her staring at me with a cautious expression on her face. 'What's up?'

She hesitates for a moment, steeling herself for something. 'Do you mind if we get a photo together?'

'We?' I frown. 'As in, you and Amber? Sure, I can get some more. Did you have anything in mind?'

'No,' Bailey shakes her head. 'I meant me and you. Just one photo.'

In all my years of wedding photography, I don't think a bride has ever asked *me* to be in a photo. Blending into the background and becoming invisible is a core part of my job, and I've never been asked to stand in the spotlight before.

'Why?'

Bailey gives me a wry smile as she takes my hands in hers and squeezes gently. 'I'm not going to push anything because it's definitely not my place, but also . . . I'm not blind.'

Amber muffles a snort from her spot on the bed but otherwise pretends to be very interested in the buckle on her shoe to give me and Bailey some semblance of privacy.

Bailey squeezes my hands again. 'There's something between you and Dane. Something real.'

'I—'

'And if there's a chance that my future sister-in-law is at my wedding right now, I need to make sure I've got at least one photo with you.' The smile on her face is completely genuine. 'Just one. So we have something to look back on in ten years and remember this moment.'

'Bailey, I—'

'I know how Dane is with relationships and dating,' Bailey says, completely ignoring my attempt at an interruption. 'But he's different with you. We've all noticed it.'

Amber nods. 'I don't think I've ever seen him so happy with someone before.'

'We're just friends,' I force out, but the words feel wrong on my tongue.

Bailey raises a brow. 'Right. Okay then. Well, as Dane's very good friend—'

Another snort from Amber.

'I'd really like a photo with you.'

My response hasn't changed. '*Why?*'

'Because you're important to Dane, so you're important

to me,' Bailey says simply. 'Even if you guys haven't figured it out yourselves yet.'

I can tell she's not going to budge on this, however ridiculous she sounds. 'Fine,' I say, dragging the word out as much as possible to make my displeasure clear. I don't think Bailey cares, though. 'Just the one.'

Bailey beams like she's just won the lottery and I pass my camera over to Amber and allow myself to be pulled into a one-armed hug with Bailey.

Amber ignores the '*just one*' rule and takes a handful of photos of the two of us. I have to pray that the smile on my face isn't as awkward as it feels.

'I meant what I said, Eliott,' Bailey says through her smile, still holding me close. 'In ten years we're going to look back on this photo and feel so glad that we took it.'

Ten years . . .

I try to picture myself ten years from now and, to my surprise, a vision comes to me quite clearly. I'm sat at a large dining table with Cash and Bailey hovering to my right, and Amber and Finn hovering to my left. Dane is tucked close beside me. He looks older – we both do, but we also look happy.

So happy.

Everyone is flicking through what I quickly realise is a wedding album. Bailey and Cash's wedding album.

I'm smiling as we turn the page and land on a photo of me and Bailey.

'There we go,' Bailey murmurs next to me, snapping me out of the daydream I'm rapidly descending into. 'You see what I mean?'

'Yeah,' I say, my lips curving upwards into a genuine grin for the first time since Bailey suggested we do this. 'I do.'

Chapter Twenty-Nine

DANE

'. . . So if you'll all join me in raising a toast to the new Mr and Mrs Reid!'

The entire terrace erupts into a loud cheer of congratulations as everyone holds up their glasses and toasts the ridiculously giddy newlyweds sitting up front. Cash has an arm draped around Bailey's shoulders and both their cheeks are flushed red with excitement and probably more than a little champagne.

'Thank you, Dane,' Cash says as I hand him back the microphone. He momentarily lets go of his new wife and pulls me into a tight hug. 'That was an amazing speech.'

'*Beautiful*,' Bailey says, standing up to give me a hug of her own. I have no idea what kind of sorcery her make-up artist performed earlier, but despite her tears, she still looks immaculate. 'Didn't know you had it in you.'

'Come on,' I snort. 'I've always been good with words. That's my whole thing.'

My attention wavers for a moment as I spot Eliott creeping round the back of the tables, her camera pointed in our direction. Bailey follows my gaze and her smile turns into something a little more smug.

'Maybe you should use that talent of yours with someone else.'

I know exactly what she's getting at, but we don't have time to get into it because suddenly our parents and Cash's mum are all approaching the table to give their congratulations to the happy newlyweds.

I slip out from the throng once I hear Mum say, '*It'll be Dane's turn next*' and head back towards my table. I'm sitting with Amber and Finn and they both grin at me as I drop down into my seat. Amber's leaning against Finn's chest and he, just like Cash, has a protective arm wrapped around her shoulders.

'Good speech,' Finn says with a nod.

'Definitely made me tear up a little,' Amber says, dabbing at the corners of her eyes with a napkin. 'It's not going to beat *mine*, of course, but you did a good job.'

'Ha ha,' I deadpan, reaching for a handful of breadsticks from the bowl between us. 'Did everyone think I'd get my speech from the internet or something?'

'It definitely crossed my mind,' Amber admits. 'Ooh! It's time for the bouquet toss.'

I watch a handful of the guests hop up from their seats and form a small cluster near where Bailey is now standing.

Amber doesn't make a move and I nod my head in the direction of the growing crowd. 'You're not going for the bouquet?'

Amber arches a brow and tilts her head up so she can catch Finn's eye. 'Do I need to?'

'Nope,' Finn says immediately, an easy smile taking over his face as his free hand comes to rest on Amber's stomach. 'You're good.'

I vaguely remember Bailey getting excited about the prospect of back-to-back weddings. I give them two months before they're planning a wedding. To be honest, I'm surprised Amber doesn't already have a ring on her finger, but I suppose they're doing things in their own time.

Not that it matters.

Anyone can tell, just by looking at the two of them, that they're made for each other.

Bailey suddenly hurls the bouquet as high as she can, but instead of landing amongst the crowd of eager and waiting women in front of her, it goes sailing through the air and lands straight in my lap.

Everyone roars with laughter but I stare, unblinking, at the colourful bouquet.

'Looks like *you're* up next,' Amber laughs.

I glance around the room. It takes me half a second to find Eliott. She's standing close to Cash and Bailey's table, her camera pointed in my direction, and she's laughing too.

I push up from my seat, the flowers skittering to the floor as I move. Someone calls my name, but I barely hear it as I make a beeline for my sister.

She's still cackling as I approach her. 'Your *face*,' she laughs. 'Oh, I hope Eliott caught that on camera.'

'Speaking of Eliott,' I murmur, all too aware that other guests are milling around us. 'Can I borrow her for ten minutes?'

Bailey raises a brow. 'You want to borrow my wedding photographer at my wedding?'

'Just for ten minutes.'

Her mouth splits into a wide grin that lights up her whole face. 'Make it thirty.'

It takes me less than a minute to cross through the cheering and dancing crowd to find Eliott. She's in the middle of photographing Cash's mum and my dad enjoying a quick dance and I feel a little bad about interrupting but . . .

'Hey.'

She pulls away from the camera and gives me a look. 'I'm working, Dane.'

'And I,' I say, pressing my hand against the small of her back so I can guide her to a secluded part of the terrace where we won't be overheard. 'I've got explicit permission from the bride to borrow you for thirty minutes.'

Eliott shoots me a look of disbelief.

'I do!' I insist. 'Bailey's promised not to do anything worthy of a photograph for the next half an hour.'

'And why would she do that?' Eliott asks.

We turn a corner and find ourselves tucked away in a little alcove. I can hear the sounds of the wedding reception waging on behind us, but it's muted enough that I can pretend we're far away. It's just me and Eliott now and I can finally say what I need to say.

'Because Bailey, and everyone else apparently, can see what I've been too stubborn to see.'

'Dane, what're you—'

I take a step closer and bring my hands up to cup her face. 'I'm not built for love.'

She swallows thickly. 'Right. You've said that before.'

'I have.' I lean in slightly. 'That's what I've always thought. And, up until recently, I didn't think that would ever change.'

Something sparks behind her eyes. 'Until recently?'

I nod as I run my thumb along her lip, enjoying the way her lips part to let out a soft, keening sigh. 'Until I met you. You make me want to be so much more than whatever I've been for the last decade.'

Her hands slide against the fabric of my shirt. 'Dane. What're you saying?'

'I'm saying that when I wake up in the morning, you're the first thing on my mind and when I go to sleep at night, you're the last thing I see behind my eyes. Matter of fact, you don't leave my mind at any point in the day.' I tilt her face upwards and hold her stare. 'You consume every last one of my thoughts and I wouldn't have it any other way.'

She lets out another shuddery sigh.

'All I can think about it how I want to be there for you. How I want to be the best version of *myself* for *you*. How I can be enough for you to want me the way I want you.'

Her hands fist my shirt and pull me in even closer. 'I already told you, you're enough for me. I don't want anything else. I just want— I just *need*— I just need *you*.'

She stands on her tiptoes and tries to press her lips against mine, but there's something else I need to say. Something else she needs to know.

'Eliott.' I hold her face between my hands and take a deep breath before I say the three words that are going to change everything between us. 'I love you.'

And then I close the gap between us. Her lips slant against mine perfectly, just like they always do, and I find myself wondering how I ever lived in a world where the feel of Eliott's tongue against mine wasn't a sensation I was intimately familiar with.

'Are you sure?' she whispers as we pull away from each other.

'I've never been more sure of anything in my life.'

She brings her arms up to swing around my neck, and she's wearing my favourite smile – the soft one, that's just for me. 'I love you too.'

Call me the Grinch, because my heart is growing about five sizes too big for my ribcage right now.

'I love you so fucking much,' she laughs and shakes her head. 'I have for a while.'

'I think I have too.'

She huffs out a happy sounding sigh. 'We've probably wasted so much time, haven't we?'

'Probably,' I say with a shrug. 'But we've got all the time in the world to make up for it now.'

Her smile turns mischievous. 'How long do we have left from Bailey's thirty minutes?'

I glance at my watch. 'Another fifteen, maybe?'

She pulls me deeper into the alcove and hitches her leg around my waist, a devilish smirk tugging at her lips. 'Let's get started then.'

Epilogue:

DANE

THREE YEARS LATER

The bride-to-be accosts me as soon as I walk through the door. She's wearing an old Great Dane Construction Services T-shirt. Her curls are wrapped up tightly with one of my scarves, and I don't think Eliott has ever looked better.

I could be biased, though – she *is* my fiancée, after all.

She launches herself into my arms and kisses me like it's been years since we last saw each other and not eight short hours. I'm not complaining, though. Even after three years, the passion between us hasn't tempered even a little and I still get excited every time she touches me.

'How was your day?' I ask, guiding her over towards the living room so we can both collapse onto the sofa.

'Not bad,' she says with a shrug. Her iPad is set up on the coffee table and I get a brief glimpse of the wedding photos she's currently editing. 'Finished most of the edits I wanted to get through today. I've just got two more clients to go and then I'm officially on leave.'

I grin and drop my head onto her shoulder. 'And then we're getting married.'

She hums lightly, her fingers coming up to twist around my locs. 'And then we're getting married.'

If you count the two-year break in between, it's taken us a grand total of five years to get here and I still can't believe that in two weeks Eliott Rayne will officially be my wife.

We're keeping it small and cosy, just like she's always wanted. A trip to the registry office with our closest friends and family, and then a small reception meal at an Italian restaurant not far from the office.

And then we're heading off on a six-month honeymoon.

Bailey won't stop moaning about how jealous she is, even after I remind her that she jets off on all-expenses paid trips about three times a year. But I suppose I can't blame her.

This *is* the trip of a lifetime.

No work. No friends. No family. No requests for favours or money or time.

Just us for six months, being selfish and indulgent, giving in to whatever whim we feel like on any given day. If there's anyone who needs this, it's Eliott and I feel a strange sense of pride knowing that I can give this to her as my wife.

'Oh yeah,' Eliott sits upright suddenly, and I can hear the

excitement in her voice. 'I got some new film today. You ready now, or do you want to shower first?'

I don't exactly remember when we started up this tradition, but it's quickly become one of my favourites. Whenever Eliott gets in a new roll of film, we make sure the first shot on it is of the two of us. We've got a pin board stuck up in the kitchen filled with photos of us over the last three years and it's one of my favourite things to look at.

'We can do it now,' I say, sliding off the sofa.

I follow her into the kitchen where she's got her camera set up on a stool waiting. I know the drill by now and wait for her to start the timer before pulling her into my side, my chin resting on top of her head.

'Hey,' I murmur as the flash starts to flicker. 'I love you.'

She lifts her head up just as the timer goes off and the camera captures this moment. Eliott and I standing in our kitchen, the home we've carved out together over the last three years.

It's perfect.

It's ours.

I wouldn't have it any other way.

She beams up at me and I still can't get over how, three years on, her smile still manages to make my heart skip a beat. 'Love you too.'

Acknowledgements

Wow. If you're here right now, *One More Shot* may be the first book you've read of mine, or you may have read my previous two novels, *One Week in Paradise* and *One Last Job*. Wherever you are in the Anise Starre library, I just want to thank you so much for giving me a chance.

There's nothing I love more than reading about Black women living their best lives, being loved on and adored and being able to contribute fun, light-hearted and joyful books in an area that is so dear to my heart is nothing but a blessing.

When I first started thinking about publishing the stories that have been ruminating in my head for longer than I can truly say, I never thought I'd resonate with so many people and reach such a kind-hearted and supportive audience.

Thank you to my husband – who is endlessly supportive and always finds great delight in talking about my smutty romance novels. Love you forever and ever +1.

Thank you to all the friends I've made in the writing community – your support and words of encouragement are second to none and I value you all so, so much.

As always, thank you to the wonderful S&S team who have done truly remarkable work to bring my books to a wider audience, and my superstar agent, Emma, who none of this would be possible without!

And thank you to everyone who has read one of my books and had something kind to say. Thank you from the bottom of my heart for taking a chance on me.

I'll be back again soon with love, laughter, joy, and just a little bit of spice.

Anise xo

Do you want to find out more?

Scan the QR code to get an extra spicy bonus chapter by signing up to Anise's newsletter.

DISCOVER MORE FROM ANISE STARRE

AVAILABLE NOW

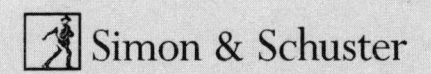

Simon & Schuster

booksandthecity.co.uk
the home of female fiction

NEWS & EVENTS | **BOOKS** | **FEATURES** | **COMPETITIONS**

Follow us online to be the first to hear from your favourite authors

bc
booksandthecity.co.uk

@TeamBATC

Join our mailing list for the latest news, events and exclusive competitions

Sign up at
booksandthecity.co.uk